MW01441936

A NOVEL OF EARLY NEW MILFORD

The Seasoning

PETER J. O'BRIEN

TABLE OF CONTENTS

AUTHORS'S COMMENTS   v

HISTORICAL NOTES   vii

PROLOGUE - *February 29, 1704 - 1704—Deerfield, Massachusetts*   3

CHAPTER I - *March 4, 1707—Westfield, Massachusetts*   16

CHAPTER II - *Same Day*   27

CHAPTER III - *May 18, 1707—Sabbath*   48

CHAPTER IV - *May 19, 1707—Town Meeting*   65

CHAPTER V - *May 20, 1707—Departure Morning*   78

CHAPTER VI - *May 20 to June 15, 1707—The Journey*   88

CHAPTER VII - *June 16, 1707—New Milford, Connecticut, Arrival*   104

CHAPTER VIII - *Later the Same Day—Fishing*   120

CHAPTER IX - *June 27, 1707—Chief's Family*   137

CHAPTER X - *July 16, 1707—Birth*   151

CHAPTER XI - *September 16, 1707—Homecoming*   163

CHAPTER XII - *Spring 1714—Takhi's Daughter*   180

CHAPTER XIII - *January 12, 1762—Woodbury, Connecticut, The Story*   189

CHAPTER XIV - *Later the Same Day*   199

AUTHORS'S COMMENTS

"To me, the greatest pleasure of writing is not what it's about, but the inner music that words make." Truman Capote

Entering my seventies, it never occurred to me that I could be an author, my interests lying more in science and historical fields dealing with facts. But during the COVID shutdown of 2019–2021, I began penning emails to my relatives and a few close friends detailing my (mostly childhood) memories as a way of keeping in touch. With much encouragement from my readers, I found I thoroughly enjoyed the creative process of writing, hard though it was.

As a young girl, my sister, Sharon, had read a story of a real girl who lived in our hometown of New Milford, Connecticut, in the early 1700s. Sharon had always wanted to write a screenplay based on Sarah Noble and asked me to collaborate with her, helping with the historical aspects of the story. During COVID, we managed to finally complete it.

While writing the screenplay, many scenes and background information occurred to me but did not fit into our screenplay format. While discussing the screenplay with my brother, Reid, he queried, "Aren't many plays based on books? Maybe you should write a book." So, with these unused scenarios in mind and the nugget of the idea from Reid, I decided to write this novel. It differs from our screenplay in that, instead of centering mainly on a single character, it more clearly describes the daily life of a colonial family in the 1700s.

I gratefully acknowledge that the subject of this book, many of the family scenarios, the pivotal inflection scenes of Takhi, and even the title are due solely to my collaboration with Sharon on the screenplay. I dedicate this book to Sharon, without whose creativity this book would never have been written. I also dedicate it to Reid for his idea of writing a book about Sarah and for his support, to my extended family members and friends who gave me encouragement, and to my son, Ned, who is always in my thoughts. Particularly I am indebted to my wife, Sally, who patiently went over the sometimes-archaic eighteenth-century prose, making it sensible.

HISTORICAL NOTES

The following characters were real figures in the history of New Milford, Connecticut. But the reader should know that the scenarios in which they appear in this book are entirely for the benefit of my historical story.

SARAH NOBLE: Daughter in the Noble family.
JOHN NOBLE: Sarah's father.
OTHER NOBLE CHILDREN: For clarity, many Noble children were omitted. Those described are historical.
DANIEL BOARDMAN: Descendent of the historical Boardman family.
ISRAEL PUTNAM: Beloved Connecticut general in the Seven Years' War and the American Revolution. Brief mention.
ROGER SHERMAN: New Milford merchant, later lived in New Haven. Served in Continental Congress, US Senate. Brief mention.
All other characters are found only in my imagination.

The story of Sarah's ordeal was apparently imbedded in the Noble family's lore very early, first appearing in print in Samuel Orcutt's magisterial history of the town in 1882. Orcutt afforded it slight consideration for good reason. The notion that Noble would bring his young daughter on such a trek seems rather improbable. After John's death in 1714, the family disappears from recorded town records that might flesh out their history for nearly a generation. There had been no mention of the family, including Sarah, in documented sources for nearly twenty years. Even then, it is unclear if this is the same family branch of the Noble clan. Sarah entirely disappears from historical records.

Noble family memories suggest that she married into the Hinman family of Woodbury, Connecticut, but there is no clear evidence for this. Many of the plot details in the story are designed to lend greater veracity to the tale. It appears that Grandma Mary actually was a resident of Deerfield, but she died some years before the 1704 assault. The tale of Sarah was first popularized by Alice Dalgliesh in 1954 in her Newbery Award-winning children's book *The Courage of Sarah Noble*.

Current town residents, familiar with the stretch of the Housatonic described, might raise an eyebrow that any fording of the river was possible near present-day Young's field. I visualized a spot farther north in the Rocky River stretch. Knowledgeable fishermen of the river might recognize the distinctive description of Straights Rock, where I spent many youthful hours angling for black bass with my father. And I couldn't resist certain anachronisms. The delightful little ditty of David wasn't written until several decades later.

Note that the narrator is an omniscient eighteenth-century speaker. The description throughout of native Americans as "Indians," while perhaps raising questions, was deemed necessary to maintain an authentic voice.

A fanciful tale that I trust does not offend,
Peter J. O'Brien
New Hartford, Connecticut, 2024

The Seasoning

PROLOGUE

February 29, 1704

It had proved an unusually sharp February night, even for these northwestern wilds of the Massachusetts Bay Colony. The forest was preternaturally quiet as if the cold caused nature herself to catch her breath. The slight breeze gave the dry cold a probing, searching quality that stabbed icy fingers into the slightest crevice, searching for an opening. When the feeble winter sun gradually rose above the tree line, the remnants of the primeval stand of white pines accepted the warmth and gradually expanded, venerable elders stretching and yawning, greeting the new day with their usual elderly complaints.

The forest resounded with sharp cracks and moans as the great stands of firs gradually warmed up. Many were incised with the large arrow-shaped gashes warning would-be loggers that they were the reserved property of the Crown. Although far too distant from any shipyard to ever do duty as Royal Navy masts, these trees were marked by admiralty agents nevertheless.

The winter of 1704 descended upon the landscape flinty and ragged in a rush. The usual January thaw, rather than a few days of balmy respite from the cold, was a quick series of ice storms that froze the upper layers of the snowpack so that it was sufficient to support a man but not his beasts. The domestic animals trod gingerly, shying back from the icy shards that their hooves created, while their owners slipped and slid on the glare. The heavy ice coating was too much for many white pines, and the snow was littered with the sacrificed limbs too brittle and burdened to endure.

A few days past had offered a new, deep coat of fresh, feathery snow. The Deerfield River was not entirely frozen over. The open stretches where the current quickened were unfrozen, the warmer water exhaling clouds of thin fog. The rising mist gradually dispersed in the frigid air, condensing into tiny crystals that the pale sun illuminated as a floating shimmer of color. A cascade of tiny flickering-colored points softly settled on the snow.

Toward the west, a thin, dark strand seen in the distance weaved its way through the clean white of the brilliantly sunlit snowy ground. At first glance, it might have appeared, without any sense of real scale, as a rusty-colored snake, improbably active in the winter, moving leisurely along, turning this way and that, advancing by fits and starts.

During the previous evening, a French and Indian raid on the frontier settlement of Deerfield, Massachusetts, had been spectacularly successful. It was to history an insignificant skirmish in a spat between faraway Britain and France, known benignly as Queen Anne's War. A dispute between European rivals over who rightly belonged on the Spanish throne spread to North America as French and English colonists each raided exposed settlements. These incursions had never been assumed to have any strategic value; their primary usefulness was in capturing hostages for profitable ransoms. Isolated outpost settlements such as Deerfield were particularly tempting targets.

The danger to Deerfield had been clearly apparent for some time, but the deep snowpack and the bitter cold perhaps lulled the sentries into relaxing their guard on that night. The surprise was nearly complete. Caught unawares, the townsmen offered little concerted resistance. Even a stout, nail-filled door was chopped away with tomahawks, which allowed the raiders to shoot through the breach. The result was disastrous: some four dozen Deerfield residents were killed. More than a hundred survivors, comprising the coils of the thin, dark strand, were marched off into Canadian captivity.

A large proportion of the captives were women, with children in tow or babes in arms. Indians were loath to take able-bodied males, who might cause mischief as prisoners. Like most New England settlements, the residents were neither rich nor poor, being small farmers who often had a skill such as cooper, cobbler, or blacksmith to provide a sideline to trade for other needs.

These were the so-called middling sort. Their everyday winter clothes, which the survivors donned as they were being herded out of their dwellings, were in muted browns or blues. An occasional greatcoat dyed with hemlock bark was a rusty orange.

A few of the captives were of the better sort, either from the educated or the merchant class, whose income was derived, in popular belief, from land jobbing or money lending. There were always the inevitable rumors of usury and other sharp unchristian practices, but this was considered, resignedly, as part of their makeup. As chickens scratched and hogs rooted, this was simply their nature. They were accorded deference and respect but were rarely liked or deeply mourned in passing.

The more well-to-do hostages, mostly women, had reflexively put on their winter wear like their more modest neighbors, but their raiment was quite different in quality and color. The linens were fine silk blends, and there was one expensive cotton cloak in green. Scattered amongst the huddled, largely brown and blue figures were also a smattering of bright-red riding hoods. These coats were warm and all-encompassing, but their bulk was scarcely suited for a long journey on foot. In those last prodded moments before the trek, hats, scarves, and mittens were hurriedly snatched up. The brightly colored items, particularly hats with feathers, soon caught the eye of the Indian raiders.

Reverend Williams, the town divine, had frantically retrieved his wig at the last moment, at some danger to himself. The Indians were primed to deal harshly with any perceived act of defiance. This impulsive act likely saved his life. Rather than being summarily dispatched as useless baggage, his wig singled him out as a prisoner of consequence and thus a valuable hostage. While perhaps a dangerous attempt to maintain this treasured proof of status, the minister soon realized that as the ranking surviving member of the town, he would need all the gravitas that he could muster in future negotiations with his French captors. He had carefully tucked away the curled wig in a safe, dry pack.

The baleful column had barely cleared the outskirts of Deerfield when Indians started seizing the finely colorful millinery that had caught their fancies. The hats were passed up the ranking ladder, where higher-status warriors might claim their prizes of choice. In a different reality, the English captives might have found the spectacle vastly amusing: Indians in traditional dress prancing about in finely wrought European attire. But these were no lighthearted larks but deadly serious expressions of worth, of victory, analogous to an enemy's scalp hanging from one's belt.

Reverend Williams watched these minor dramas unfold with a keen, discerning eye. In his late forties, he was not a pale, ascetic divine but a hearty, vigorous man in what he liked to reckon as his prime, dark-haired with only a hint of gray under his official wig.

Reverend Williams quickly noticed that the French officers carefully kept the various disparate tribal contingents safely separate on the trek. As a result of longtime intertribal animosities, the different Indian groups might set upon their traditional enemies as readily as they might savage the English.

It took Williams some time to recognize the French officers for what they were. He had never met a Frenchman, but they were nothing like the effeminate, sleek fops that he expected. These were lean, hard men; their very features were sculpted by years of service. The reverend's early attempt to appeal to the commander as one civilized man to another was curtly dismissed. By the time the remnants of the column reached Canada, Williams would come to appreciate that the French commander's authority was tentative at best. The disparate tribal groupings might wander off on their own quests if the command decisions were not to their particular liking.

Family groups clustered together on the march, comforting as best they could the whimpering children. A young woman walked alone. She was snatched up, on her way to the necessary, very early in the assault by the Indians, who later provided her with a miscellaneous collection of clothes they had gathered during the ransacking of Deerfield. A beaver hat drooped over her brow, nearly covering her eyes. A faded blue woolen greatcoat nearly reached her ankles, impeding her movements while keeping her warm. The heavy boots fit rather well and were much warmer than the casual ware she had slipped on for the trip to the privy. The buckles were silver with an ornate clover pattern; she'd seen them before but couldn't immediately recall the owner. If still alive, he'd surely be wearing them.

There was no sign of her family amongst the prisoners, neither her husband nor her sister. Perhaps in the initial commotion they had been alerted and fled out the back kitchen door through the woodshed. In the dark, maybe they were overlooked, hiding amongst the stacks of wood.

A speechless anger kindled gradually from a tiny ember to a raging hate that nearly quenched her fear. Her eyes narrowed as her forehead muscles tensed and drew back. The plump, round cheeks thinned and flattened as her lips pursed into a rigid pucker. Suddenly she halted and emitted a scream that echoed through the valley.

"No, I won't," she screamed as she heaved her pack into the snow. Two Indian tenders descended upon her with tomahawks drawn, ready to inflict their intended purpose. Instead of cowering, she faced her towering tormentors and shook her clenched fist and screamed with shrill venom, "No!" Startled, they froze and regarded her thoughtfully for a long moment, finally turning to each other and bursting into hysterical laughter. When the gale seemed to pass, the younger of the two suddenly poked his companion with an index finger, shouting in a mock female voice, "No, no!"

One of her minders retrieved the tossed bundle and forcefully thrust it on her. The light, laughing face of just moments past was transformed into a mask of deadly purpose. She was about to toss the burden away a second time when an old woman nearby caught her eye and shook her head silently. The girl's courage was spent, the rage gone cold; she hefted the bundle and trudged along. Throughout the long march, a number of Indians, intrigued by this curious episode, made it a point to watch this particular English woman very closely.

This brazen act of defiance was a godsend to the old woman. The turmoil and uncertainty halted the column momentarily and provided her with a much needed, if brief, respite. They were barely outside the settled limits, and she gasped for breath. Once, on the crest of a slight, snowy rise, her vision turned all to white while she had become dizzy and feared she would faint. All the dark colors of her townsmen's outlines faded to shadows, only slightly more distinct than the snow. They seemed to be all fading away. She gave the appearance of sturdy health, despite her years, which had probably saved her life.

But within was a faltering constitution. This weakness crept up on her gradually, and her strength so slowly slipped away that it was scarcely noticed at first. She realized that she would never make Canada and pondered the manner of her exit as she slipped and stumbled along the path.

Deerfield would certainly send out a party of militia, but when would they appear? They would proceed cautiously, ever vigilant against an ambush. There seemed to be only two choices. If she continued, she would die in the dark, untamed forest on the way north. The rescue party would not venture far into these wilds, as they knew these were the natural home of the Indians. Her body would lie by the wayside covered with snow and of interest finally to forest beasts when sustenance was wanting or when the melting snow revealed her remains come April.

If her end came upon settled, cleared ground, her body would surely be found and treated in a proper Christian manner. She grasped frantically in her mind for a more agreeable path, turning over increasingly to unlikely ends. But when the sparsely cleared fields disappeared and the darkness loomed, she serenely made her choice.

The pack that she carried was not heavy, an indulgence perhaps tendered in deference to her advanced age. It was a soft burden, merely a bundle of cloth. With her foot, she cleared a level spot on the path and put the packet down. Sitting on the bundle, she smoothed out her dress, arranged her hair, and sat erect with her eyes tightly closed, waiting. The sharp pain, so recently an unwanted companion, pounded in her breast with a strong drumbeat. And then, as if by magic, it stopped. Reverend Williams chanced to look back and noticed in the distance one of their captors on the path straddling one of his flock.

He realized that negotiating their ransoms would be more difficult than he initially thought, since they might be apportioned out to a variety of tribes. And the Indians may not agree to give them up for any price, particularly the children. The Indians seemed to have a warm place in their hearts for children and allowed their sinful natures full reign with scarcely any watching. Rarely under godly control, the children's natural wayward spirits were allowed full flood by the Indians.

At a meeting of ministers during the past year, a colleague from Maine reported that many previously kidnapped children did not want to return to family and church, preferring to remain with what was now their tribe. Ominously, the numbers of babes choosing to forsake the Indian community lessened as the time of their captivity lengthened.

Reverend Williams paid little attention to the path or his flock as he moved north. He had a plan to record their ordeal, mentally transcribing the details of the journey and the horrible travails. *The Lord's Righteous Few Grievously Tested by Evil and Saved by the Fulsome Grace of God* seemed a fitting title.

His reverie was broken by his young daughter, Eunice, tugging on his greatcoat. At eight, she was a robust girl given to needless fantasies that were long a worry to her parents. Always conjuring up strange futures and fabulous events, she was, even her mother admitted, a strange one. "Father, what will become of us? Will we ever see home again?"

The minister replied without a moment's thought as though repeating a line from one of his sermons. "The Lord will provide. We are captives now, but we shall be redeemed."

He retreated into his own thoughts once again and decided that *The Captives Redeemed* was a more proper title. He briefly pondered how well Eunice might fare living with Indians but soon dismissed the thought as an unprofitable idyll. But what if they were separated? She might be seduced into darkness.

An old man a few feet behind, privy to their conversation, muttered softly, "Redeemed? If we live long enough." That he was alive at all was something of a mystery. The old were dismissed by the Indians as useless burdens and usually killed as a matter of routine.

As the burning town of Deerfield receded slowly from the sight of the bedraggled column, silence gradually returned to the snowy riverbank. The crunching footsteps faded, and the children's wailing slowly trailed off to a soft buzzing sound like some distant bee swarm. On the path lay the old woman next to her bundle. Her hazel eyes were wide open, as was her mouth, as if frozen in place during her last breath. There was no anguish on her face; the expression was, if anything, one of surprise. A bloody strip across the top of her head attested that the scalping had been both perfunctory and hasty.

Skin so pale that it nearly blended with the snow was only brought into relief by the bright blood.

• • •

The sun had not moved more than a few degrees across the sky when new footfalls broke the silence. These were more measured and cautious, with even a sense of delicacy. The remaining militiamen of Deerfield were following the French-led band. Cautious, with primed muskets, they proceeded gingerly. On each side, flankers were active, trying to head off an ambush. The main column following the well-trod path, despite best efforts, outpaced the flankers as they were slowed by the unpacked snow. In the lead were Moses Marsh and John Noble.

Moses was a Deerfield worthy of middle age used to sedate living. Florid in face, with a well-fed girth, he worked with steady determination to follow the pace. His companion, John Noble, while nearly the same age, was rangy and weather-beaten, a more visual companion to the French officers a few miles ahead than his English companions.

With prematurely graying, sandy hair that belied his forty-two years, John had spent his long-past youth as a free-spirited trapper living for years in the wilderness. To supplement his own trap line, he had visited Indian villages to procure particularly favored pelts. He was known and accepted by various tribes, not entirely trusted but familiar. Now and again carousing with French trappers, he had picked up a passable knowledge of their language. Though of the Papist persuasion, they were amongst the most profane and irreligious men he had ever met. They were, however, unfailingly good company, and he counted several as fast friends.

Now agreeably settled with a wife and family, John was sometimes drawn to his former life. Though much was forgotten, the survival lessons of those days were well remembered. While Moses fretted over his tight boots, John's eyes constantly evaluated the landscape for dangers.

Even from a distance, John recognized the form of his mother-in-law lying in the track. Moses, without his spectacles, was slower to realize who the inert lump in the snow was. "I'm so sorry, John. Take her home. I'll continue the pursuit with the band."

Moses was the leader of the town militia, but his rank was awarded on status and popularity alone. He had little experience in this type of warfare, and John was reluctant to leave him to his own devices entirely.

Pausing to catch his wind, Moses continued, "Don't leave her here like this. Take her back to Mary and the children. We're close to being upon them now."

"Don't outpace your outriders for any cause," John warned. "If one or more escapes and approaches, no matter how well known or dear, do not run to greet them. It is likely an ambuscade."

As the militia receded into the distance in the gingerly chase, John inspected his wife's mother for wounds. Carefully scanning the open ground around him for any sign of movement, he uncocked his musket and firmly grounded it in the snow, butt first. Lifting Grandma Mary, his wife's namesake, he slung her over his left shoulder. Retrieving his musket, carefully cocking it once more, he began the journey back from whence he came.

The adrenaline-charged outward rush of the soldiery had made good time before caution congealed the pace. The return trip was at an even slower pace as though creating, quite unconsciously, a stately dirge of footsteps. Grandma Mary's arms swung back and forth gently, keeping a grave rhythm with his steps.

In the distance, John heard a volley of muskets, another, and then more intermittent firing. John knew the pattern only too well. They had been ambushed, finally managing to get off an ineffective volley, and then retreated. More likely than not, the more sporadic gunshots were Indians picking off the fleeing militiamen.

• • •

The Noble family, John, Mary, and the three daughters, were in Deerfield on a long-delayed visit from Westover, Massachusetts, a more settled town to the southeast. Their sons were left at home to carry on the winter tending of the livestock. Mary had feared that this might be the last opportunity to see her mother due to her mother's ill health. Weather and snow be damned!

By a stroke of Providence, the family was socializing with friends at some distance from the Deerfield town proper and was alerted to the raid in good time. Returning later, slowly venturing down the main street of the ruined town, the family clustered together in an illusion of safety. John had bolted some time earlier at the first musket blasts.

Mary paid little heed to the burning houses and the occasional corpse sprawled in the street. She craned her neck in a vain attempt to see her mother's house. If it was on fire, the flaming outline would lighten the night. Her mother's house lot was dark, save for the flickering shadows cast by burning houses nearby. Inside, the residence was a complete shambles, but at least there was a sound roof.

There was no sign of her mother. Mary took some solace that, in spite of the casual wreckage, there was no blood. She must be a captive. There was still hope. Mary paced back and forth across the disordered kitchen while her three daughters sorted through the wreckage, culling out usable and mendable items.

Over and over, she muttered, "John, where are you? Where are you?"

Every few moments she pulled the great iron kettle away from the door, scanning the long street for any sign of her husband. The door latch had been shattered when the raiders burst in, and only the heavy kettle prevented the wind from playing with the old door like a cat with a toy. The three daughters watched their mother as she made her laps back and forth across the small kitchen.

She was suddenly at a loss and indecisive, an unusual state for her. Mary ran an ordered world. If it couldn't be managed, it was either an act of God or else not worth a further thought. These were things she couldn't take charge of.

•••

John carried his slight but fragile burden up the disordered main street. Personal effects and clothing were scattered along the street as though thrown about by puckish imps out on a lark. Most of the doors were broken down or caved in, many of them marred by hatchet marks. He was surprised by the amount of fire damage. It was clearly in the marauders' interest to scoop up their spoils and make a getaway quickly before neighboring militia bands gave chase. John was perplexed that they would risk the time to destroy the town. At this time, he did not fully appreciate how complete the raiders' victory was.

The dead would be collected and returned to their families, if any survived, for the final ministrations, the preparations for burial. With so many lost, the burials would be hasty, without the usual communal gathering. Lacking also would be the comforting solemnities of the minister, now apparently in captivity.

Mary slid the kettle aside and peered once again through the open door down the long street. A distant, solitary figure was loping up the lane with a bundle. Instantly, she recognized her husband by his distinctive gait. Leaving the kitchen and stepping into the cold air in only her housedress, she sighed in relief at John's return.

Standing on the threshold, holding the door closed behind her, the bundle over his shoulder slowly came into focus. A piercing, nearly preternatural shriek, "Mother," echoed through the town green as she recognized the simple butternut-colored skirt that was her mother's trademark. John came to a halt as Mary, coatless, ran toward him. He remained expressionless as she wailed and caressed her mother. As they approached the house, she tearfully tried to arrange her mother's hair as it swung to and fro.

Suddenly, she emerged from behind her husband, grasped his free hand, and in a clear, determined tone, commanded, "Put her on the long table, John. There is much to be attended, much mending before she is fit for the ceremony."

The old woman's body was laid out upon the oak farm table in a dignified sleeping position while her daughter fussed over her, talking to herself, straightening this seam or that hem, muttering, "Perhaps the camlet dress." Gingerly, she pulled some tresses aside, revealing the scalping slash. "A bonnet will cover most of this. Perhaps a veil." Her tears suddenly wiped dry, Mary's voice returned to her customary even and matter-of-fact tone.

Quietly John warned, "Mary, the times will not permit the entire finery that you want or have come to expect. Few hands are left, and more important tasks beckon ahead of burials. Mourning must be put off for more timely needs."

"John, my mother has been heathenishly murdered, and I will prepare her for a proper Christian burial at all costs! This is above all mortal concerns."

"Mary, look at her scalp. There is but little blood. We know that she was ailing with not long to live. That is why we came here in midwinter, to say our last farewells. Mary, she was a sick old lady who decided on her course and simply sat down to die in her own time in her own way! She was dead before the Indians came upon her."

"John Noble, do not talk to me about wounds or no! They killed my mother, and all the soothing, oily words that you may offer will never change that. To my dying day, I will believe this truth."

John turned as the kettle scraped across the floor. The door, forced from the outside, swung open, and a diminutive old woman strode into the kitchen. Her name was Faithful, her mother's longtime companion and a fixture in the house. There was some debate over her true age as there was no one alive in town who remembered. She didn't appear to age but instead became gradually smaller over time. John once offered an observation over dinner that the cost of her coffin was becoming less dear all the while.

Ignoring John, Faithful moved past him and hugged Mary. Breaking the embrace, she surveyed her deceased friend of many years. Silently, she relived so many memories, happy, sad, even triumphant. The silly capers of their youth flooded over her. Snapping out of her reverie and wiping her eyes, she carefully observed the wounds. "Too big for just a bonnet or cap." Turning to Mary, she suggested, "Perhaps a riding hood?"

On his way out the open door, John picked up the kettle and positioned it as best he could so that the door was only ajar. The three daughters, Elizabeth, Mary Jr., and Sarah, had left soon after the arrival of their grandmother's friend. Faithful was a sharp old soul who made no attempt to endear herself to any of them. The girls were standing near the house, basking in the warm winter's sun. With the hearth fire long cold, it was warmer outdoors in the feeble sunlight than indoors.

Elizabeth was doing her best to soothe and console Sarah, while Mary, a few steps separate, was scanning the wreckage with a sharp eye. John approached his daughters from behind and startled them by gathering them together between his arms.

"My Three Graces, life plays out as a rolling stream of both arrivals and departures. Some are pleasant and some are not. They are the nature of things. They are what they are and must be enjoyed or endured in turn."

John had always referred to his daughters as "My Graces," eventually settling on "My Three Graces" with the arrival of Sarah. It was always something of a family mystery where the phrase came from. John never explained, replying to queries with a sly smile. Young Mary, as was her nature, was suspicious. It seemed to her somehow improper.

In truth, in his youth, John ran into an old French trapper on occasion, who, properly motivated with brandy, would regale the campfire company with ancient tales, by turns lurid and preposterous, of heathen gods and their goings-on. Amongst the others, the story of the "Three Graces" lodged in John's memory. Although he had long since forgotten the finer details of the tale, he did retain a fondness for this term of endearment.

Surveying the weather-beaten boards of the nearby barn, John released his tight hold of his girls and muttered, "And now, I must undertake a proper box." Without a suitable supply of fresh lumber, he would have to strip away usable barn boards for a coffin. Too many dead, including the sawyer. None of the girls cared for their dead grandmother's disagreeable, longtime friend, who was even now arranging her corpse. They preferred to watch their father as he inspected the south side of the barn. He probed the boards, looking for open knots.

Sarah puzzled out loud, "What is Father doing?"

"He's looking for sound boards with no empty knotholes for the coffin," Elizabeth finally explained after an awkward silence. "The ground is frozen hard, digging is most difficult, and if grandmother is aboveground for too long in this weather . . ." Elizabeth's face then went blank while vainly searching for fitting words.

It was Mary Jr. who finally completed Elizabeth's thought. "She'll begin to drip."

CHAPTER I

March 4, 1707

Three years had passed. The Noble house in Westfield, Massachusetts, was a modest affair, though not shabby by common reckoning. Clad in unpainted pine clapboards long since turned black by many winters, it was the typical two-over-two. The kitchen and best chamber were divided by a massive tapering chimney on the ground floor. Above were two more chambers or bedrooms, one on either side of the massive flue. The upper chambers were never finished off. The original intention was to cut into the stack for fireplaces, but the tapering chimney still protruded undisturbed into both rooms, one for the daughters and the other for the sons. Even without a firebox, the fieldstone stack was always warm, a blessing in cold weather but a curse in high summer since a fire was always working down below for cooking. The family must be fed, and even the low summer cookfire heated the upper chambers.

In her early forties, Mary's black hair was just beginning to streak, and her thin frame was year by year filling. In her youth, she had sharp, angular features that might unkindly be described as hawklike but became softer and fuller over the years. The bloom of her youthful years had scarcely faded, and it was often remarked that she was still a very handsome woman.

THE SEASONING

The eldest daughter, Elizabeth, was everyone's favorite. At fourteen, she had a sweet, open, round face and thin sandy hair. She was one of God's creatures that everyone loved and trusted instinctively. Cheerful and capable, she was her mother's sturdy right hand. She was not petite but solid and strong. A man looking to make a proper match might approve of her as being made of such good wood.

Mary more than once confided to her husband that she worried about Elizabeth's trusting nature. Soon, she would be entertaining a young man. For privacy, the courting couple would be allowed in the parents' bedroom. When there was any winter bundling under the blankets for warmth, with a separating bolster of feathers between Elizabeth and her beau, Mary would keep a sharp ear out for unseemly noises. She had no intention of allowing any goose feathers to waft about obscenely.

A few years younger was Mary Jr., a double of her namesake parent when her mother was young. She had lustrous full-bodied black hair and elegant, striking features. She was the most quick-witted of the siblings, able to deal with nearly any crisis with dispatch. Her outspoken sharp tongue was the topic of some gossip. Older brother Stephan mused only half in jest about the particular hone that she used to keep her tongue in such fine form. Unlike Elizabeth, Mary Jr. viewed the world with suspicion, always assuming that the worst was more likely than the best to happen. She was rarely disappointed, which hardened this belief. In her light, since the world was an unpredictable and even cruel place, she must always be careful to manage its vagaries to her benefit. Cause and effect and the hardheaded balancing of possibilities were the keys to a good life.

Sarah, the youngest of the three, was born as a tightly coiled spring and rarely ever unwound. Nervous and twitchy, she drove her mother to distraction with her fears and fantasies. When she was nine, she was hardly what anyone except the family would describe as a cunning, beautiful child. Painfully thin and angular, her bony knees and elbows, when flexed, were nearly arrow points. She was uncommonly agile and fleet of foot, however. Her long, bony fingers could, with surprising speed, deftly catch any fly that landed on her ham slice or cheese. Sarah's thin blond hair seemed to defy any sort of management no matter how much attention was expended.

Even at the supper table, the unruly strands might waft about, agitated by the slightest movement of the diners.

Alarmingly, all Sarah's adult teeth gushed in at a rush over only a few months, and her little mouth was simply too small to easily house them. Her lips were distended to accommodate the crowd, and Sarah, painfully self-conscious, rarely flashed a full smile, being mortified at her misshapen mouth. Mary briefly took to referring to her younger sister as The Basilisk until their mother firmly put an end to it. One of young Mary's little friend's family had fragments of an ancient book referred to as a bestiary. Mary was amused at the resemblance of her little sister to one of the fabulous beasts. Her mother calmed Sarah by explaining that this was just a phase and that her head would, in time, grow up to match her teeth. Sarah's achy, lanky legs were another phase, mere growing pains.

In cold weather, when the daughters were hatching a plot to avoid their mother's ever-twitching ears, they would climb up to their cold chamber and recline against the sloping warm masonry, warming their back parts while planning their designs. In truly bitter times, they might pull a quilt off the bed and cover themselves against the chimney to trap the heat.

At one of these secret meetings, Sarah, whose diminutive body fitted the chimney slope to perfection, started rubbing the masonry with that quizzical look that her sisters had come to recognize as signifying the advent of one of their sister's curious fancies. To her siblings' astonishment, Sarah wondered if they could stay warm leaning against the chimney, why couldn't the masonry be modified to include a flat platform with the warm smoke passing under it? Then they could sit on a warm stone bench.

In the time since the horrors of Deerfield, expected changes had occurred in the young women. Elizabeth had lost all traces of her adolescent past and was what she would be for the remainder of her life. Mary was every bit the beauty that her younger years had promised. Sarah was taller but still sharply angular. Now at age twelve, her teeth didn't deform her lips any longer. Brother Stephen mused one morning at the breakfast table that her head seemed bigger now or perhaps her teeth had shrunk. Her mother was correct. She had grown into her teeth. To everyone's surprise, Mary didn't seize the opportunity to tender a humorous quip.

THE SEASONING

The sisters, lying together in a featherbed on this bitterly cold March night, were entombed under a mound of quilts of different materials, designs, and sizes. Some were heirlooms, but most were cobbled together from scraps of long since forgotten clothing. Heaped up on the bed, the sheer weight held the sleepers fast. To exit the bed during the night required considerable forethought and effort. Elizabeth and Mary were on either side, and the youngest, Sarah, was snuggled in between. Age conferred certain privileges, and the older siblings decided to claim the outsides. While not as warm, it was much easier to slip out and respond to nature's demands.

The pale light of the full moon flooding in the single small window provided only a cool, dark illumination to the chamber. A thick incrustation of ice on the panes cast eerie shadows over the bed. There was not the slightest movement from the sisters. The weight of the quilts dampened even the slight rise and fall of their slow breathing. The blankets were pulled up under the sisters' noses and curled around their cheeks. Beneath their noses were spreading fans of ice crystals, indoor snow, as hours of breathing froze on the bedcovers.

Suddenly Sarah bolted upright and emitted a shriek, an unworldly wail, that the family had grown to know well over the years. Just as suddenly, she fell back and sobbed.

"Again and again, it has come again." Elizabeth rolled over and gathered her sister up.

"Sarah, it is only a dream, a dream."

"But it was so real," Sarah protested. "The blood, the hair, and Grandmother stretched out on the table."

In her usual soothing tones, Elizabeth cupped her sister's cheeks, explaining, "It was only the night hag seizing your sleep again. It was just a horrible dream."

"Elizabeth, all I can remember is that terrible day. It swirls about in my mind and crowds out all else. In my memory, her smile is gone! Nothing remains except her frozen death face."

Softly Elizabeth cautioned, "By and by, the sad memories will fade and more joyous thoughts of Grandmother will come back. There will come a day when you will smile recalling her awestruck confusion over your lye bread."

"Hard as stone and sharp tasting," confessed Sarah, "but it burned with a pretty flame in the fire." Both girls chuckled over the episode. Sarah had, through inattention while processing a pail of wood ashes for pearl ash, let some of the crystal lye lees in the bottom of the pail mingle with the leavening liquid.

"Sarah, kneading over bad memories serves no purpose and gives no peace. Give them up." Suddenly, Elizabeth jerked, and in a loud voice demanded, "Cut those toenails! I've warned you before. They are as daggers."

"But, Elizabeth, Mother's scissors always seem to do my toes mischief."

Mary, listening thus far with sleepy disinterest, finally piped up sharply to this silliness. "Then chew them off like we all do."

With a slightly airy tone, Sarah responded, "That is not genteel or ladylike!"

With a snort, Mary quickly spat out, "So speaks the duchess of Westfield!"

With her emotions spent, Sarah slowly fell into a quiet sleep. These dreams had, if anything, become more frequent lately. Often, it was not Grandmother who appeared in her sleep but a spectral snow-white horse with glowing eyes that loomed out of the darkness.

Elizabeth, now entirely awake, fretted over what was to become of her younger sister. Sarah was so fidgety and nervous, flitting from this thought to that with no constancy. A mere butterfly. It was often mentioned in the family circle that, at times, she could be such exhausting company. When Sarah was in one of her states, it was as if all the air in the room was suddenly sucked out, leaving everyone gasping for breath.

Mary listened to her sister's laments with resignation. It was always the same travails. In the past, Mary had always been sharp with her during these episodes, pinching whatever part of Sarah's form was most available and scolding that this was long past happening. Constant grieving changed nothing and brought on only melancholy. Better to banish it from her mind and clear her thoughts of it.

At length, Mary came to feel that these night terrors had become a part of Sarah's very nature. It made no more sense to hector her about them than to reprove hogs for rooting in the kitchen garden. Blessedly, her sister's breathing settled into a quiet rhythm.

Often this past winter, Sarah, after one of her visions, might shimmy out of the featherbed, making for the west window. Using her fingernail, she would etch a picture of her tormenter in the frosted window glass. They became more fully done in time as Sarah became more skilled in working the details. Mostly they were ghostly horses glowing in the moonlight. But sometimes it was a little creature on its haunches. Seen against the moonlight, Sarah was a mere silhouette devoid of features. With her silent breaths visible in the cold air, she presented an eerie, witchy aspect. By afternoon, after only a short period of pale sunlight, the frosted images were melted away, ready for the next vision to appear.

When Sarah first took to her occasional scratching at the window, Mary thought the mouse had returned. In early fall, when sensible creatures prepare for the cold, a mouse took up residence in the featherbed. Its presence was betrayed by soft rustlings and gnawing at night. And then suddenly, it was gone. Brother David wondered at breakfast one morning if the mouse departed in search of a quieter nest.

Mary idly scanned the wanly lit room. Nothing was finished off. Father never did get around to it. The walls were open, and thin beams of moonlight filtered through the gaps in the pine siding. The roof shingles butting up to the chimney stack admitted rays of cold light across the featherbed. Mary easily reckoned the evening hour while the beam gradually migrated across the quilts as the moon moved across the sky through the night. It was now only a few hours before the household would start to stir.

Mary briefly pondered why clear, still nights seemed so much colder than cloudy nights. Tonight was the coldest in a good bit. She soon dismissed it as a useless thought as it was cold in all events regardless of the cause. Knowing why did little good. With a chuckle, she tucked away the query for future use at mealtime. Sarah, no doubt, would have a fanciful answer to the question that would amuse the family.

Mary remembered that it was her turn to empty the chamber pot this morning. Thankfully, it was unlikely that Sarah would shimmy her way out from the quilts to pass any more water. With any good fortune, there would be a frozen amber block in the chamber pot that might sail out of the window into the snow while Sarah was not looking. Sarah had the most unsettling habit of telling Mother nearly everything.

The rule was such that Sarah would crawl over whichever of her sisters was still awake when nature was insistent. Mary reflected that the girl must have a bladder scarcely bigger than a chestnut. If both older sisters were asleep, she had to slither her way up to the headboard for an exit, but the knees and elbows always made their marks all the same.

Mary had given some thought to trading her outboard sleeping position with her younger sister, but that would mean sleeping next to Elizabeth. And Elizabeth was a thrasher, flailing about through the night and moaning. Mary considered her bedmates with dismay, one a screamer and the other a moaning dervish, sighing that she may never have a featherbed all to her own. She would leave this communal bed in time directly to her future husband's without a pause.

Father, in cryptic comments, had hinted that he was likely to take one of the children with him when he left to prepare their new land pitch to the south in the Connecticut colony. Certainly, her brothers were needed to manage the farm in his absence. David, the most scattershot of the boys, was a possibility, but he was strong and a willing worker and would be needed to tend the crops. Mary reckoned that this left only one of the girls.

Mother relied on Elizabeth so much for everything, even the slightest of chores, that she did not believe her father would care to provoke the inevitable fuss by choosing Mother's steady right hand. There was no other logical choice other than herself. She looked forward to handling the family business arrangements and could easily manage the household matters until the entire family arrived. She would order affairs to her own liking, smiling as she savored the thought of her mother's praise. This would be an adventure, freeing her from the humdrum daily routine of her life in Westfield.

Before drifting off to sleep, Mary briefly considered her father's unpredictability. Some of his decisions made no sense at all to her, although the results were more often favorable. His thoughts did not seem to follow the short, straight, logical line from here to there but often meandered from this zig to that curve, arriving in a roundabout path without sense. Rarely was the path that of an arrow.

Sarah, his favorite of all the girls, had a mind that capered about like that. *Sarah?* No, he wouldn't do that, would he? Mary tried to tally up the pluses and minuses of this possibility but was too exhausted and gave it up. There were no pluses, only debits.

In a nearly identical sleeping chamber on the other side of the chimney, the three Noble sons were only barely roused by their sister Sarah's piercing screech. At the beginning, years past, of course, they had bolted upright in confusion, but now, after so many repeats, they heard her cries less and less. Like a babe sleeping in its cradle unaware of the raucous confusion in a busy kitchen, their dreams ignored the commotion.

The middle son, Stephen, who just recently came of the legal age of twenty-one, drowsily muttered, "Indians again," before drifting off, but not before sleepily brushing the sharp ice off the quilt under his nose. Brother John on his left was his elder by two years and observed, "I don't reckon that Grandma Goodwin made that much of a din when she was scalped!" The youngest son, David, barely fifteen, occupied the outboard bedside nearest the window. With a mock serious tone, he said, "This time, I note she didn't rattle the window glass. Perhaps that's the future path? Could this be an improvement?"

The elder sons were very much younger versions of their father: tall, lanky bodies with fair complexions and light straw hair. John Jr. was retiring and diffident even as a child. He rarely initiated any action but felt more comfortable reacting to events as they unfolded. Pondering all the possibilities, opportunities often disappeared before the event could be seized. However, he did have uncommonly good horse sense.

Stephen was altogether a different animal. Decisive, even rash at times, he grabbed at every slight advantage with little thought to the long-term consequences. Their mother described them humorously, but perceptively, as her twins in the looking glass. Each strength and personal fault of her two older sons was balanced by the other.

The youngest, David, was unlike his elder brothers, being dark-haired and more heavily built. To the despair of both parents, he seemed entirely incapable of the slightest foresight of any kind, always assuming, with an engaging smile, that everything would somehow work out for the best. He had, however, the most beautiful and powerful tenor voice, which he put to good use on every Sabbath.

In the congregational church, the custom was, from the earliest settlement in New England, that every family sang the selected hymns in whatever melody struck their fancy. David's clear and pure tones more than once seduced nearby pew mates to drift over to the Noble family's choice of melody. The resulting cacophonous din was regarded as quite natural since salvation was intensely personal and each family group talked to God in their own way, which also included the sung voice.

A recent surveying commission dispatched by the general assembly to try to lay out the disputed far western border with New York contained a number of high church Anglicans. They described the music emanating from the Meeting House on any Sabbath day as much like the caterwauling yelps of a sack of wet cats.

David's innocent countenance was in perfect symmetry with his personality. He was inclined to credit anything told to him as the truth and to believe the best in everyone. On many occasions, he served as his sister Mary's cat's-paw. His sense of mirth was so aligned with Mary's that, although he knew that she was leading him down a puckish path, he followed her with no hesitancy.

Sleepily he mused that father would take Sarah with him when he left for their new land pitch in Connecticut. She was the only one of them who could be spared. And then they might sleep with no interruptions. Neither of his brothers responded.

The first-floor chamber directly beneath the daughters' room was the space long reserved for parents John and Mary and whatever babe needed suckling as well as more warmth. Directly abutting the kitchen, it was the warmest of the bedchambers, having finished plaster walls and a ceiling that deflected some of the drafts from the room above. It was quiet, with little of the moaning winds that blew through the garret chambers above. Mary was what one might call a sound sleeper, but she had a nearly preternatural open ear for any sounds from the rooms above. Her whole being did not seemingly ever sleep, but a certain portion of her was always alert for unusual sounds from above. Mary's eyes snapped open at Sarah's first scream.

"Oh Lord, not again!" Sighing loudly, she listened closely, hoping this was but one of her short episodes, dreading the possibility of a lengthy weeping ordeal. She heard only soft conversation from above and, relieved, turned to her husband. John had not stirred, lost in the slumber of the dead. In the beginning, he would rouse in such cases, but now slept through them all. And yet if a pinecone rolled down the roof or a branch scraped against the siding, he bolted up, instantly alert. The more Mary thought this over, the more her annoyance blossomed. Regarding his softly snoring form, she began to vigorously poke his ribs.

"John! John! Wake up! We must talk!"

His eyes never opened. "Now?"

"Yes now! Sarah had another visitation."

"That is hardly news, Mary."

"But they are increasing. We must get away from this place . . . to a place with no Indians to plague her. We cannot go south to the new allotment. It would be a calamity."

"The frights are not increasing by my reckoning, but I do admit, they are becoming more vexing. How would I continue my trade in pelts without the Indians? The whole notion in all cases is nothing but a false hope. No matter where we went, Sarah would bring the visitations along as unwelcome guests."

He rolled over onto his back and clasped his hands together on his chest. He had never once opened his eyes since Sarah's howl. "The lass needs seasoning. I shall bring her with me when I lay out our new farm."

It took Mary a moment for her husband's announcement to finally bloom in her mind. Heatedly, she warned, "No, John Noble, you will not spirit my babe away into the wilderness. I will not let her be lost, swallowed up into Satan's Kingdom. It will be the ruin of her." In the dim light, she noticed that his placid expression was unchanged. With an alternate argument, she pivoted.

"Take David! I can spare David. In the time together, you can finally straighten out his bendable nature. The trip will strengthen and order his wayward character."

"It shall be Sarah."

"But David would be of more use."

"Yes, but Sarah has the greater need."

"Will you give some care to my concerns?"

"I will think upon it, I promise."

With that, she sank back into the bed with a heavy sigh and pulled the quilts up to her nose. The decision was already made and set in stone. She knew full well that her husband's verdict was as hard and fast as a ruling from the Great and General Court in Boston. Lo these many years together, she'd learned all too well that when her husband uttered the promise to "think about it," it was a wordy cipher for "no." Later, she came to believe that her heated words that night had caused a misfire. Perhaps, without her scolding, he might have taken David.

During their conversation, the infant nestled between them made hardly a noise; that was not unusual in the least. She was a strange newborn who hardly even cried. The flailing little arms, expected for her age, rarely moved. At first, her skin was a sickly yellow. That had passed, but the snuffling runny nose did not. She made her presence known generally only by wet, gurgling snorts as she sought breath while nursing. So frail at birth that they sent for the minister to perform a hasty irregular baptism, she lingered with only gradual improvement. Mary insisted, despite the divine's reservations, on the name "Preserved." With the exception of Elizabeth, the children were distant to their new sister, as well they should be. There were doubts that this little stranger would stay with them long.

Fears that the spindly child would not survive the journey south was the logic for John to travel on ahead of the family to prepare the site as best he could. The rest of the family would follow when the girl was hardier. John regarded this as an opportunity to tie up the loose threads of an earlier life. What would he find of old companions? Returning nearly alone to the stage of his past might finally work a lancet into an old boil. While the family sensibly assumed that he would choose one of his sons as a companion, he knew from the start that it would be Sarah.

CHAPTER II

Same Day

As in all New England households, the kitchen began to stir at the slimmest glimmer of daybreak. The designated offspring was carefully teasing out the remaining live embers from the mound of ashes and delicately tending a growing fire that would warm the kitchen and cook their meals through the long winter day. They followed an age-old rhythm that was reenacted daily as nearly a religious rite. It was described simply as "kin and kaint." One rose when one "kin" see and retired to bed when one "kaint."

It was a source of regional pride that the northern colonies were populated by solid, prudent, middling men. No foppish Church of England grandees here, but God-fearing small landowners who provided for themselves and minded to their own affairs. This smug belief was mostly accurate, though it omitted the many indentured servants and bonded apprentices who were deemed to have no role to play. Also passed over in this comforting fiction was the thin scrum of the educated and wealthy who wielded significant clout and were invariably granted deference.

The Nobles were part of the "middling sort" but just barely. To describe John Noble as a farmer was technically accurate, but the term meant little in practice. Nearly everyone grew their own sustenance by necessity.

Even the reverend Edwards bent over his plow in the spring and, like his neighbors, swung his scythe with a hypnotic rhythm in his wheat field come the harvest. This was much like a pious chant, and it wasn't unusual for men to lose themselves for hours in this mindless repetition. He also struggled to process the thirty cords of wood needed each year to heat the farmhouse and fuel the great fireplace. Some years the congregation might award him firewood as part of his salary.

Like his flock, the grave divine scoured the forest in the fall rounding up his hogs for the November slaughter. Let loose into the forest after the harvest was safely put away, the hogs gorged themselves, fattening on the abundant mast of acorns, chestnuts, and hickory nuts, giving them, according to local belief, a far superior flavor to English porkers. Timing was crucial. Left free too long, they quickly turned wild and were lost to the pork barrel. It was a yearly source of amusement to watch the reverend, shorn of stately wig and his ministerial robes, stumbling through the underbrush in search of a particularly elusive hog.

If pressed for an occupation, a man might explain that he was a housewright, a cooper, a blacksmith, or a tanner. They farmed to eat but lived by their trade. The income from their skill paid for what they could not make themselves. A cooper might trade a good, tight barrel for iron tools or shoes for his children. One might get by farming alone, but it was a precarious road if there was no product to trade.

John Noble was such a man. He was, by all accounts, one of the best trappers to be found, but the fur trade was shifting farther to the west year by year as settlements increased and the animals played out. Moneyed interests were also at work buying up pelts at prices that he dared not match. Agents from concerns in Boston and Hartford scoured the countryside as relentlessly as locusts. With such a large family to maintain, he could no longer simply decamp and move on as was his custom in years past.

In the Noble kitchen, eldest son, John, teased the remaining live embers out of the ashes to kindle the day's fire. He soon had a vigorous flame working in the large hearth. It was spacious enough for a goodwife to nearly walk into, provided, of course, that her head cleared the lintel.

The masonry mass never cooled, even when the fire was stone cold. In the frigid months, it was a generous grotto of warmth.

Outside chores done, family members would often line up as near as they dared facing the masonry, basking silently in the heat. Presently, they would turn, as if by silent consent, as one might flip hoecakes and expose the other side. It was at this stage that animated discussions of the daily events were often shared. Nearly unconsciously, while in animated discourse, they invariably rubbed their bottoms absent-mindedly, spreading the welcome heat about as a sort of soothing ointment.

It is the very nature of things that every advantage was inevitably paired with its evil twin. Despite longtime experience in the choice and placement of the wood sticks, there was always the occasional unruly log that might expel a flaming ember onto the floor. A pail of sand was kept near at hand for this peril, but some householders felt more prudent in spreading a thin layer of sand on the floor nearest the hearth.

Last spring, the aged Mrs. Gilbert, while preparing the evening's meal, suffered an attack of apoplexy and fell into the hearth. She was duly discovered by her husband, Luke, at the end of the day's plow. A recently elected justice of the peace, relishing and preening in his newfound authority, caused much comment when he insisted on presiding over an inquest over her death. Giving little heed to the high regard in which the town held the widower or simple common sense, his reelection was unlikely.

The oldest Noble son, with a lively fire in hand, edged some embers aside into a mound to heat the spider, a large, long-handled skillet on legs. Nestled on the bed of embers, the heavy iron skillet heated slowly. His mother, from long experience, judged if the time was right to add the bacon merely by running her palm over the long handle. This skill was as nearly magical to her son as her ability to decide if the bake oven was hot enough by simply thrusting her hand into it and counting out loud. Biscuits required one count, quick breads quite another.

John Jr. swung the crane over the fire and reset the adjustable trammel so the pot of corn mush would be at the proper height over the heat. Set too high, and breakfast could be delayed long enough that squabbles would surely break out. Both cats and siblings proved noisy and sharp when hungry. Too low, and he would be confronted by his mother in a hard-eyed mood, thrusting a pot of scorched cornmeal under his face. The bill of fare in late winter was nearly always monotonous. The food put by from the fields—squash, sweet potatoes, onions, pumpkins—was long gone, either eaten or spoiled.

This room was the warmest chamber in the house and was little different from many other kitchens in town. The centerpiece was a long, unfinished trestle table, surrounded by painted, armless chairs. The perimeter was an untidy clutter of barrels of victuals: Indian meal, salted pork, and baskets of chestnuts and hickories. Nearby, the great spinning wheel was nestled with a smaller Dutch spinning wheel and a lap loom that turned out thin strips of coarse cloth for common purposes.

As Mary began to set out the table, her brood, one by one, their morning chores attended to, drifted into the kitchen. She made a mental note that she hadn't noticed any of her girls passing through the kitchen with a chamber pot. Daughter Mary must be up to her old tricks again! She never could decide what vexed her most, the act itself or the fact that young Mary considered her mother so dim that she wouldn't notice. Such disgusting behavior might be common in the mother country, where householders pitched all manner of revolting things into the streets, but this was upright New England, a place of pious gentility.

The wooden trenchers serving as plates for the porridge and bacon would need renewal soon as they were becoming ever the harder to clean, despite a scrubbing with lye soap. They shone with a greasy glow. The knives and spoons were serviceable, and Mary was insistent on clean napkins of coarse linen with every meal. She was not yet completely successful in impressing upon her children the importance of not wiping their greasy fingers clean on their clothes.

Mary had recently heard from one of her lady friends of a new fad sweeping England, an eating tool called a fork. As far as she could make out, it was a dainty little version of a hayfork but in metal used for stabbing bits of meat and such. She dismissed it quickly as a pointless affectation, particularly once she learned that the notion had come from Italy. Doubtless, the Pope and his red-clad minions used them, jabbing at their luxurious fare.

While idly setting up the meal, she noted that the cheese, only yesterday removed from its press, showed clearly the toothy sculpting of at least one vermin from overnight. When her son John appeared from the cellar with a large jug of cider, she was reminded to set the earthenware mugs on the table. At this time of year, the cider was well past the cloying sweet stage and was perfectly dry and sharp. An ample draft of this drink fortified the whole family for the day's labors. She remembered that she needed to remind young John to unbung one of the smaller barrels soon so that she might have a good supply of vinegar for the springhouse scrubbing.

Immediate morning chores attended to, the family members wandered into the kitchen one by one and drifted into casual conversations with their siblings already seated at the table. Elizabeth, while bantering with brother Stephen, held up her trencher to a raking light and, between giggles, casually scrapped off a spot of suspicious dark residue with a spoon.

Their father, quiet until now, mused out loud, "And where is Sarah? She is holding up the meal." The family rarely waited long for an absent diner nor thoughtfully put aside any food for a latecomer. The meal was done when all was eaten by those present.

No sooner had Sarah's mother explained "at the necessary" than Sarah burst through the door. She had every intention of standing for a bit before the hearth to warm her parts that were recently exposed to the cold, but she sat in her accustomed seat under the expectant stares of more than a dozen eyes. In the following silence, her father tendered the mealtime prayer.

"Heavenly Father, we give thanks for the meat and drink that You have so graciously provided us to sustain our feeble bodies. Amen."

What followed was nearly akin to pandemonium. Amidst shouts, banter, and laughter, the tabletop was adorned with a flurry of hands brandishing by turns spoons and knives. The separate dishes seemed to levitate about the table as if by magic. As predictable as John's prayer was, their mother's caution that "your sleeves are not napkins" seemed always to follow with the same regularity.

John intoned the same prayer at every meal for their entire marriage, but Mary, over time, reluctantly accepted the fact that it got more abbreviated with each passing year. It had been so long since she had heard it in its entirety that she was not sure herself of all the proper lines. On a social call to her friend Prudence Messenger, she once compared the situation to a stick of wood being whittled down by a sharp blade and wondered how small it might at last become. Prue, always with a puckish temperament, without a moment's hesitation suggested, "Lord, good pork. Amen."

As was the custom of the house, the kitchen became entirely silent save for the clanking and clattering of utensils. Each family member observed nothing but their plates staring at them with a singular intensity. Mary, in exasperation, loudly raised the question, "So, we are dining with the swine now?" When the collective stomachs were sated sufficiently that the angry gurgles were tamed, snippets of conversation began to drift across the table.

John finally broke his silence, mused that the sorrel mare was in season. "We should give some thought to a profitable breeding."

Stephen and John Jr., seated next to one another, exchanged sly grins. Savoring their secret knowledge, they sat silently in ostentatious innocence until their father, in mock casualness, put the question, "There is a droll tale to tell, if I'm not mistaken. And good news as well?"

Young John could no longer hold in the news and blurted out in a rush, "Abijah's prize stallion went astray last night and—"

Stephen finished his brother's thought, "And came for a visit! And did his work to a fare-thee-well. And we need not even pay for the jump! I hear he gets ten shillings for each frolic."

John pondered this unexpected good fortune for a moment and asked, "Were you able to corral the stallion?"

His son shook his head sadly and admitted, "No, he was off before we realized the possibility."

"Too bad," their father muttered. "We might have charged Abijah a few pence for board."

His wife, listening to the conversation, turned to her husband with a broad smile. "Yes, John, why poke him in the eye only once when you have the chance for a second go!" The entire family laughed aloud. Such small triumphs were rare enough that they were greatly treasured.

John lapsed into concentration with his extended index finger tapping gently against his pursed lips. Abruptly, he turned to his older sons and, with that same finger tapping the end of his nose, instructed them, "When you're at the tavern next, tell the tale and make great sport of it."

"Abijah Steele will be sour about it," was Stephen's quick response.

"When is he ever not? If he takes offense now, he cannot deny the bloodline later. The foal may fetch more than the dame. But take care that Abijah is not at the inn during the telling." John explained to his puzzled sons that, "The cut will be all the sharper if delivered by more than one source and friends."

"They are to be sold, then?" inquired Stephen.

"When the crop is sold, the accounts settled, and provisions laid by. Use your best judgment. We'll have greater need of a brace of oxen than spare horses." After a brief pause, he continued, "When the crop is well set, consider selling it standing."

Young John immediately cautioned, "We'll take a loss."

With a peculiar grin that nearly always foretold clever reasoning, his father explained, "Perhaps not. The contract holds that we may stay until the end of the harvest. The new owner may pay well to be rid of us earlier."

Turning to her oldest daughter and changing the subject, Mary casually inquired, "Where has young Isaac been keeping lately? It's been a while since he was at the door last."

After a pause, Elizabeth admitted bitterly, "With Ruhamah Payne." The table went eerily quiet, not even the metal utensils dared speak. This was very hazardous thin ice that required careful thought before testing.

Finally, David took the plunge. "Well, Beth, don't fret, you know how to weave! That's all a thornback needs."

The tension suddenly broken, the room erupted into laughter. The gaiety swept across the table, and even their father, at the head of the table, chuckled. His face was impassive, but his shoulders shook and telltale mirth danced across his eyes. Mary backhanded David across the back of his head with such force that his smiling face nearly plunged into the corn mush.

"David Noble! How dare you. How dare you compare your sister to a spiny little fish that's spit out! Don't mind them, Elizabeth. You have many fine and true points. You'll make a very good match with the right lad."

Suddenly young Mary brightened as if recalling a droll tidbit and blurted out, "Patience delivered her son yesterday."

Her mother, collecting the wooden dishes, shook her head while pensively observing, "And only four months wed."

Young Mary, in a theatrical tone of voice, declared, "It was a miracle!" Raising her arms up as if beseeching heaven, she went on, "It was truly a vouchsafe miracle of the age."

Her mother, already out of sorts from David's teasing, turned from her cleaning, and in the thin, brittle tone that never failed to invoke fear from the entire family, cautioned her daughter, "Mary, take care, you are treading into impiety." With those few words, the soft tittering ceased.

Still removing some burnt residue from the pan, she turned to her husband and wondered, "Do you suppose that she'll be brought before the court for . . . ?"

When she hesitated for merely an instant, her namesake blurted out in a loud voice, "For fornication!" The girl instantly realized that she was in grave danger of poking the hornet's nest once too often. She buried her face in the remains of the breakfast, avoiding eye contact with her mother. The expected cuff to the back of her head never came. Her mother was far too preoccupied with something else.

Shaking his head, her husband doubted it would come to that. "I believe that Justice Ashbel will close his eyes to the matter since he and Phoebe . . ." Becoming silent, his smile alone finished his thoughts with far more eloquence than words ever could.

In a sudden rush, the memories of those days so long past flooded back into Mary's thoughts. As if in a trance, she inspected all the dusty details with newfound fondness. She was consulting a long-lost book squirreled away on a shelf and not referenced for years. "I had forgotten all about that."

Young David, following his parents' cryptic conversation, tried to puzzle out the story. He was quite sure that it was a good one. Turning to her brother, Mary leaned over as she whispered in his ear, "Really? Really?" His face brightened. Mary, watching that her mother was not listening, whispered softly, "Oh yes, in their younger days they rogered each other like rabid minks! They were the talk of the village."

David was amused and somehow quite satisfied that Ashbel, in spite of his misdemeanors, was now dispensing the proper courtly remedies. If the grave justice had come up in status despite various faults, then David might also, contrary to Mother's finger-wagging warnings.

Sarah said nothing throughout the clamor and clatter of breakfast. She had little interest in the gossip and banter of the table but was absorbed in carefully examining every detail, however minute, of her latest sweat dream. She was convinced, totally without reason, that if every dream was studied and compared to the others before, an answer, a meaning, would present itself.

Confiding these notions to her mother proved a mistake. All it got her was a scolding to put down this type of heathen thinking. She might as well consult oracles or seers or fortune tellers. God's guidance and grace was the only true answer. As much as Sarah revered her mother's judgment, she had doubts in this case.

While Sarah paid little heed to the usual early-morning nonsense, she detected a certain brittleness between her father and mother this morning. It looked calm and placid, but the surface was made of the thinnest crust. They must have had words the night before. The girls were all privy to their evening disagreements. The daughters' bedroom was directly above their parents' bedchamber after all, and only a layer of floor planks separated the two rooms. As the floorboards dried out toward winter, the cracks between the planks opened wide enough that a gentle shower of dust filtered down to the room below.

They might giggle at their parents' spates and equally as well pull the quilts up over their ears to muffle their more private sounds. Sometimes the words were quiet and compressed, spit out with an ominous hissing tone. In such cases, the following mornings were quiet with little of the accustomed chatter between them. Sarah knew that there was a serious disagreement the night before, even though she was fast asleep. Mostly, the issue was sorted out between them over breakfast, often with a family announcement, but rarely the boil was left unattended until a suitable private moment.

• • •

Carefully trimming a moldy spot from a slab of cheese, Sarah watched her father intently for the expected announcement. The cheese was luxuriantly furry, and while digging out the green and orange mold, she was startled to hear Father's voice. "I've decided to take Sarah with me when I travel on ahead to our land division in the Connecticut colony."

John spoke slowly and with exaggerated enunciation. This was often his practice when he had made up his mind about something and would brook no further argument. Mary was silent, though her opinion was perfectly expressed by her energetic scrubbing of the greasy spyder still scorching hot from the bacon frying. David leaned back and smiled at his brothers in triumph. Save for lacing his fingers together and cracking his knuckles, "I told you so" was his only comment.

Daughter Mary sat, her hands clutching the table, as her face turned the brightest scarlet. Her very ears throbbed with the heat of mortification. She could scarcely credit that her father had chosen Sarah, one of the most hapless creatures that God had ever created. What was he thinking to pass her over so? Why did he do this to her! All her carefully considered plans of accomplishment were melting away. Mary could never prove her worth now.

To suggest that Sarah reacted quietly did not even rise to the level of a half-truth. Her slender body was entirely frozen. Years later, her siblings argued over whether she had even blinked. As immobile as a stone statue, they said. Sarah was as powerless as one bewitched. She was conscious of the room and her family, but the conversations were far away and distant. Disembodied, she floated above the room, which receded, becoming smaller, and presently she was a mere observer, not party to events. She was intrigued that all the conversations appeared to be so far away. The effort to speak seemed futile, her voice being so distant that she could scarcely make out her own words. This drift state was never fearful or unpleasant. Rather, it was soft and soothing. At times, when she was in a nervous state, she might nearly be able summon the sensation at will.

Sarah was barely conscious of her name being called, then once again more loudly. Her trance was shattered suddenly by her mother's commanding voice. "Sarah, cease your idyll and fetch a pail of milk."

Startled into consciousness, she was suddenly aware that all her siblings were about their business and that her parents were staring at her with a mixture of alarm and resignation. Dashing for the door, Sarah was nearly outside before she stopped and awkwardly turned to collect the bucket. As the door closed, Mother turned with a snort. "If that child mislaid her head, it would be a time before we noticed."

"John, why? You'll be taking her away from all she knows—the church, her companions, brothers and sisters, the comforts of home. And me!"

"This is not about any of those things. She has a need."

"But the heathens, John! You saw how addled the mere mention of the journey made her. I fear that she will lose her senses altogether."

"Mary, the world has many parts."

She stared into space while pacing, unconsciously kneading David's greasy napkin. Suddenly turning, she said, "John, what I fear most is that we lose her completely. The minister has long cautioned against the siren songs that darkness sings. So many of Deerfield's children were lured away from the path and became savages. Even the minister's dear daughter Eunice has become one of them. Sarah's thinking is so awry at times that I fear for our girl's soul."

John listened attentively, carefully tamping the shreds of tobacco into a well-worn clay pipe. It was once snow white with a long stem. Various mishaps gradually shortened the stem, and many burns as well as greasy fingers had long since sullied the purity of the bowl. Cinching his leather tobacco pouch tight, he rose and retrieved a small flaming fag from the fireplace to kindle his pipe.

John, as long as Mary knew him, was always a man of careful, thoughtful movements. Each footfall and gesture seemed deliberate and measured. When deep in thought, his movements became almost delicately artful. Through a cloud of pungent smoke, the pipe stem in his hand looped and coursed gracefully through the air as a brush might trace an imaginary portrait.

"Mary, of all the people I've ever known, you above all others should be able to harbor the proper faith." Long since, she had realized all the signs of a lost cause when he had made up his mind and replied with affable vagaries. It was all set.

"You are leaving Stephen to settle our affairs here? Why not young John? He is the elder."

"Stephen has the better head." This casual remark unexpectedly inflamed a long-endured niggling sore that never would heal. Just when it seemed skinned over, it was rubbed raw anew by some trifling event. Like a barnyard fowl constantly worrying a minor wound, increasing it by degrees.

"And I do not! I once had my own book credit accounts . . . well managed. In my own name, I traded in cloth and fancy lace goods. I had bills of hand and even demand notes. Even now, I do not need a reckoner book to tally sums. But the moment I wed, all that faded like an echo, and I became a mere feme covert. Even now, after so many years, when I enter Aaron's store, I can sense him making a mental tally if the purchases might meet with your approval."

With her ire now past a simmer, she wagged her finger in his face and threw out a question that was more nearly a challenge. "Do you ever consider why widows of sudden means rarely remarry? Everything is lost before the sound of the 'I do' fades!"

This was an old rancor. Mary was a sensible wife in most cases but occasionally went off track in her purchases. Of course, she had privileges at Austin's store like every other town goodwife, but prudently she was subject to limits. The exact amount was flexible depending on the need.

Mary rose into a towering rage when she first realized that the merchant Aaron was also an arbiter of her spending. Over the years, this was an issue that, by unspoken agreement, they both carefully treaded around. John clearly remembered her final question that she put to him in a quite disarming, nearly sweet voice, "So, John, how many masters do I have?"

Often, he found that judicious temporizing solved many a thorny point. Put off for a sufficient time and deftly avoided, they might agreeably disappear on their own. Unfortunately, this was not one of those times. With only a nod to Mother, he gathered his coat and left, closing the door quietly on his way out.

• • •

THE SEASONING

Deep in thought with a milk pail in hand, Sarah slowly shuffled toward the barn, trying to make sense of her vision. She'd had them on numerous occasions in the past but never as intense as this morning. At first, she was alarmed and fought them, trying to claw her way back. But now they were a pleasant escape from troubles. All her fears, for a blissfully short time, were washed away. They must have meaning, she told herself. Surely, they were a portent, but the answer to the riddle was always lacking.

Sarah never confided in anyone, not even Elizabeth, about these spells. They were far too private. As well, she feared that her family would judge her as drifting into an addled state. Sister Mary, with her sly grin, would doubtless imagine a schedule where Sarah would be parceled out to various relations in turn when her wits were lost.

Sarah scuffed along to the cow barn as was her wont. Her mother often scolded her for not lifting her feet when she walked. And, in truth, Sarah did indeed cause her shoes much unneeded mischief. In exasperation one evening at dinner, her mother complained of the continuing cost of Sarah's footwear and curtly ordered her to "take big steps!" when walking. The amusement, dying down, was followed by various thoughts if this might really work. David mused that the family might cause quite a sensation all striding together into the Meeting House in their "stepping over puddles" gaits.

Entering the barn, Sarah carefully positioned the stool and pail near the cow's bag. The milch cow, expecting her, turned and bellowed in complaint of her sore udder. With a pitchfork, the girl shoveled several forks of hay to the elderly animal. Long past her milk-producing prime, Sarah's father was even now deciding if the cow was worth her keep. The next year would probably have her as barrels of salted meat.

A slight rustle in the piled hay, and there was a quick stab with the fork. The center tine struck home. Sarah carried the rodent still impaled on the fork to a small window and shook it off the tine into a large dung heap.

This particular cow was a "kicker," known for being jittery during milking and very likely to lash out with a swift hoof. The tiniest provocation, a clink of metal, a loud voice, or a slamming door could set her off. Sarah stroked the beast's head as it ate the timothy hay and slowly, quietly mounted the stool and positioned the pail.

Sitting far back on the stool to avoid a maiming blow, she gingerly clutched a teat in each hand. This was a stage when the old cow would usually react. With the first rhythmic pulls and squeezes, she turned, still chewing hay, to decide if all was well. When there was no response, Sarah quickened her pace and rested her forehead against the broad, warm flank. Presently, for comfort, she pressed her left cheek hard to the flank and worked out her plan.

Mother would be approached first. Sarah would stress the danger of the journey and her fears. This was not an untruth. Not even a partial truth. The trek presented certain dangers that even her father admitted. And thinking too deeply on the ordeal raised little bumps over her body. She would fan her mother's fears about the Indians. This was the best avenue.

Father, however, was rarely swayed by timid thoughts and might need convincing that she would not be suitable. Sarah would convince him that another of her siblings would serve his purposes better. Mary was smart, cleverly sly about bending people to do what she wanted, and expert in almost everything of worth. With a stab of jealousy, she recalled Mother referring to Mary with pride as "capability herself."

As almost an afterthought, she wondered if David might be put forward as an alternate possibility. Nothing came to mind immediately. She realized some considerable artful crafting was required to put forth an argument in favor of David. He was so lightheartedly wayward that holding a cross thought against him was beyond any hope. Perhaps that was the key. The journey would put steel into his person and turn his spirit to a more somber, manly bent.

For a full eight days, Sarah practiced and refined her oration. Discarding this word or that as too strong or unsuitable, she treated the weary old milch cow every morning to the latest refinements honed the night before in the featherbed. The large brown bovine eyes stared dully ahead despite the rolling improvements to her words. Sarah did notice that any sudden loud declamation might cause a hind foot to jerk in readiness for a strike. At last, she was ready, confident that her arguments were unassailable.

• • •

THE SEASONING

There are days in May, not many, that are perfection itself. The soft, warm breezes promise an easing of winter's gray grip, and the sun seems gloriously awake after its long sleep. Perhaps it was this gift that gave her confidence to slip quietly into the kitchen.

Her mother was hunched over a bread tub rhythmically kneading the week's batch of dough. The wooden tub, carved from a single short split log, had sloped basin-like sides, making it convenient to roll the dough back and forth. Sensing her daughter's presence, Mary turned, holding her sticky flour-incrusted hands apart.

It is well known that sticky fingers automatically cause the nose to itch, and without any thought, she relieved the annoyance. Sarah nearly giggled at her mother's flour-smudged nose and left cheek. It was such a small thing, really, something that Sarah had seen many times, but this time she was totally put off her pace. All the words that she had so carefully practiced in the cow barn drained away as though through a colander.

"Yes, what do you want, Sarah?"

"Mother, I am uneasy about the soon journey. The reason is lost to me."

Mary had expected this interview or one much like it. She was surprised by the delay, however, expecting her daughter to raise an immediate alarm. She became curious, believing that Sarah was now hatching an ornate fancy to avoid the decision.

"Your father feels it is for the best, but I, too, am concerned. A turning in the road. It will be a changeling experience for you, surely. But your father is clever about such things and will undertake it well. He knows the best of it."

Sarah, all the air pressed suddenly out of her, confessed, "I fear that my dreams will be all the worse for it." This was an argument she never shared with the old cow, but in the end, it was the crux.

Her mother cautioned, "Often, we are bolstered by such trying times. Fears faced are often calmed. The grace of God will always watch over you both."

Sarah tried to collect her wits to frame a reply, but there were no thoughts. Her mind was dry of ideas. Nodding, she turned and slowly opened the door.

Mary did not even watch Sarah leave before she turned to continue working the dough. Hefting the shiny mass, she slammed it down into the tub, mauling and abusing it with a ferocious vigor as she applied the final turn. A last hurl, and both fists were buried in the dough.

She had spoken her husband's words just as surely as if they were copied down. She could not argue with the clarity of his thinking, but a greater part of her was gripped by an old, longtime fear. Leaning over the tub, her fists still buried in the dough, she conjured up a prayer. "I hope you are right, John Noble."

Sarah stood a few paces from the work barn, trying to decide if she should take the case to her father next, which was part of her original plan. Dismayed nearly to tears over her mother's response, it all seemed so futile. She had counted on her mother as a natural advocate, and yet her mother had strangely tempered her fears. Sarah stood in front of the barn for some time, trying to collect and organize the remaining shards of her carefully crafted appeal. Like one might gather up bits of a broken vase, she wondered if there was still a chance to mend.

With a deep breath, she slowly approached the barn, fists clenched. John was thoughtfully organizing categories of necessities he would take with him when he traveled light to the south. A second group would follow with the entire family later. The last were tools not needed or too bulky to ferry south. These would be gradually sold off and, with some luck, would help cover the cost of the large four-wheeled wagon that would transport the family to the new home lot.

The price paid had been agreeable. It was a well-used machine, even though somewhat elderly. John was wary in dealing with the jobber, Silas Coe. For a second time, he made a mental note to warn Stephen to check the left rear wheel before he took possession. Silas had promised to replace the two damaged spokes as part of the cost. Silas was a man of sharp practices who needed close watching. No one had ever accused Silas of dishonesty, yet to a man cautioned a careful eye.

John had six promissory notes from five different local hands for small amounts in his possession. But, when word spread of the family's imminent departure, his creditors would surely rush to redeem his own notes of hand before they were gone. He was quite certain that he might tender his notes to Aaron Austin in exchange for a debt swap. Aaron would square up all the sums. And perhaps there might be a plus on the book.

He was aware of Sarah's approach but made no recognition. Like his wife, he was expecting Sarah's elaborate complaint. As was his longtime practice, he preferred initial silence, gaining the upper hand, while leaving the other party to reveal their cards first. Sarah's line of thought, while often convoluted, was always well reasoned. He was surprised by her tentative, fumbling start.

"Father, I believe that David would be of more use to you at Weatanock." Even at this late stage, the family used the Indian name as John knew it. As yet, they had no clear knowledge of the town's proper future name.

With scarcely a pause, he said, "Yes, he would, but you shall go."

"Or Mary, she's such a clever girl." Her earnest tone drifted into pleading. "Perhaps, or Elizabeth?"

Softly, he added, "The nub here is not utility, is it, but fear?"

"I am unready," pleaded Sarah.

"Less so than you think. Sarah, you are endowed with all the proper parts, all the needed bits. Complete the puzzle. You must step out from childhood. You are not my small wren any longer."

That night, cosseted in the featherbed between Elizabeth and Mary, Sarah dissected the disastrous events of the day. Perhaps it was a mistake to directly confront her father after her mother's dismissal. Maybe she could have conjured up another speech with more success. But done was done, and nothing was to be undone.

She glanced at Elizabeth's calm face. She was truly in the slumber of the blessed. To Sarah's left, Mary was moaning softly, her mouth working as if to speak, her eyebrows in constant frowning movement. She was dreaming. All Mary's dreams seemed contested. Sarah wondered whether she remembered any of them. At least they didn't wake her with a screaming start. Sarah wondered if Mary had her own night hags.

Sarah dozed off while designing a plan to change her father's mind. There was still time, after all, before the departure, and she took comfort in the fact that he had not uttered the dreaded, "I'll think upon it."

∙ ∙ ∙

The weeks of increasingly warm weather softened and mellowed the anxiety of the decision. It was still there nestled in the pit of Sarah's stomach, its lair, sly and crafty, just waiting for a trigger, a prick, to awaken. It was always an inconsequential thing, a word or look that roused the *fear* again. Watching their daughter, the Nobles became increasingly confident that the worst was behind them.

Many years in the future, Sarah would recall, quite improbably, that the incident took place on a Saturday morning. She had lately taken to tidying up memories of her childhood, tucking in or folding over outlier details. Elizabeth nearly always seemed to remember the same stories from a different angle. Mary, becoming more with age what she was as a girl, snorted that Sarah was conjuring up details to make a more pleasing effect.

Sarah firmly avowed that the truth of it occurred on that warm pre-Sabbath day. Skimming off the unspent charcoal bits floating atop a murky bucket of water, she peered in, looking for the telltale crystals in the bottom. She was allotted this unskilled task ever since she could recall. It was simplicity itself: ten parts water, one part wood ash, mixed together and allowed a day to "work." When the lye crystals settled to the bottom, the remaining liquid was decanted into a kettle to be reduced over the fire to a powdery bread leavener: pearl ash. She had done this so often that she scarcely paid any heed to the motions. It was as second nature to her as carding wool.

Her mother was sitting in her favorite chair, silently mending stockings. The chair was amongst martyred Grandmother's meager belongings. In truth, Mary didn't much care for the color, as she often explained to visiting friends. It was coated in a most curious green that brought to mind the insides of caterpillars. Deerfield had a known fancy for such colors. Even so, she was quite taken aback when she first saw a substantial dwelling house on the main street of Deerfield completely painted yellow.

Newly arrived visitors were often struck by the feet of the chair. Instead of standing fore square on the floor, they were tenoned into two curved lengths of wood resembling the rails on a sleigh. Indeed, John called it her "sleigh chair." The maker or source of this sleighing chair was never known.

Grandmother professed different stories depending on the importance of the company she cared to impress.

For Sarah's mother, it was a soothing respite, particularly when she was engaged in tasks of no great thought. During solitary moments, lost in the rhythmic cadence of her feet, she might relive the past reveries of her girlhood, sailing to the fabulous mythical realm of Prester John, that Christian king of exciting legend. But, most of all, the chair was distinctive and hers alone.

Hearing the splash of the liquid decanting into the kettle, she raised her eyes and cautioned, "Sarah, mind the lees. We want bread, not soap!" Facing away from her mother, Sarah rolled her eyes and made pantomime faces mimicking Mother's hectoring expressions. In the years since, the coming mishap became something of a favorite family tale to be brushed up and trotted out to regale dinner companions. She despaired of ever moving beyond it.

Nestling the well-charred kettle into the embers, Sarah spoke abruptly to her mother. She hadn't intended to ask the question. After rehearsing the point many times during sleepless nights, she knew, of course, what the response would be. Despite her resolve of silence, it burst out on its own like a loud passage of wind at a Sabbath meeting.

"Mother, are Indians happy like us?" She had fully expected annoyance. Her mother was one who had an opinion about most things and was rarely at the loss to offer them. And they were ready at hand. Surprisingly, her mother looked puzzled at first, followed by an unusual thoughtful quiet. Finally shaking her head, dismissing the notion as wholly unprofitable, she explained curtly, "I don't have time for this nonsense. Don't you have things to attend?"

The moment had passed, and Sarah slowly stepped into the sunny dooryard. The door didn't latch properly and gradually swung open again, bathing Mary in morning sunlight. She would have to speak to John about it. The door moved in its track when the ground froze up and moved again after the spring thaw. Winter and spring, the latch was needing readjusting.

Mary relished the sunlight, particularly after the hard season, but she could not abide the wandering animals. Basking in the warmth, she turned Sarah's fanciful notion over and over in her mind. By degrees, it became more unsettling, though the reason was dark to her. At length, she wanted to put it aside and did so with a shake of her head and a nearly silent observation, "What a queer notion."

•••

Like most New England farms, the Noble homestead was comprised of a number of buildings, generically referred to as "houses," mostly modest in size, devoted to specialized uses. There was the dwelling house, the cow house, horse house, and perhaps swine house. On that mild morning, John was in a structure simply called the barn. It was a repository of tools and equipment, and a workshop. All the edged tools were laid out, and he was applying a sharp hone to each in turn. He intended that everything should be in perfect order before he left.

Nearby was a contraption that he had been working on for some time. Originally a light two-wheeled cart, he had extended the bed and added a canvas hood against the weather. They needed to travel light to avoid overtaxing the horse along the way.

Even absorbed in his work, John knew Sarah was nearby. He heard her long before she came into view. The scuffling footfalls were a sign that her errand was troublesome and reluctant. Quietly, she perched on an upended drum of oak that served him as a workbench and watched as the broadax received a honed edge. These unspoken times were not unusual. It was in character for Sarah to sit nearby for long periods without a word passing between them only to suddenly rise and leave.

Pausing, he said, "You present a troubled countenance."

"Father, are Indians happy and sad like us?"

The soothing rhythm of the stone slowed as John chose careful words. "They are happy and sad in many ways like us, and different in equal measure. They rejoice in their families and grieve the losses. A fall day and a good harvest or hunt are equally welcome."

"And the differences?"

"The loss of the lightly touched world of their memories. We tame what God presents; they accept what is."

"But are we not the chosen of the Lord?" He said not a word but stared her fully in the face and smiled. Sarah knew immediately that this was not the time for the answer, and it would come later in good time.

CHAPTER III

May 18, 1707

The Sabbath service was the social highlight of the week, lasting the better part of the entire day. The morning and afternoon sessions were split by a long noon pause. During this interval, the midday meal was prepared. If families lived close to the Meeting House, they might retire to their residences. Families from distant farms usually nestled in with friends near the Meeting House. Some few who could afford it erected Sabbath day houses nearby. Lightly built, they provided a warmer place to cook the midday meal and to socialize.

But most of all, this break in the religious services was a time for socializing. The entire town, excepting suspicious dissenters, came together to renew old ties, visit and gossip with friends, and consummate financial arrangements. In strict observance, no unnecessary work was allowed, but inevitably land was traded, horses sold, and victuals purchased. The minister's ban on Sabbath day work was often ineffective. Business makes its own time. If the shoals of children, newly released from the minister's grip, did not entirely respect the sanctity of the day, their shrieking antics were grudgingly accepted as inevitable.

The Meeting House itself was not much different in its particulars on the outside from the many private dwellings that surrounded it, except perhaps for its size and the more numerous windows. Eschewing the use of candles, it was lit only by daylight. The use of candles, besides the expense, raised theological issues: too close to the practice of the bishop of Rome. The town's supply of the militia's gunpowder stored in a nearby closet also argued against any open flames.

The Meeting House had recently received, after a long delay, window glass for all but the south side. Funds were short, and the sunny side would have to wait. The clapboards were as yet unpainted, but discussions were in hand to color the building. The color white was already voted down. Lead white, the pigment, was dearer than the society was willing to bear. The search continued for a more appropriate and cheaper alternative.

A sexton, mustering up the suitable gravitas, stood at the Meeting House door ringing a handheld bell to summon the latecomers. The interior was a large, open space filled with rows of backed benches facing an ornate pulpit. The pulpit towered over the space, a figurehead of sanctity.

The congregation had a near reverence for the spoken word, the sermon. Listening avidly to the minister's long orations, a turn of phrase or telling metaphor would be a common point of conversation for the coming week.

While the benches might be identical, the seating was not random, and was a strictly controlled expression of hierarchy. The educated, the well-to-do, and those in greatest esteem were seated closest to the pulpit. It was commonly accepted that as a family improved their situation year by year, the seating committee would move them nearer the pulpit. The Nobles were seated in the middling rows.

At the last Society meeting, the contentious issue of appointing a committee to reseat the Meeting House was discussed. As longtime residents left or died, the house needed reseating at times to more fully reflect the social standing of the congregation. Newcomers also expected suitable accommodations reflecting their worth. As families came up in the world, it was proper that these changes should be reflected by being seated closer to the pulpit. A viewer gazing down from the gallery was presented with a map of the social order of the town's families. The selection of the seating committee was approached warily, rather like gingerly poking a dangerous animal to make sure that it was certainly dead. Many enmities were stoked and friendships lost by the decisions of the committee.

At that meeting, Dr. Brinsmaid proposed that the rows of benches be pulled up and replaced by permanent pews. With growing enthusiasm, he unfurled a large chart of the Meeting House with discrete pews of various sizes limned in. The many smaller cubicles with awkward access were commonly referred to as "eel pots." Only in the back of the hall would the benches remain. As part of his proposal, he suggested that the pews be sold to families, allowing them to be passed down as property from generation to generation. The resulting windfall might be used to finish and beautify the Meeting House.

The notion was not accepted by John, who viewed it as an omen of the future. Perhaps not soon, but in time, the tangible regard the town might award his family, moving them closer to the pulpit, would disappear. The path forward would be blocked by a fortress of oaken pews. Initially, John had questioned his decision to move south. But Brinsmaid's proposal, which clearly would stir up the town for years, clarified his feelings.

It was Mary who had broken the news of the seating committee's decision to John. Her circle of friends knew the gist of any meeting even before the clerk recorded it in his leather book. The import was so obvious to them both that no discussion was needed. Mary's misgivings about the move became instead sad resignation.

The chattering of the congregation rebounded off the bare walls, making conversation quite impossible unless the speaker leaned into the listener. The hall fell silent at the entrance of the minister in full regalia, the space taking on a reverent sanctity with his mere presence. Mounting the ornate curving staircase to the towering speaker's platform, Reverend Edwards scanned the congregation with silent gravity. Starting with a low, near musical voice, he began:

"*Then Jesus was led up of the spirit into the wilderness to be tempted of the Devil. Matthew 4, verse 1. The wilderness is the realm of the Devil. Jesus teaches this in this passage. Creatures of darkness, ravening beasts, and the ungodly prowl this land. Temptation is at every hand: cunning, smiling and soothing, and agreeable to the senses. Like the purring cat on the hearth, toying gently with its mouse, evil is biding its time until our destruction. When we turn from the path, God withdraws his protective hand. Our journey to salvation must pass over the cauldron of Hell. The Bridge over the abyss is slight, mere threads of yarn upheld only by the hand of God. When your faith falters or is lost . . ."*

The minister's voice was rising nearly imperceptibly in intensity as the sermon unfolded. His arms splayed out suddenly, startling his listeners, and he began to sway back and forth from side to side. As if mesmerized, the congregation's bodies began to mimic his motions.

"*The bridge starts to sway . . . to and fro. Eternal death is at hand.*"

Sarah sat with hands clenched into tight fists as the crescendo of the sermon faded from her senses. All the soaring words and wailing moans were now a faint drone. Retreating into herself, she despaired. *He is addressing me, surely. Can I follow the true path being away from all I know?*

Sarah's parents sat side by side on their allotted pew, the sons on their father's right, the daughters arranged on their mother's left by seniority. She caught only momentary glimpses of her brothers. Mother sat rigidly erect, as if frozen, but with tears flowing in rivulets down her cheeks, puddling and soaking her collar. Elizabeth, covering her bowed face with both hands, was unrevealing. Mary was entirely impassive as if immune to the truths of the sermon.

Sarah wondered if sister Mary's hooded eyes were telling enough to attract the attentions of the prowling church wardens with their twitching staffs. They were known to nudge awake drowsing sleepers and sharply rap the ankles of miscreant little boys with their rods. Sarah didn't suppose, however, that they would wade into their family row to bring Mary about. But the very thought of the possibility was of some comfort.

Sarah's father listened to the sermon with interest, his eyebrows responding to the minister's soaring eloquence. *He is truly unafraid! He shall be my guiding star. His judgment is true.* She was stunned when he only partially stifled a yawn. *He does not credit the words! He does not believe!*

The thunderous finale to the sermon awoke her from her reverie.

". . . you will be consumed in the hellfire. Our earthly pain ends in a cure or our death. The searing agony of Hell is infinitely worse. There is no end. There is no time. We are tormented in an endless present. Our flesh sears and chars. Our eyes steam and bulge. Our entrails boil. There is no respite, no succor."

The raft of hymns that followed didn't cheer Sarah as was customary. The singing nearly always gave her hope and a lightness of spirit. But not on this bright Sunday. The line of one of her most favorite of psalms, "The Lord is close to the brokenhearted and saves those who are crushed in spirit," rolled off her tongue dry, without taste. Furious images raced unbidden and uncontrolled through her mind. Multiple arcs of a tomahawk followed by loud cracks. The blade becomes bloody. Disembodied screams. A child is snatched from the mother by a shadow.

• • •

The evening meal was as noisy and boisterous as usual. The dire warnings of the morning were put aside, carefully locked away for some future inspection. Only later in bed did the emerging pattern of future events start to make sense to Sarah. Like a fancy bit of cloth on a loom, the true design only gradually becomes clear as more is woven. She was to be tested. The minister avowed that all would be tested in turn. And it was clear to her that her ordeal was in sight.

• • •

The following day, John was bitterly blaming himself for the delay in departure. He had been inattentive for too long in tidying up the loose threads of his affairs. They should have long since been on the road.

The alterations to the two-wheeled cart, extending the bed, caused eccentric handling and balance. Instead of resting lightly on the shaft tips while unhitched, it canted backward, resting on the bed gate. After some thought, he altered the shaft rest and positioned it under the bed. As he hitched up the mare, he took some consolation that the changes worked to his satisfaction.

But John had spent too great a time on these niggling tasks. It was careless inattention. On the periphery of his vision, he spied Sarah trudging across the door yard with a bushel keg of wood ashes. She was a slight girl but wiry and well able to tote her share. Seeing the rig set to go, she gave him a puzzled expression.

"Off to Austin's for supplies." Sarah's face brightened. After a pause, her father nodded. He was in a bilious mood this morning, and Sarah, if not always calming company, was usually distracting. Instantly, she dropped the pail and sped toward the cart, even taking the great strides that Mother suggested.

Wriggling around in the seat excitedly, she watched as her father shook his head while watching the overturned pail slowly rolling down the slight incline toward the barn. With only the protests of the seat springs audible, she dismounted and retrieved the pail. Scooping up the spilled ashes, she deposited them in the barrel and returned the lid. She paused only a few times to brush the ash off her dress and shoes before mounting the cart.

With a deft twitch of the reins, the cart pitched forward. He was quiet on the journey to the store. Assuming that he was annoyed at the spilled ash, Sarah decided to mouth the words herself that she knew were surely coming.

"Mind the task at hand. Keep the eyes on the purpose. Finish one step before starting another."

He turned and looked at her for a moment. While he did not smile, his eyes were less cloudy. "Wise words to follow." But they talked sparingly and only of trifles on the way to Austin's.

Austin's mercantile business was operated from a dwelling house and a later addition tucked along the narrow end. A separate work area was about thirty feet away. The general store offered nearly everything needed for most households. Of particular note were bolts of fine cloth leaning against the parlor wall. Elegant varieties of quality fabrics, some patterned, were one of Austin's specialties. Invariably, customers entering the shop, before all else, would inspect the fabrics and wistfully stroke the soft cloth. Above the yellow-painted door, the sole portion of the building colored, a large sign proclaimed:

PETER J. O'BRIEN

AUSTIN GENERAL STORE
JOBBING AND UNDERTAKING

Aaron Austin had three strapping sons whom he rented or jobbed out to neighbors for various tasks. The lads might hay, pull stumps, or deliver wood according to customer whims. Recently Austin had taken to undertaking the raising of barns.

In the center of the sign, the painter had added a fanciful rampant creature. It was a most curious beast. Ever since its installation, there were shifting schools of thought as to just what it was. Did it have four legs, or was there a fifth hidden by the tail? Did the snarling face threaten with fangs or tusks? The forked tongue further deepened the mystery. Aaron never confessed his opinion, leaving the mystery to serve as his lucky business talisman. Sarah didn't even glance at the sign as they entered the store. She had long ago dismissed it as an "impossible beast."

Although the store and dwelling were little more than a few hundred paces from the Meeting House, Aaron was wary of inviting neighbors to relax and warm up between Sabbath sessions. According to a friend's telling, the minister was overheard wondering out loud if forbidden business was being transacted there on the Lord's Day.

The store's interior was overflowing with nearly every desire, both luxurious and homely, that local families might possibly imagine. All stacked or shelved in immaculate order, they were viewed with near reverence. The counter was twelve feet long and wide enough that a bolt of cloth could easily be unrolled for inspection.

After a buying trip to a Dutch merchant on the great river in New York, Aaron had his eldest son turn out a number of fancy chair legs. Split in half, they were glued to the front of the long counter. Arranged in patterns and painted black, Aaron fancied that his shop rivaled anything to be found in Boston or Portsmouth.

The proprietor, of middling height, was soft of form, reflecting his less strenuous profession. His face, perfectly round, was nearly always wreathed in a smile. He was affable and gracious to every soul he met, even those few he abhorred. This raised a degree of unease in some. If he was unfailingly polite and pleasant to friends and foes alike, how were his true feelings to be judged? With long association, most neighbors could discern the face of the merchant from that of the friend. The eyes seemed to sparkle the more for his friends.

Sarah, ignoring even the heavy scent of spices, made straight to the rolls of cloth.

The proprietor brightened as father and daughter entered.

"John, it has been some time. I hear that you're moving on. Are the wagging tongues truthful?" At John's nod, he continued, "I'm surprised. I thought that you were well settled here. What is your calendar?"

"Sarah and myself will leave after a fortnight or so." Clearly startled, Aaron, in a skeptical tone, asked, "Sarah?"

"Yes, Sarah. The rest will follow when our affairs here are finished, the stock and crop being sold."

"You'll be going by way of Hartford, then?" This was clearly the obvious route, well settled and as safe as possible. He casually pulled aside his tally book to record new transactions.

"No, we'll follow the Indian trails west and south along the rocky river." This was so unexpected that Aaron stared at John in silence for a few breaths to ensure that there wasn't a mishear. John finally nodded.

"But, John, I wonder if a safer route might . . ." Out of the corner of his eye, he noticed that the girl no longer stroked the silks but was drinking in every word. She was a curious child who possessed the uncanny skill of making herself near invisible when she chose. With adults forgetting that she was nearby, she often picked up bits of conversation not meant for her ears.

"I require two pounds of powder and six flints. Also, two cones of sugar." Depositing a small lidded wooden keg on the counter, he added, "Your finest flour, and, Aaron, no vermin."

Aaron reacted in mock horror, and both laughed as they recalled a droll episode of a year past. Opening the sealed keg, Mary had been besieged by a swarm of flour moths.

"Any lead? No?" With that, two pounds of powder were carefully weighed out on the steelyard and deposited into a leather pouch. Father inspected the flints and sugar cones while his purchases were added to the store daybook.

"These cones seem smaller than the last." Aaron looked up from his accounts and shrugged. With a smile, John observed, "If I didn't trust your truth, I might wonder if you didn't set your son to run them through your lathe to skim off an extra profit."

Responding in a like tone, the shopkeeper, without glancing up from his account book, explained, "Not possible. The sugar gums up the lathe blade!" John would come to miss Aaron. He gave as good as he received.

"We might reckon my account for the last time while we're here." Austin retrieved a separate volume, turned to Noble's page, and added the new charges.

"Four pounds, twelve shillings is the tariff. Bills or in kind?"

"I'll settle in bills."

"If you have any salted pork, I'll reduce it."

"No, we'll need it all."

"The bills? Connecticut, Massachusetts, or Rhode Island?" Austin greeted the response, "Rhode Island," with a deep sigh. While most colonies in New England made at least a pretense of backing their bills of credit with something tangible, Rhode Island ran her printing presses with the lascivious abandon of a shameless bawd. By solemn agreement, all the local colonies agreed to value each other's bills equally, but, in practice, each merchant gave them his own estimated worth.

The quick recalculation yielded a new sum of five pounds, three shillings. John carefully and laboriously checked the arithmetic, noting Mary's charges. After a satisfied nod, he carefully amended the page with a signature, date, and final reckoning notation. "Done!" Slowly, he fished out a small wad of Rhode Island notes and tallied up the tattered bills on the counter, shuffling through the entire pack to satisfy the final three shillings.

"I suppose I'll see the rest of that assortment before Mary and the children finally depart."

"Very likely," John confessed with a wry smile.

Sarah was entranced by a bolt of green silk, caressing it lovingly, walking away several times only to be drawn back by the hypnotic luster of the fabric. Austin noticed that Sarah was drawn to it and asked, only partially in jest,

"An excellent choice and much in demand. So, madam, how many yards do you require?"

She recognized the jest for what it was. The mere possibility was far beyond even the realm of fantasy. Responding to the tiniest speck of hope, she caught her father's eye. He nodded to a prominent sign over the counter. The ornate lettering advised:

> *LADIES AND GENTS MAY LOOK FOR LOVE*
> *BUT BUY FOR CASH IN HAND*

Sensing an opportunity, Aaron added, "John, I have a bit that's not too dear." He reached under the counter and produced an eighteen-inch strip of the very same green silk. John nodded, and Sarah snatched the fabric, bolting for the door, fearing that any delay would allow a change of mind.

"How, Aaron?"

"Madam Brinsmaid bought fifteen yards but refused to accept the end. She judged that it was soiled and frayed by my customers' idle attentions."

Abruptly, the conversation veered. "Stephen will act in my stead after I'm gone and has full right to speak for me."

Aaron, cautiously considering the possibilities, mused, "Not your eldest, then. And Mary?"

John responded slowly with exaggeratedly enunciation for emphasis, "Yes, she will be prudent."

"Yes, I understand." Aaron wondered how many hot sessions were in store for him with Mary. John had poked a hornet's nest, and others would endure the swarm. Leaving through the open door, John turned and casually informed the shopkeeper, "When Stephen comes in, inform him that he is to pay for the silk. It will be his departing gift to Sarah, as far as Mary knows." Aaron laughed at this parting shot. John did not do anything by halves.

Sarah scarcely noticed her father approaching the cart. Her newly found treasure presented so many possibilities that she was quite befuddled. She arranged the silk slip as a sash, then a belt, but finally decided that a headband would suffice until a proper hat was in hand.

• • •

In the days that followed the visit to the store, John found himself more and more disquieted by the coming migration. When a near neighbor offered a bearskin one morning, he eagerly accepted it, although he had politely refused similar gifts for some years. Long ago as a young trapper, he found the witless task of cleaning a fresh hide, carefully scrapping the fat off, a soothing respite, a time to think upon pressing problems while keeping busy. The young bear had thought to feast on spring lamb. Lean after a long winter, the fat was scant. John would rue the lack of bear fat in the coming months.

Working up the rutted pathway that was the road, a solitary figure approached, and it was only when it was a rod distant that he recognized the gaunt figure of Consider Hopkins. John's spectacles served well enough in reading the Scriptures but were of little gain when he was out and about. He would need sharp eyes on the coming journey. And he would have only Sarah. Recalling a line from Isiah, "and a child shall lead them," he shook his head.

Consider was a spare man to the point of being cadaver-like. With deeply sunken eyes and hollow cheeks, he had changed little since his youth, excepting only the loss of hair and patches of overlooked beard here and there. One Sunday, it might be in a cheek hollow, another under the chin, and yet another under the nose. The common opinion was that he had a looking glass with many spider cracks.

Consider laid up great esteem in town, however, named for having uncommon good sense and a hard head. He was tax collector twice, an office only for the brave since the incumbent was held personally to account for taxes not collected. In recent years, his age had released him from militia duty, but he never failed to toast the parched militia with a mug of cider brandy as they mustered near the tavern.

In his later years, Consider made a name for himself as a wolfer. The colony offered a handsome bounty on them if both ears were produced as proof. As was customary with some families, he was named after a perceived manly virtue. His Christian name, Consider, matched his being with the perfect fit of a pair of old shoes. His wife, Mindwell, however, was known to often stray from the virtues of her given name.

"Good morning, John. Up to a disagreeable task, I see."

"It will end up as a very agreeable travel robe, though."

"My last one became filled with vermin and stench."

"Who tanned it?" Although John certainly knew the answer unbidden.

"You may guess." Both men smiled.

Consider was uncommonly pleased about something, and that pricked John's curiosity. The old man was, after all, a refined scowler. "Are you the bearer of happy news, Consider?"

"Indeed, I am. I have a pouch filled with ears, ten in total."

"Five wolves in one hunt? How?"

"I found a den with a bitch wolf and four pups!" Carefully opening the leather sack, he shared his treasures. Peering in, John fingered the ears one by one, two large and the remainder barely a quarter of the adult size. "One of the pups was black, I see. Do you suppose that the selectman will certify all five for a bounty?"

"Why would he not?"

"Well, he might suppose that the whelps, even if weaned, would not survive the female's loss and accord you only one set of ears."

"John, you would cloud over a summer's day! But there is another matter. Are you going to the meeting?"

"Likely."

"Mindwell has worked herself into a froth over this Indian rumor . . . I myself am troubled. Do you think there is any peril?"

Running the scraper over the bearskin, John dismissed the danger with a laconic, "Slight."

At this, Consider reacted with surprise. John, of all the men he knew, was ever cautious and had, moreover, a great knowledge of Indians. Envious rumors were bandied about by people of ill will suggesting that John's youthful time with them was not always spent following godly pursuits. "How so, John?"

"Their main strengths are cunning and surprise. That would be forfeit coming so deep into settled parts." He was momentarily distracted by his sons, John Jr. and David, who were preparing to butcher a freshly taken deer. Hung up on a rack spread-eagled, this was to be young David's first solo attempt. Older brother John was there for supervision and intervention if events took a perilous turn.

Distractedly, he shouted loudly, "David, mind the business. Remember what I showed you." He had only slight hope that his commanding instructions would be heeded for long.

When his attentions returned to Consider, the old man continued, "But the takings would be greater than in the outer settlements."

"Yes, but harder won. The party would have to pass up easy fruit. With the country alarmed, they would face a warm welcome. I believe that they would be content with fewer prizes for fewer losses."

Nearby, David briefly examined the curious knife in his left hand, although he had seen its use many times. The tip of the blade was a sharp hook. Starting from the anus, he carefully opened the deer's belly, keeping the dull side of the blade inward and the sharp hooked edge outward. With slow, hesitant cuts, he gradually opened the abdomen, leaving the thoracic contents undisturbed. Finally, the large, multichambered stomach suddenly sagged out of the cavity, smooth and gray. With a triumphant grin, David waved the knife in the air, celebrating his victory.

And as his father had feared, at this point, the work went awry. Despite his brother's warnings to take some care in teasing out the viscera with the hooked blade, the younger boy started working with nearly theatrical flourishes of the knife as though it had suddenly become a saber. When Consider and John had first heard the voice, they were so puzzled that they didn't recognize it, at first, as a song. But presently, they realized that David was singing!

A fox may steal your hens, sir
A whore your health and pence, sir
Your daughter rob your chest, sir
Your wife may steal your rest, sir
A thief your . . .

This episode, embedded in family lore and doubtless richly decorated over time, maintained that, at the end of each line, David dramatically slashed at the carcass on each "sir." The sprightly air, which he savored privately away from any adult disapproval, was never concluded. At the final "sir," the stomach was cleanly slashed, the contents spurting out with force.

It is well known that smells endured for an extended time often recede from the senses. A cow's droppings, so fresh that even flies have not found it, or the steaming corner of the sty favored by swine, scarcely rise to notice when they are daily inhaled. The smell of freshly baked bread is soon lost to the baker.

The spilled gut of the deer was not only more pungent than mere barnyard odors but also very much a novelty. Both John and David, with watering eyes, clapped their hands over their mouths, attempting to hold down their gorges as they ran to the fence. Side by side, leaning over the top rail, both expelled vomit with brisk abandon. When his breath returned, John Jr. turned to the younger boy, grinning. "Well, that was quite a lark, wasn't it?"

Watching from a distance, John admitted, "I remember doing that."

"But only once," Consider added with a grin.

"Let me see how much mischief was done here."

As John walked toward the deer, Consider, in an afterthought, piped up, "Will you be at the meeting?" John nodded without turning.

• • •

A short distance away in a busy kitchen, Mary was attempting the possibly fruitless task of tutoring a neighbor's daughter in arithmetic, namely multiplication. She had assured Eleanor's father, Jacob Ensign, that any child could master the subject. Skeptically, Jacob suggested that payment for the tutoring should be governed by how well Eleanor learned. Feeling trapped by her own words, she could only agree to "see how it goes." She knew full well that the point would rise again.

Eleanor was only a few years older than young Mary and was certainly not slow but simply failed to see the need to master sums. She could add up and take away but could not be convinced that multiplication was of any use to her. Even the word itself seemed to tangle her tongue in a knot. She had taken to referring to it as "breeding sums."

Eleanor's most striking feature was her flame-red hair, always worked into complicated braids piled up on her head. In contrast, her blue eyes were as pale as her abundantly freckled skin. These freckles were, on more than one occasion, the subject of speculation amongst the Noble sons as they drifted off to sleep. What, exactly, did the parts of her speckled person look like under her shift?

Sarah and sister Mary were absent-mindedly organizing the midday meal, listening to their mother while she drilled Eleanor. The simple lunch required little effort, merely cold-boiled mutton, cheese, and bread and butter. Sarah was more particular than the rest of her family, heartily disliking the mouthfeel and taste of the fat that still clung to the sheep joint. She carefully scraped away the fat with the blade of a knife. She never understood how it could be so savory when hot and so repellent when cold. Considering how unpleasant the candles made from sheep's fat smelled, she considered it a wonderment that anyone ate it.

"Eleanor, I promised your father that I would teach you to reckon without a book. Seven nines?"

"I forget. It's so hard to recall," the girl wailed. Scrapping the joint, Sarah muttered softly, "Sixty-three," earning her mother's glare.

"Take one number at a time and work it through. One nine is itself. Two is eighteen. Move up the ladder and learn them well. Then go to another number. This is not Hebrew to wrestle with, Eleanor."

Mother propped a white-painted wooden panel up against a chair back and, with a shaped charcoal, wrote a notation: "I want you to recon two pounds, ten and four by eight." At the sound of John's voice calling her name, she rose and motioned to her daughter. "Sarah, see to this while I'm gone." Pulling up a chair, Sarah sat next to Eleanor, and both stared at the numbers: 2/10/4 x 8.

"Do you know how to start?"

Eleanor gazed at the numbers with as much comprehension as if it really were Hebrew. "It is hiding in my head."

"Remember, the little sums on the right pine to become pounds." As if a dam had suddenly broken, Eleanor brightened. "Yes, yes. The four pence breed with the eight to become thirty-two!"

With self-control, Sarah managed to bury a laugh but not a smile. "And this mob of pence?"

"They aspire to become shillings. Twenty-four of them turn into two shillings and add to the ten. The eight pence left are foundlings, poor dears." At the sound of a distant handbell, the lesson paused and Eleanor's light mood drained from her face.

"Is it a warning bell? My mother warned me of an Indian raid. Deerfield! They will murder us. Sell us to the French. Keep us as squaws forever!" Clasping the girl's hand, Sarah explained in a calm voice that she judged soothing, "Eleanor, it is merely the early call-to-meeting notice. Don't let your fears rule you."

"How do you stay so calm?" Quite curiously, her father's announcement that she would be his companion on the journey to Connecticut set Sarah's mind finally at some ease. She was not so much calmed but rather becalmed. The uncertainty was finally removed, although the storm still lurked just out of view to reappear in time. The white horse had come to her in a recent dream, but she did not awake.

Leaning forward to Eleanor, she advised in a low, conspiratorial voice, "I have a plan," prompting a loud cackle from sister Mary.

"Handle your fears in bits!"

"Bits?" Eleanor, as confused by bits as arithmetic, shook her head in dismay.

"Fears can be fanciful or real. The fancies may run wild if allowed. Stifle them as only apparitions until they are real. Face the real as they appear, in bits day by day." Sarah had gradually worked out this strategy in the evenings after the announcement of her departure while wedged between her sisters in the featherbed. While unsure if it was sound, any plan was better than none.

With a practiced and elaborate casualness, sister Mary strolled by Eleanor and fingered her lush red curls. Sarah had seen this stagecraft of Mary's all too often before. Silently dismayed, she waited for the game to begin.

On cue, in a soothing, silken tone, Mary advised, "And they do so prize colorful hair. Red and yellow. You two would be a valuable pair."

Sarah, nearly sputtering with rage, turned to her sister sharply. "Mary, cease this toying!"

Eleanor, being entirely innocent of the nature of the sibling drama unfolding, suggested, "Sarah, don't you think you should learn to use a gun before you leave?"

"But we have only the one."

Mary, springing on Eleanor's suggestion as a suitable finale, suggested slyly, "Perhaps Father could learn you the use of his Indian tomahawk. They are useful to crack skulls."

Sarah was aware that she was merely a stringed lute upon which Mary might play any tune at her convenience. Despite her vows, all too often, Sarah found herself trilling to the plucked notes. With a thin screeching wail that startled Eleanor, "Mary, cease your devilry now," flooded from her throat. Mary exited with exaggerated casualness, a thin smile of satisfaction on her face. After a few minutes, when Sarah's breathing returned to normal and the veins in her neck settled, she realized that Eleanor was gone.

Her fears poked by Mary's taunts, Sarah was initially oblivious to the rising chatter around her as the family settled in for the midday meal. The journey was a few days off, and she could sense her fear awaking. Only her mother's commanding voice shook her from her reverie. "Sarah. Sarah . . . Sarah! Where are you?" The girl's eyes, open but unseeing, suddenly snapped into focus. Embarrassment rose from her cheeks, culminating in both ears as she suddenly became mindful of the entire family, now seated, staring at her. These episodes, which her mother referred to as "spells," were common enough that they had long since ceased to be a curiosity.

CHAPTER IV

May 19, 1707

Mary gave her husband her dark look and slowly shook her head. This stare was well known to the family and never failed to arouse anxiety in the target. The glare had several levels of intensity. Her head tilted back with a raised left eyebrow as a warning. This was followed by the slow headshake. The table was silent, awaiting the ultimate level sign, a quick saber jab of the left index finger. When it became clear that it wouldn't be unleashed, the room was once again alive with voices. John was expecting such a last-minute stratagem and addressed Mary in a voice that barely rose above the din. "I know this is for the best."

"John, what time is the meeting?"

"Now."

"You'll be very late if you don't hurry."

Absent-mindedly, John regarded a bit of mutton impaled on the end of his knife, admitting, "Little loss." Sarah finished her meal with dispatch and was cleaning the cards to work up some remaining wool. Even carefully trimmed of the fat, she wasn't tempted by the meat.

"Father, the meal will be quicker if you join it all together!"

"How so?" he wondered. She jumped to her feet and thickly buttered the bread slices. Placing the mutton slice on one piece of bread, then the cheese, she placed the second bread slice butter side down and cleanly cut the assemblage in half. When her creation started to tilt, she pressed down firmly on the bread with both hands.

"Just so! No knife or napkin needed. Fingers are clean, and the whole can be eaten on the way."

If she had entered the dooryard leading a bridled unicorn, her father would have been only slightly more astonished. He eyed the combination with suspicion, carefully probing the layers with his knife tip. Facing Sarah with a wordless question, she replied, "It came to me." He never did grasp the whole, but ate it down layer by layer.

His wife knew him well enough to see that he was dawdling, playing out the time in the hope that the meeting might already have decided the issue. John had avoided all offers of public office for reasons that escaped her. This required considerable cunning, for in a small town, there were many posts to fill and only a small number of men professing the freeman's oath to fill them. Wistfully, she recalled that she had hoped the office of first selectman would be in his future. Lately, John had consented to election to ensign of the town militia band, but that amounted to little more than marching for a few hours up and down the town green a few times a year followed by an even longer sojourn in the tavern.

Finishing the meal's final layer, John rose, nodded to Mary, winking at Sarah on his way out. Through the door side window, he was in full view walking toward the green. With Sarah busy carding, Mary decided to favor her sore back with a rest in the sleigh chair. Of late, a night's sleep was not as vouchsafe as it was in the past.

Catching herself dozing, she awoke with a start and, with eyes still closed, commanded her daughter, "Sarah, I would like you to . . ." Her voice trailed off when she realized that the girl had flown. "Now, where has that child got to?" Just barely visible through the window was the scarcely recognizable figure of her husband disappearing over the slight rise. Next to him stood Sarah, waving her arms and posturing, filling his ears no doubt with her notions. "After her father. I should have known."

John did not need to look back to know who was trotting up behind him. Her footfalls were well remembered. Sarah sidled up beside him as they walked along and launched into a stream of words, complete with dramatic punctuations in the air.

He knew from experience that this was not an intended conversation but rather a soliloquy of flitting thoughts. Fragments of ideas, jostling and stumbling over one another, all striving for release. Eventually the stream of words would taper off as a steaming kettle quiets when taken off the heat. He nodded and smiled at what seemed likely points.

They approached the Meeting House silently, both kneading their own thoughts. In his mind, John had already departed from Westfield, having little interest in this minor town tempest. Sarah was busy preparing a plausible response to her mother's annoyance at her sneaking out. She had watched her mother's drooping lids carefully and had silently crept out the door when she judged it safe. Feeble as it was, she decided that "You didn't tell me not to" would have to suffice.

The sight of small knots of men milling near the front door of the Meeting House was an unwelcome sign that the meeting had not started. John nodded acknowledgments to the loiterers, settling into a bench near the door. Sarah veered off and joined the groups of children of various ages that were gathering near the still unwindowed south side.

The children's level of interest varied. Some were actually curious as to the meeting's details. Others, usually well turned out, were hoping to strike a romantic spark in certain directions. The greater part of them simply wanted to meet friends. If their fathers rose to speak, they listened with pricked ears, ready to bask in the reflected glory of a point well put.

John sat next to Silas Goodwin. On the Sabbath, with families present, they were separated on either end of the row. But now, with the empty spaces, they sat side by side. He knew Silas only slightly. Their two farms were far apart, and they did little business together. Silas had a small fulling mill on one of the lesser streams scouring the oil out of sheep's wool. The liquor mixture needed to remove the lanolin from the raw wool caused the fish downstream to be scarce. Livestock soon learned to avoid the stream.

Eliphalet Brinsmaid, recently something of a local grandee, was milling around at the front of the house. John and Silas looked at each other. Silas was the first to comment, "Our moderator, I would think."

The hall ran quiet when three men, the board of selectmen, entered. With practiced gravity, the first selectman took the lead, announcing, "I now call this special meeting of the electors to order. Do I hear a nomination for a moderator?"

A voice from the assembly that neither man recognized obliged. "I nominate Eliphalet Brinsmaid."

"Is there a second to the nomination?"

After a pause came a muffled, "Aye."

"Are there any other nominations?" The hall went silent. "No? Do I have a motion to close the nominations?" A pro forma series of "ayes" sewed up the decision.

"All in favor of Mr. Brinsmaid for our moderator say aye." A few murmured "ayes," and it was done. The housekeeping complete, the new moderator rose and surveyed the electors with a gravity suited to the occasion. Eliphalet was a physician lately from Salem. A man of wealth and taste, he lived well enough that townsmen assumed that he came from a family of substance. The clacking tongues finally decided that he was an heir to a shipping company. As usual at such times, Eliphalet donned his go-to-meeting attire. The most splendid part of the ensemble was a bright-red silk weskit with solid gold buttons.

Respected for his medical skills and ability to soothe frightened children, nevertheless, he was a man hard to warm up to for reasons never fully agreed upon. Over several mugs of flip in the tavern, Otis Cook, widely regarded as the village idiot, gained a degree of momentary regard in succinctly describing the conundrum. He likened the good doctor to bear grease, very handy to have around to lubricate wagon axles but quickly wiped off the fingers when the task was done.

Eliphalet, speaking as moderator, began: "Westfield, we are gathered here to face a dire threat to our town. Reports are that the northern tribes in the pay of the French may be near. We must be prepared! Eris is on the wing. She means us ill."

As the assembly tried to make sense of this alarming news, in the front row, an alarmed man turned to his seatmate with a question, "Who's Eris?" Before shrugging, he guessed that it was "some Roman god, or maybe a goddess, or a Druid?"

Seth Merrill, a few rows back, seethed at the moderator's opening warning. A housewright, he'd settled in town decades ago, hoping to find work. He was not a young man even then, but the years had spared all his senses excepting hearing. Unable to follow his trade, instead, he faithfully served in the office of town fence walker, pacing off the enclosures in town, ensuring that good neighbors stayed as such.

Enraged at what he considered brazen slander, he leapt to his feet. "That is a damnable lie! She is a goodwife at home at this very minute. She's not flying anywhere, nor would she hurt a soul." As it was well known that Seth often mangled what he heard and acted hotly on word bits, seated neighbors pulled him down, explaining that it was not his wife, Iris, in question but Eris.

The moderator, sensing that he was losing control of the meeting, searched the audience for Jacob Adams, the captain of the town's militia band. Not seated in his accustomed row, Jacob was lingering at the back of the hall perched on the steps leading up to the gallery. A heavy-set man, his face seemed perpetually frozen in a scowl. In his presence, nearly everyone, without thinking, weighed each and every word carefully. A terse speaker who rarely wasted words, as if believing that God allotted him only a particular number of words in his life, Jacob was reluctant to waste them on nonsense. He was one of those men who was expert at everything he put his hand to. Anything new was mastered with ease, and he acquired the nickname Capability Adams.

"What does the captain of our militia say?"

Jacob rose with effort as one knee recently took to lameness. "We will send out riders and post sentries until we know the nature of the danger."

"And the far houses?" piped an anonymous voice. Generally, these meetings were solemn and orderly affairs, where everyone with a notion to speak respectfully awaited a nod from the moderator before rising. However, when the matters were heated or controversial, decorum was often put aside, drowned out by shouts.

Jacob, now fully limbered up, walked up an aisle closer to the front to respond. "They must look to themselves for the moment or else come in. The danger of an ambuscade is too great."

A surge of dismay sloshed back and forth from wall to wall across the room in a tidal wave. Men turned from side to side and pivoted to talk excitedly with nearby friends. From the vantage point of Moderator Brinsmaid, the spectacle was akin to the ripples that a handful of pebbles might cause when thrown into a still pond.

A faceless query pleaded, "Do we have enough powder and shot?"

Before the meeting, Jacob had done a careful inventory of the munitions stored in the small armory room of the Meeting House. The results were disquieting.

"We have enough for eight volleys. More if we load light."

"That will not do! Why are we so lacking?" There was a distinctly inquisitorial tinge to Brinsmaid's question.

"If you recall, sir, the money for powder was voted down at the last annual meeting." Jacob let go of his words at a slow pace and, just for a moment, the scowl softened into something that might pass as a smile.

The doctor realized immediately that he had blundered into a situation of his own making. He was being hoisted upon the point of his own spear. Clearly recalling speaking out against the purchase of more powder at the last meeting, he awkwardly pivoted, "That will suffice. If not, we shall call on neighboring towns."

The militia captain, carefully meting out his limited allowance of words, replied, "If threatened, they will not give up their powder."

From the increasingly unruly chorus came the demand, "What does John Noble think?" When John didn't immediately respond, Brinsmaid addressed him directly, something he had never done since coming to town.

"Mr. Noble, I've been given to understand that you've spent much time amongst the Indians and indeed are able to think like them. Have you sensed any signs of a raiding party nearby?"

John ignored the sly insult and admitted, "No, I have not. But if mischief was planned, I would not."

"Would our Indians warn us then?"

"In a fashion. If raiding parties were near, they would not be. I would heed their actions more closely than their words." Turning to reclaim his bench, he paused and asked Brinsmaid, "What is the source of the alarm?"

"An acquaintance heard of it at an inn while traveling," Brinsmaid admitted. The tension in the hall melted away as men dribbled out of their pews, making for the door and shaking their heads in relief. When the fears were finally calmed, every man would later claim in the tavern that they were skeptical all along.

Walking into the sunshine, Silas turned to John in disgust. "Rumor! All this from tavern tittle!"

Amused, John observed, "Silas, rumor is a swift mare, the truth a lame mule!"

As the last few men left the now empty hall, the moderator tried to make sense of the fiasco. "Are we to adjourn? Do I hear a motion to . . . This is most improper." Exasperated, he turned to the board of selectmen for support, only to realize that they had also flown the building by way of the rear exit.

While both by turns annoyed and relieved at this false alarm, the men did not disperse but gathered around in small groups using the opportunity to share news with friends and strike bargains for needed victuals and services.

"John, I hear you are moving on. Why is that?" The young man addressing him was new to town, and for some reason, John couldn't recall his Christian name.

Nodding toward Brinsmaid, now chatting on the steps, John said, "New pastures." The young man was oblivious to John Noble's well-known personal quirk. As he regarded the local grandee, he sucked air through his upper front teeth. Although he rarely raised his voice when angry, he frequently was known to hiss when provoked.

Innocently, the young fellow continued, "I hope we meet again before then. Let me know when you sell up. I'd like a look." Aaron Austin, overhearing the exchange nearby, smiled. Newcomers in town were hapless to discern the elaborate weave of relationships. If they were clever, they volunteered little.

John answered, "My son Stephen will handle the sale after I depart. I'll tell him of your interest. But it might be settled at auction." He made a note to sound out Aaron if a quick auction or the more time-consuming sale by sale would be best.

∴

The entertainment over, the tightly clustered hive of children and adolescents mobbing outside the open windows slowly dispersed into more natural groups. Some knots were near neighbors of long friendship. Others were budding young women in plumage.

Their counterpart was a cluster of young men eyeing these girls and discussing quietly their more interesting points. These talks were usually carefully phrased and respectful. Since the particular interest of any lad was not always obvious, an amusingly lewd comment might cause some trouble.

While previously paired off couples withdrew discreetly to a distance, the singleton groups of both sexes were parted by an unseen but formidable fence. Crossing this invisible line required a period of time in order to prepare words as well as courage. It was not always successful; foul weather or the early departure of a parent might cut short any mingling.

Thankful Brinsmaid, daughter to the town physician, was at the center of a group of girls who curiously not only didn't live near one another or have a great deal in common, but, in truth, heartily detested one another. The lure of Thankful, as hypnotic as fresh meat to hornets, was her confident air of gentility, bordering on aristocratic grace. Her dresses, crafted of the finest fabrics that Austin's could provide, enhanced her worth. Her tresses were, without fail, elaborately braided and piled up on her head, held in place by hairpins capped in red beads. When Sarah once idly mused that her hair would never look so fine, her mother snorted dismissively, "That family does little all day except preen!"

Sarah, standing off to one side as an observer, did have to admit that Thankful was a pretty girl who seemed born to her clothes. Regretfully, Sarah remembered that she once tried to become a member of Thankful's coterie, but the girl's hurtful ridicule was too painful to endure.

Much later in life, when Sarah was pondering if a memoir was even proper, she traced out in her mind the outlines of the scandalous episode about to unfold that day. With amusement, she dismissed Thankful's cloud of followers as only myrmidons, the mindless, anonymous followers of Achilles recounted in her favorite volume, *The Iliad*.

The square in front of the Meeting House was only rarely empty of activity. The town stocks and official message board were located here as a town site. The most common and well-known place to conduct regular livestock auctions was in the square. Individuals with church or militia business crisscrossed the open plaza regularly. Mostly bereft of grass, consisting of poorly drained clay soil, it was often muddy and slick. Churned up by the footfalls of men and animals, their footprints often remained as shaped puddles for days. The ground lying nearest the Meeting House was then the sole safe place for shoes and hems.

Catching Sarah's eye, Thankful lifted her dress just high enough to clear the mud and carefully made her way around the obstacles to approach her. "Sarah, I hear you're leaving very soon for a new town. Maybe your family will do better in a place where no one knows you."

"What do you mean?" Sarah was wary but puzzled.

"My father says that after all these years, your father has scarcely risen to middling rank." Thankful basked in the admiring laughter of her cluster of associates. Turning to the group, she couldn't resist a parting barb. "Well, it is true, you all know it as well as I."

Never losing view of her, Sarah slowly approached her tormentor, heedless of the ground. She missed most but not all of the puddles. Sarah had no intention of debating such a quick-witted girl. Thankful, however, relished the image of Sarah's sputtering rage as her words were twisted and turned against her, becoming a binding cord of her own making.

Thankful was petite, porcelain delicate, and already a fully formed woman. She would look the same as now on her distant wedding day. She had no awkward gangling parts that needed hiding. Finally, face-to-face, staring Thankful down, Sarah had not a wisp of an idea of her next move. Her uneven growth surges of the past year had not only rearranged her face more agreeably but gave her curiously long, slender fingers.

Later, she explained her actions that day cryptically: "Her face, it was her face." Suddenly, her hand, moving faster than Thankful could avoid, lashed out and clasped the girl's face in her palm. Although an instinctive reaction, Sarah hesitated for only a lash blink before she pushed Thankful backward into the mud. The soil was slick enough that Thankful slid several feet across the mire.

The suddenness of the attack left Thankful quite speechless, but only momentarily. Extricating herself from the sucking mud required coming to her knees and pushing away with her hands. "My dress! My beautiful dress! Look at what you've done. You have ruined it. You wretched girl."

To Sarah's receding form, she laid out a stinging curse, "Sarah Noble, you will never be a lady!" Catching her breath at length, Thankful examined her muddy hands with horror as if they were no longer parts of her body. From her earliest memory, Thankful had abhorred the slightest foreign sensation on her hands. She avoided certain fruits when overripe, as she could not abide sticky fingers. Even working the lard-laden floury crusts of a pie was unwelcome. Resignedly, she rubbed her fingers over the front of her dress, carefully cleaning her hands as best she could. She resisted the urge to run her fingers over her hair to assess the damage and stalked off through the puddles, a woman in a fury.

As Sarah approached the dry ground to join her father, her mind bubbled with possibilities for explaining the fracas in the best light. He had certainly heard Thankful screaming out her name. That was assured. It was sufficiently loud as well as alarming that all the negotiations and gossip mongering were, for a moment, suspended until no threat to life nor limb was apparent.

Since her father likely had not actually witnessed the spat, several explanations were possible. Recognizing her father's silhouette, Sarah approached, standing next to him while he bade families farewell. As was usual in such cases, they were not brief. It was always the same. The conversation invariably drifted from the weather to crops and finally to horses before her father expressed their goodbyes.

Sarah was quiet on the walk back to the farm. She decided to let him bring up the matter. Thereby, she could judge what he knew as well as the nature of his humor. Her response would follow accordingly. It wasn't until the Meeting House had receded from view that he spoke. "The Brinsmaid lass was peeved."

With as casual an air as she could muster, she said, "She was angry that her dress became soiled." Sarah initially considered an elaborate well-polished tale but decided on simplicity. "She fell. Her hair might need washing."

"Yes, that's often the case." After a pause, he turned to his daughter, warning, "Your mother will have words about this."

"Will you . . ." She trailed off, never finishing the question that she already knew the answer to.

"She will know by Sabbath day next at the latest. By voices who were not there. Probably sooner. Even now, the crows are gathering."

"What must I do?"

"Sarah, you are no longer a child. You are well able to direct your own affairs. Think upon it. A proper path will appear."

Father and daughter walked in silence until the farm came into view around a bend.

"Father, I cannot be mild with such as Thankful. The fire rises within me. How can I learn forbearance as you have?"

"By the doing of it. Sarah, making an enemy needs little effort. Unmaking is often hard. Consider carefully if there is sufficient profit to it. Friends are of many shades. Enemies are of a single color."

A sigh and a timid question were tendered. "The dress?"

"If they press the matter. They have the right."

Sarah suddenly brightened as she realized that they were to begin their journey the following morning. With only the slightest good fortune, she would be safely away before her mother heard the tale. It would be months before she would face her, and her ire would have cooled by then.

This lighthearted interlude quickly faded as she sadly weighed the untasteful choices that she knew loomed: her mother's short but hot burning rage or her father's quiet but long reproach. As she knew it would, the less painful path beckoned.

John slowed, halting when they reached the rail fence. He had approached his modest homestead through this very gate hundreds of times over the years. He knew that this would be the last such approach, and he took care to fondle the sight.

"Life is made up of the comings and the goings." He wasn't speaking to Sarah; indeed, he wasn't addressing anyone but himself. Her father was known for his occasional, usually cryptic and spontaneous adages. Mary referred to them lightly as his "oracle musings." Sarah made an effort to remember them but was never able to tease out the meanings.

• • •

The evening meal was entirely uneventful. Sarah was both relieved that her mother did not yet know and dismayed that she would then have to raise the subject herself. How to start? Lightly or contrite? For most of the meal, she reviewed and edited the details of the encounter in her mind, carefully disguising points not favorable to her view. As was her custom, her mother retired to her sleigh chair after the plates were cleared away and rocked.

Suddenly, she opened her eyes and spoke softly, "Sarah, do we have something to discuss?"

"Mother, I—"

Her beginning was silenced by a dismissive flick of her mother's hand.

"I need not hear of the mud wallow. Done is done. It cannot be taken back. At the Meeting House, did you act as a Christian woman ought?"

With tears welling, Sarah admitted that she did not. The quietest shakes of the head always seem the most sorrowful.

"Proper gentlewomen do not scratch and claw or wallow about in the mud like swine! You were not raised in this manner. What came over you?" Sarah's only response was a vacant stare. "I will not mention this mishap again unless your future actions recall it. If Thankful is here tomorrow, you will apologize. And, Sarah, good, honest words. She will expect it."

Mother's closed eyes signified that the matter was ended. Sarah, trying to salvage some small dignity, slowly walked toward the stairwell and the asylum of her bedchamber. She had scarcely climbed the first steps before she was halted by her mother's words.

"What dress was Thankful wearing?"

"The blue one with the white lace trim." Since her mother was out of sight, Sarah waited a moment, listening if perhaps more details were wanted. After a moment of silence, she climbed the stairs, carefully avoiding the uneven crack in the seventh step that lay in wait for a false footfall.

Mary, never breaking her chair's rhythm, took to smiling. Sarah was so relieved that the burden was lifted from her heart that, lying on the featherbed, she never realized how artfully it was all so arranged: the kitchen, unaccountably, was empty save for Sarah and her mother; Thankful was nearly magically informed of the coming apology, and her brothers disappearances on vaguely pressing errands.

CHAPTER V

May 20, 1707

The next morning the kitchen was eerily quiet. There were none of the usual sounds of banter and teasing. The rattle and clatter of plates and cutlery was intermittently punctuated by the sharp pop of a sap pocket exploding in the hearth. Cherry logs were apt to send sparks into the room. Taking up most of the available space were last-minute supplies for the journey. Early that morning, salted meat had already been hefted into the cart. Bedding and other sundries were heaped on the floor. John's and Sarah's garments, previously so carefully stored, were retrieved from chests and stuffed into coarse sacks.

Space and weight were limited in the cart. Tidiness was sacrificed. Soft articles were wedged into any spare space. Left behind were all the heavier tools excepting those that were absolutely necessary. The mare, John knew, had little stamina. Fearing that she might break down along the way, he eliminated nearly everything. For the past week, Mary's suggestions that he should pack this or perhaps take that were met with the same response: "Don't want."

He had mulled over the notion of purchasing a suitable ox to pull the cart. This was often the preferred strategy for such moves, as their great strength was useful in clearing the home lot. Waiting for a sharp bargain that never came, he resigned himself finally to the horse. A horse would afford him more mobility when they reached their allotment, though he was hard-pressed to believe that there would be a need.

Mary, meanwhile, assembled the coming midday fare, a meal she knew that neither her husband nor Sarah would sample. She had made these meat pies so often that she did it with no conscious direction. Her hands, as if of their own accord, trimmed the crusts and filled the earthenware vessels. Without taking her eyes away from the silent table, she plunged her arm up to the elbow into the scorching bake oven, judging the temperature. Not perfection but passable.

Sliding the heavy pots carefully into the open oven, she turned, viewing the disorderly heap of belongings on the floor with dismay. She had finally come to terms with the move south. The farm here in Massachusetts was too small and far too stony to provide them with anything more than a straightened livelihood. On an earlier scouting expedition, John had carefully paced out the available lots in the new town in Connecticut and had chosen a fine one at the top of the future town green. The land was plowable and, although he wasn't entirely sure, he thought that it extended all the way down to the banks of the river, known as the Housatonic by the Indians.

While the move was settled in her mind, Mary was lately vexed by the image of the empty chairs. Within mere hours, the symmetry of the family table would be askew. The shoulder-to-shoulder ring would be broken by two vacant chairs. She, for a time, had thought to pull up the chairs and store them in the barn. In bed last night, however, she decided that such reminders of absent members were more proper. She chided herself over these silly trifles, but they were rarely out of mind.

Her eldest son finally interrupted the silence. His soft observation, "Today is the day, then," was greeted with embarrassed coughs and furtive glances. His father, in a measured voice that he hoped was near normal, announced, "I want to be packed and ready before the goodbyes are said."

Sarah, descending the stairs, had barely reached the landing when her mother bolted upright and scolded, "No! No! No! Sarah, this is settled.

You will *not* wear your good skirt on the road. Elizabeth's old strip skirt is perfectly serviceable."

"But, Mother, I look like a patchwork quilt."

"There is no one to preen for along the way!" With the dismissive wave of her mother's hand, Sarah turned and trudged up the stairs, stumbling over the seventh step. Shimmying out of her skirt, she inspected the handed-down garment with dismay. Elizabeth was taller and the hem was too long. And she was so much bigger down there. Convinced that she was wearing something akin to a tent, Sarah resolved not to view herself in the looking glass on any account.

In exasperation, Mary exclaimed, "That girl! She wanted to take my fine dog-skin shoes with her. First the shoes and now the dress. Has she no sense?"

With the mention of the shoes, John was suddenly reminded of the years gone past. The rambling hunts with his favorite dog, a fine black and tan hound, flooded his memory. He had two pairs of fancy shoes made from her skin at the end, one of each color. The black shoes were long gone, and the tan pair were nearly spent as well. Although they made fine shoes, dog skins had little durability.

"That bitch was a fine hunter, as I recall. The best I ever had. What of the skirt?"

"The bottom strip was worn, and I replaced it. I had only scraps to spare, so the colors differ."

Mary turned to her husband. "John, I intend to take on a few more pupils while you are gone."

"The ready money will be useful. Or salted pork."

Sarah slowly retraced her steps down the staircase, the perfectly poised picture of dejection. The wide bottom strip was part red, followed by yellow and ending in pink. Actually, not pink originally but faded from some color now long forgotten. She walked purposefully, neither stopping nor uttering a word, while crossing the kitchen. Gingerly, with a deep sigh, she opened the door and went out.

Mary, only now realizing that there was far too much yardage hanging about Sarah's thin frame, waved her hand airily and maintained, "She'll grow into it."

John, from long and hard experience, decided that a jocular retort was unwise. "But she'll be easy to track" seemed mild enough.

In rising, he reached over and offered Mary a playful pinch, causing her to glance about, ensuring that they were alone. Opening the door, he was greeted with brilliant sunshine. John Jr. had nearly finished hitching up the mare to the extended cart.

Sarah's father realized that, with the rough going along the way, both of them would need to walk. The horse was a healthy beast, but it was a heavy haul. He dared not trust his daughter at the reins. Spying Sarah at the helm, the animal was very likely to decide on a mind of its own. The horse seemed to quickly judge her tentative nature. Kicked once some months ago, Sarah was wary.

The dooryard was filling up with neighboring families and longtime friends hovering quietly for their turn to bid a final farewell. The goodbyes had, of course, been repeated over and over at various times for the past months. But this was the end, the final ritual of departure.

Another group, however, was in mind of another purpose. Knots of men, most unknown to the family, were evaluating the property and carefully judging what the stock might fetch and the value of the tools. A casual passerby might read the crowd as all of the same, but they were not. Only upon close inspection were the fine feathers revealed as those of vultures.

After a gruff hug from the shopkeeper, Aaron blurted, "I wish you all the best. I shall miss you, John. First Isaac Messinger and now you. Soon, I fear that most of the good sense in this town will reside with the horses."

"These past years have indeed been agreeable. Mind my direction concerning Mary's spending. I would appreciate you guiding Stephen through the auction of the farm if it comes to that."

"I will do so, John, but guiding Mary will be more fretful." As John turned to walk away, Aaron caught his hand in a silent shake. "I will, of course, deny to one and all. But if it gets about that I'm acting as Mary's minder, it would be very injurious to my trade."

Detached from the amiable shopkeeper, he slowly offered his farewells as he worked his way toward the family. Some were warm and extended; others were short and brittle. Most were what might be seen as proper only. John motioned to his three sons, gathering them together.

"You are now the men of the family. I expect you to act with due prudence. I will no longer be here to hone smooth the results of your missteps."

The two elder sons murmured assent while David promised brightly, "Father, I will conduct myself as always."

John paused for a moment, pondering if this was another of his jests or simply more addled words from his youngest son. "Strive for betterment, then."

"Stephen, consult with Aaron regarding any difficulties. He will expect it. If you feel the need to disregard his counsel, remember that he has always been a true friend to me."

At Elizabeth's touch, he turned and hugged her fast. Despite her vow, she could not stem the rush of tears. "If I am wed soon, I may never see you again."

"You will see me again. That is a solemn vow. As you well know, weddings often require a spell of time to unfold. There is time . . . unless other events are at a full gallop?" The jest seemed to brighten her face into a smile. "But take care how you manage your affections in the time before you. Take a husband here, and here you stay."

Young Mary, listening nearby, knew that a final appeal was insensible, but it was an itch that she finally had to scratch.

"Father, I should go instead. I am older and less fanciful." When her father did not respond, she tendered a quiet possibility, "Perhaps we might both go?"

Unexpectedly, her father cupped her cheeks in both hands. This was in itself rare, as Mary did not favor being fondled and never did even while still very young. She would often shrink back from the slightest caress.

"No, Mary. We cannot carry provisions for three. Your stalwart nature must serve your mother. You have insights that Mother lacks and" with a sly grin "clever cunning."

•••

Sarah, meanwhile, was idling away the time until her departure, speaking last words to a cluster of girls, some friends of various shades and some not.

The heartfelt farewells had long since passed between them. The conversations on this day were little more than dry husks long since drained of feeling. Eleanor, however, remained in mourning.

"Why do you have to go so far away? My reckoning will suffer."

"Eleanor, Mother is much more skilled than me."

"But she can't make me laugh. Will you ever return?"

"I'm certain I will."

As if prodded by a soundless cue, the young girls all nodded assent and murmured the lie together. Everyone excepting Eleanor knew the truth that they would never see Sarah again. Once the cart vanished down the dust-powdered road, she was gone from their lives. The comings and goings of families was a part of their common existence, every bit as much as the arrival of lambs in the spring.

Unspoken was the knowledge that assembled words were often more than just the simple truth or a lie. Between the two was a subtle weave of intents and ends. Soothing assurances gave comfort to Eleanor, although all the girls knew deep in their souls that the promise was little more than a translucent wisp. Friends and families on quests for new beginnings in fresh lands to the west were as lost to them as if they were nestled in their graves. Eleanor, not in union with the fiction, demanded, "When will you return?"

"I do not know." Sarah's answer was not the pure truth but edged closer to that side of the scale.

Even while consoling Eleanor, Sarah glanced furtively at Thankful a dozen paces away. Unusually, she stood quite alone. The usual chorus of supporters was blessedly absent. There was no audience to thrill with a performance. Detaching herself from the well-wishers, Sarah slowly approached.

"Thankful, I fear that I have caused you a great meanness. I did not act as a proper woman ought. For that, I feel deep remorse and shame. I sincerely beg forgiveness and humbly seek your good feelings." Thankful's stony face slowly softened to a thin smile. When it so broadened that her teeth were exposed, Sarah stuck out her tongue languidly and turned away abruptly.

As the well-wishers and profit seekers gradually ebbed away, the Noble clan clustered in a ball as if seeking protection from an unseen peril. Clasped hands not proving sufficient soon became soft hugs. Finally, Mary took her husband in hand. The long ritual of goodbyes was concluded the night before. She stiffly squeezed his arms in a parting gesture.

"John, it's been some time since your trapping days. I scarcely know how I shall endure."

"It cannot be helped. The time will pass soon enough."

"Too slowly, I fear."

"The family will be of great support to you in this time."

"Not in all ways." They both smiled at the hidden meaning.

"They are strong. Lean on them heavily to ease your burdens." Speaking louder so that his brood might hear the words, "Mind there will be a reconning at the end."

He mounted the cart and with a gentle flick of the reins, it finally began. The children and lingering friends slowly followed the cart, gradually falling away as the wagon crested the slight hill. Mary remained rooted, never moving even a step from the ground of the last farewell.

•••

The route inevitably brought them through the village and past the Meeting House. Roads were few, and it was the easiest connecting path south that the cart might manage. They had passed this way more times than their memories could count. Often passersby would acknowledge them with a wave and a smile. Sarah knew all the families along the road, each face and even some of their deepest secrets. On this occasion, however, their passing was met with only grave nods and solemn eyes. She suddenly had the most unsettling sensation that she was a mourner at a funeral. No, it was not that, she realized! Was this the way friends and neighbors might nod to her own coffin?

"I will never see any of my friends again. Or anyone left in Westfield." Brightening up, she added, "Or Thankful. I will never reflect upon her presence ever again."

The bright, giddy flash soon faded from her face, remaining little longer than the brief spark of a late summer's lightning bug.

"I do not like goodbyes. There are too many."

"That is the way of it, Sarah. The pages turn. The pages must always turn."

THE SEASONING

• • •

Mary stood in the dooryard staring down the road long after the cart faded into the distance. Only when the last dust mote finally settled did she slowly walk to the house. Her namesake was distractedly setting out the late meal. The meat pies, long since retrieved from the oven, were quite cold on the table.

Daughter Mary, judging the oven cool enough, slid the pans of bread dough to the back for proofing. She greeted her older sister descending the stairs with an impatient, even demanding, nod. Elizabeth waited until her mother had settled into her musing chair before gingerly handing her a small, scrolled letter bound up with a ribbon.

"Sarah wished that I deliver this when they were gone." Her mother had expected something of this sort from Sarah. She would question Elizabeth about the letter later. Although still early in the day, she had not the strength to chisel the truth from Elizabeth just now. It would keep. A quick tug of the bow and the letter rushed to uncoil.

Shaking her head sadly, Mary recalled how hard she had worked to craft Sarah's writing to the elegant level of a scribe. The striking capital letters and the flowing alphabet, alas, seemed entirely beyond Sarah's skill. The ability to record a handsome deathbed last will and testament was a profitable skill, and families were not reluctant to bear the cost. Sarah learned the required legal words so easily, but scanning the letter, the results were always thus: the footmarks of tiny birds capering across the page. Her needlework was wretched as well.

Before Mother dared begin to decipher Sarah's words, she shouted across the kitchen, "Elizabeth, bring me your father's spectacles."

"He took them, I believe." With a snort, Mary wondered of what use they might be to him in the wilderness. Squinting and moving the note near and far, she read the letter to herself.

Mother, it was my intention to say this to you but every time my crafted words became a jumble in my head and my tongue went mute. I am saddened that my actions and my carriage have disappointed you so. When next we meet you will discern a great improvement, I promise. I have every hope that I shall be hardened off by the travails to come.

Your obedient daughter, Sarah

Mother gazed absently into space. Softly, she said, "Sarah, my wonder child. 'Tis a wonder what you'll be up to next."

As their mother slowly read the letter, the two sisters, with scarcely a conscious thought, gradually drifted near one another. The expected energetic reaction did not appear, and their mother slowly rolled up the letter and carefully retied the ribbon. Curiosity was more than balanced by fear of unleashing their mother's ire. Each was silent, awaiting for the other to brave the storm. Finally, young Mary could stand it no longer, and in a soft voice poked the question, "Mother, the letter?"

The answer, infuriating, as no doubt was the intent, was only "Yes."

The two sisters slated to remain in Westfield had been dividing up Sarah's chores once their father's plans became clear. The arguments, often heated, ebbed and flowed over a period of weeks. The tense compromise was a sort of rotation where neither was permanently burdened with the most distasteful of them. Sarah had refused to listen to her sisters' bickering back and forth. Was minding the milk cow more onerous than dealing with the swine? And if one was worse, how to compensate? The talk was unsettling; it was as if she was no longer, and they were dividing her up.

This was the first day of their uneasy agreement. They both left the house toward their respective toils: Mary Jr. to the nervous cow and Elizabeth with a slop pail of cheese pressings for the hogs' dining. As they gradually parted, Mary shouted to her sister, "Mother will never reveal the letter. Do you suppose it's a scandal? Why didn't you read it?"

"It was private to Sarah."

"Yes, but if you became privy to it, it would be private to us also."

The evening meal, the first without Father and Sarah, was best described as curious. Not sad, not even somber, but somehow lacking the expected pace and rhythm. It was every bit as boisterous, but the repartee was careful and guarded. This was new ground, and the hazards were not yet clear. The empty chairs, as missing notes, skewed the melody.

Near sunset, Elizabeth walked slowly to the roadside fence. This was her favorite place of contemplation. Very much more on this day, as Father and Sarah had traveled this path mere hours ago. Sister Mary watched her through the kitchen window for a time before joining her. Elizabeth leaning on the top rail, deep in thought, was heedless of Mary's approach. "Their leaving?"

Elizabeth was startled out of her pensive thoughts and shrugged.

"Isaac, then?" prompted a nod.

"You must look further afield."

"I don't care to. I know him and am easy with him. Our thoughts align, and between us there are few rough spots that scratch."

"Consider Adam Wilcox." Her sister's reply was swift and heated.

"No! His eyes are too close together and look in different directions at once. When I speak to him, I cannot tell where he looks. And his hair lays on his head like a barn rat. His very laugh makes me shiver."

"Minor defects in a man with such fine prospects. He is to finish at Harvard this year. Word is that he will ascend the pulpit here as minister soon after. He will provide you status and a life of ease."

"I don't crave a man with fine prospects above all else."

"So, here you are, waiting at the sliprails. For how long?" This was a long-standing debate between the two sisters, one without resolution. Annoyed, Mary walked back to the dwelling. In her quest for perfection, her sister had foolishly insisted on overlooking the perfectly sufficient.

CHAPTER VI

May 20 to June 15, 1707

The first few days of travel were something of a lark for Sarah. The settlements along the way were tidy and well-tended. She made a game of imagining the nature of the inhabitants as they slowly passed by the dwellings. In her imagination, grand houses sheltered merchant grandees with sleekly handsome, well-tailored sons. Small weather-beaten cottages always housed poor widows with hungry children.

When overtaken by boredom, she dozed. Reading favorite Bible passages was not possible. She soon found that the rough road brought on nausea after a very few verses. She dismounted the cart when the road opened onto a sunny stretch and walked alongside the cart picking berries. She knew to carefully shun any bright tempting fruit growing in full shade. Any berry with milky juice was also suspect.

John was grateful that the going was easy. The path was dry with few difficult grades. They made good time, even allowing for stops to rest the mare and allow grazing. Despite carefully parsing out the daily oats, he had no faith they would last the entire trip. The oats could run out just as the grazing became sparse.

THE SEASONING

On the third day, Sarah noted the position of the sun in the western sky, motioning to her father. For the third time in as many days, he gave the same reply: "Soon."

The cart moved slowly enough that it took some time before the large, sagging inn was fully visible. It would not be even slightly truthful to describe it as a grand old building that had fallen on hard days. In truth, it was never grand even when it was new. More delicately put, it was a structure whose fabric was raised with great casualness and little expense.

The most striking aspect was a large sign announcing the Red Lion Inn. The major part of the sign was taken up by a painting of a large rampant red lion, snarling on hind feet with lashing claws. Sarah realized that it bore some family resemblance to the unknown creature gracing Aaron Austin's sign back in Westfield.

She was skeptical but quizzically turned to her father: "Here?" The previous night they had lodged in a gentle establishment of good reputation. Her father was at first reluctant to pay the cost, but a threatening storm tipped the scales. Sarah slept with the proprietor's younger daughters while her father shared a bed with three strangers. While it occasioned some grumbling from his bedmates, he refused to remove his boots. They were a fine new pair, and there was more than a slight chance that an early riser might take a fancy to them. John quickly decided that the Red Lion was likely far less accommodating.

Loud, raucous voices became even more boisterous when a well-clad gentleman lurched out the door of the Red Lion, leaving it unlatched. After several failed attempts to mount his horse, one of his fellow imbibers managed to finally get him seated. Reeling in the saddle, he leaned heavily against his horse's neck, arms flung to either side. He was suddenly quite asleep, and the mare calmly trotted unbidden along the well-remembered path homeward.

"Too frisky and too dear," Father replied. "This is not for us."

It was only when they were nearly past the ornate tavern sign that the faded lettering became legible: "Entertainment for Men and Horses."

Nodding her head in puckish seriousness, Sarah decided that, "I would not be allowed there in any case."

Puzzled, her father wondered, "Why is that?"

"They entertain men and horses only. And I am neither." She was quite pleased with her witticism and was disappointed when her father didn't react. Finally, he promised, "We shall stop for the night at the crossroads."

• • •

While the term might conjure up a grand intersection of busy highways, this intersection was, in reality, a scarcely noticeable crossing of meandering paths. It was near dusk before the horse was attended to, the bedding arranged, and the fire stoked.

"Sarah, we go west from here, and the path will be rough and steep. We must walk a good deal to save the horse. Your soft shoes will not stand the usage. Best to wear your substantial boots."

Stricken, she remembered in a rush that she had left them behind. An errant step while in the hog sty led her to stumble into their dung corner. Scrapping them clean as best she could, they were left to dry on the stone wall near the barn.

"I forgot them in Westfield."

Without even a hint of annoyance, he allowed, "Best then to save your shoes by doing without."

Sarah started to protest that her stockings would be ruined but thought better of it. She realized that she would be without them also. Best to save them for an agreeable presentation when Mother arrived.

Slowly filling his pipe, Father continued, "The habitations will soon become fewer and fewer and finally cease. We must never be out of sight of each other. That is the first rule. You may lose your way very easily. Never ever out of my sight!"

"Is Mother right, then? Is this dangerous ground?"

"It can be . . . made more so if untutored in its ways as you are. You will not see what must be seen and heeded. You must always be in my view. Do you understand?" She was startled by the quiet vehemence of her father's words. They carried the greater weight because he so rarely was this solemn.

Their meals of simmered salt pork and hard bread were already becoming monotonous after only a few days. The cheese blocks were even now clearly showing signs of growing furry coats. Sarah meant to save up her daily cache of berries collected along the way to share with her father. However, she seemed to nibble most of them away during the day despite her good intentions. Best to also eat the pitiful amount left.

That night, Sarah queried, "You were not moved by the minister's last sermon?"

John, taking time to carefully craft his response, allowed that, "The reverend says a great many things rightly, but we all have imperfect knowing."

"How do you see the world, Father?"

Another hesitation. "As a looking glass on creation."

"But the evil and savagery?"

Father exhaled loudly. "To everything, there is a season."

With a pensive smile, she picked up the passage: "A time to kill and a time to heal . . . a time to weep and a time to laugh." It was one of her favorite verses. The lovely symmetry of the poetry was compelling. Although certainly part of the Word, she was troubled by the meaning.

Her mind gradually became blank, empty of any thought as if in a trance, mesmerized by the embers of the lowering fire. The winking coals and spurts of flame became by turns different faces, some happy, others fierce, ever shifting in the fire. Her father's voice sharply calling her name brought her back.

"Sarah, this is what you must not do. While in your dreams, you are senseless; you do not see, you do not hear. The world happens around you unfelt."

"It is hard to stay out of it. I drift there for peace."

Poking the fire, she continued, "Some of the children captives of Deerfield refused to be ransomed. Were they possessed?"

"Possessed? There were reasons likely beyond our understanding. Perhaps the new families cherished them so that they would not give them up. Perhaps the children grew to accept the new state as good."

"That is not possible! They must have been beguiled. They cut their flesh and colored the wounds." There was a hint of disgust in her voice.

Startled as well as amused, he countered, "Who?"

"The Indians!"

"Some do. Not all."

Sarah was annoyed that her father should shrug off such a revolting practice so lightly. Unwilling to put the matter aside, she offered the final retort, "And their captives also! Why do they do it?"

He had witnessed Sarah's mother working herself into such a righteous froth on many occasions over the years. The main difference here being that Mary always waved her arms around with vigor.

"Many reasons. For pride or rank . . . or even beauteous fancy." Father's hope that Sarah might savor the wit was sorely disappointed.

She could not hide the disgust that ran over her face. "Heathens!"

"Sarah!"

"Yes. I know. I must mind my words."

Cupping Sarah's face, Father softly warned, "Much more, child. Much more. You must mind your expressions also. Your face is an open book that all eyes may browse upon. Strive to become a blank page of interest to none. An unmarked sheet tells nothing. You will soon see many such masks. Strive to become one of them."

Affecting an impassive face, she promised, "I will try." The serious, solemn vow wilted with her smile.

"It is time to retire." John reflected that his words alone were too weak; she needs to experience.

• • •

As her father had warned, the farms quickly became fewer. Suddenly, as if crossing an invisible border, they stopped. The familiar world of open fields, barns, and livestock was gone. They stepped off the edge of their world into the unknown.

While John was drawing water from a small rivulet one dawn two days later, Sarah reflected on the previous day's progress. Observing that he was occupied, she pulled his bound account book from the pouch. From her small cloth bag, she retrieved a vial of ink and a stub of a quill. She trimmed it down so as to be less noticeable. She remembered that the old gander she had plucked it from was loudly cross at the outrage and delivered a smart peck.

THE SEASONING

Turning to the bottom of the very last blank page, she began her account. Writing from bottom to top, from right to left, she hoped that this was a puzzling cipher:

My adventure begins. I am both frightened and giddy in equal measure. The old forest is so strange, the trees so great. The path is lit by blinding sun patches here and deep shadows there. The soothing sounds of livestock and home are gone. Commonly so quiet and still, strange shrieks echo through the forest. All evils may lurk here. But if I prevail, it will be the doing of me. I know the dreams will cease then. I feel this is true, but I know not why.

Out of the corner of her eye, she saw her father approaching and quickly put everything back in its proper place, fumbling to close the ink vial. She was relieved when none spilled.

"Busy with something this morning?"

With a casualness that she hoped was not telling, she yawned. "I was searching for one of my childish trinkets."

• • •

Gradually, day by day, the strangeness of her new world became a habit. Objects once cautiously poked and prodded now scarcely warranted a second glance. The journal entries lagged as the exciting newness waned. The days assumed a comforting sameness.

On one of these muddled days, impossible to order in her journal later, the morning began as usual. She scampered off the path on her quest for berries. She had so tired of their journey fare that they need not even be ripe. The sourness of the fruit itself was a welcome difference. After some days, her father's warnings and her replies became chants: "Stay in view," followed by, "Yes, I will."

Sarah became intrigued one morning by a large burl on an ancient maple tree. It took the perfect shape of a sheep's head. She couldn't help but reflect on what a wonderful bowl it might make. A true treasure. She suddenly became aware of a spent cookfire at her feet and sprang back with a start. With a stick, she probed for live coals and then felt the ashes for signs of heat. It was long cold.

John decided to stop there for the night, which struck her as odd since it was still early in the day. Perhaps he was tempted by the sunny patch with lush grass. The sack of oats was ebbing away.

"I have found a spent Indian fire."

"This is an old trail. There are many. What kind of fire was it?" Sarah was crestfallen. The exciting discovery was apparently disappointingly common. She could recall not a shred of the dead fire's nature. She had mingled everything with the probing stick.

"How old is the trail?" she inquired.

"As long as the Indians have been here. Long before us. It is their doings. It divides and rejoins like a sleepy river. We are on the longer, easy path. We must conserve the mare."

The tent unlimbered and staked, her father handed her a pail with a terse, "Water."

"I wish to bathe also."

"No, mud today. Draw the water first."

The country near the Indian path was alive with small streams, mostly mere rivulets, good for drawing drinking water if attended carefully or sating the horse but quite unsuited for bathing. This trickle near the trail was little different from the others, excepting that it lazed contentedly over bare rock, debauching into an open bowl shape scoured from the solid rock. As though a great hand had scooped out a smooth hollow, the tiny stream, over time, filled a clear pool that was deep enough for Sarah to sit in water nearly to her neck. She could have savored a long soak.

Filling the wooden pail first, she regarded her nearly black feet. They were calloused from hard use, and her jagged nails were crusted with dirt. Still shuffling, but now without shoes, her toes bore the signs of painful stubs. She peered intently into the clear water, scanning for unpleasant company, and slowly lowered her feet in. Her breath caught by the coldness of the pool, she quickly weighed against a full soak. Sitting with both feet soaking to the knees, she worked with the flat seed of a pinecone prizing the dirt from under the nails. The afternoon spring sun cast the canopy overhead in curious relief, each limb and branch melding into a tapestry.

Losing interest in the mud under her nails, she fell into a favorite reverie. Faces were conjured up in the foliage and as quickly disappeared only to be replaced by others. Each face was so particular and complete, she was at a loss as to why none ever resembled any of the faces she knew. Nor did any betray a feeling. A large face gradually formed in the branch web near a gap in the leaf cover. It scowled and throbbed as the leaves were stirred by a gentle waft.

The daydream shattered, she sprinted the short distance to the campsite. Slowing to a walk, she paused to regain her breath only to reverse her steps to retrieve the water. Carefully picking up the pail, she hurried to the path. The pleasant arcadian glen so restful before was now an unsettling place.

At the daily evening meal, now for sustenance only and devoid of enjoyment, Sarah suddenly wondered, "Why do we not see any game? A deer or squirrels? Something better? I would crave a fat turkey."

"We move with telling noise. Our coming is announced long in advance."

"We should move more softly, then?"

John, with a slight grin, gestured at the burdened wagon.

After a short pause, she said, "How do you judge the Indians? They are so strange and fearsome. I cannot fathom them." This was not a question that Sarah would have ever posed in Westfield. Indians were certainly there but on the edges, shadowy figures that did not require meeting.

"The same way that I would understand a heathen Moor. By caution and careful looking. If unsure, do nothing. Say nothing if in doubt. But always sharpen your eyes. Their natures are as changeable as our own."

These were disturbing new concerns for her. At home Indians were the "others," feared, even scorned, but given little thought otherwise.

"Do you count any as friends?"

"A number I respect. Fewer I trust. But friends?" This was a thought that had pecked at his mind for many years. He paused to form up his words so that Sarah might understand.

"Hearts are hearts, and deep friends open their souls. Sarah, I have had the privilege of sharing a friendship with a few." Holding his index fingers parallel, he said, "Our worlds move separately but never seem to join."

Changing the subject, "Why do you never address Emily by name?" Nodding toward the horse, she asked, "Or even your favorite hound?"

"Where is the need? They are beasts of the fields. A name does not matter. They come and go and are soon forgotten. A name creates an unprofitable memory."

"And the nameless stillborn babes?" Father sensed that the conversation was drifting along an unwanted path, but despite it, seemed compelled to offer a safe homily.

"They lack the naming ceremony."

"An unnamed sorrow must pass more easily, then?"

John Noble was a man often blessed by Providence. Luck seemed to trail behind him as a faithful pup. At difficult or dangerous moments in his life, salvation would appear from the most unexpected of saviors. On this occasion, the long, childlike howl of a mountain lion deflected the need of a reply. Sarah, without a conscious thought, moved closer to her father.

"Now there is a creature to be respected always! They are beings of fine judgment and careful patience. Prey so large that they may cause them wounds are avoided. All others are watched and stalked until a weakness is seen. The ambush always silent from behind."

"Are we of interest to them?"

"Yes, but small and unwary prey the more so."

• • •

Sarah lost track of the sequence of events in later years, but it was on the very next day that the wagon creaked past the open field. Her father became aware of it first, a two-acre stretch of open ground with no trees. Knee-high black birch saplings were already beginning to advance inward from the edges. Nature was reclaiming its own.

When his daughter became aware of the open ground, she shrieked with glee, "Let's stop here for the night! The night breezes will keep the bugs away. And finally, I may see the stars." It was certainly time to camp. The high ground to the west nearly obscured the setting sun.

"No. This place is not for us," was her father's laconic reply. "Sarah, look at the ground with searching eyes."

In time, she would learn to critically see without her father's prompting, but that would come much later. She squinted at the open ground with intense concentration. Finally, she asked, "This is long-tilled ground. Indians? But where are they? It's late in the planting season. They should be about."

John, with a raised eyebrow, slowly shook his head. The evening meal was a somber affair. Sarah was quiet awaiting her father's explanation for the empty field. But it never came. His once-a-night tobacco indulgence became four. Wreathed in smoke, he spent the night looking into the darkness, pondering the village with no fires.

While preparing to retire, Sarah could stop herself up no longer and asked, "Father, what became of them?" John slowly shook his head as he had earlier. But now she knew it was not just an admission of ignorance but of loss. Sleep came hard to her that night. A whole village scooped off the earth as if by some giant hand. She lay awake kneading the various causes. But none of them were pleasing or soothing. The sly little imp nestled in the pit of her stomach started to stir again. This was a dark and fearful place, bathed in innocent sunlight. She was gladdened the next morning to leave it.

• • •

Sarah lost count of the days. They were all the same. Although measured in weeks, the days seemed endless. The grand adventure had long paled; the curious sights were no longer new, and she had taken, where possible, to riding in the cart. She was dirty and gamey in both her apparel and her person. She came to suppose that snakes were gifted by their ability to shed their old skin. Their overnight pauses at streams presented either clear icy pools or muddy puddles.

Idly inspecting her calloused, dirty feet brought back the memory of Emily's reshoeing just before the departure. With a curiously shaped but devilishly sharp tool, the blacksmith had cleaned away all matter of filth from her hooves. Sarah chuckled out loud at the thought of a smithy working over her equally fouled feet with the knife. She quickly caught herself, however. Lately she had gradually come to feel that she was being greatly put upon during this journey. This sour mood was becoming almost agreeable, and she was loath to lose it to momentary mirth. The feeling of being wronged by fate flooded her with a sense of righteousness. A black rose perhaps deserving cultivation.

"Father, how much longer?" There was a slight scrim of impatience in her tone.

"Soon." He was leading the horse afoot but did not require her to join him.

"You promised that two days ago."

"Then it's more soon, isn't it?"

"My dress is soiled. I am soiled!"

"If we press on, we may reach a stream with a small pool."

She asked in a voice only she could hear, "Is it warm? Is it clean?" She let it go finally. What would be would be. With the remaining half-filled sack of oats for a pillow, she drifted into sleep.

John, scanning the high ridge to the north became aware of a lone horseman observing them. A tall man in Indian attire, he might have escaped notice except that he wore a bright-blue hat. He was too far distant to judge the exact nature of the head covering, but John certainly knew the wearer. The leather garments were not threadbare but easy, conforming to the Indian's frame by longtime habitation. Silently, the horseman disappeared over the ridge. Climbing into the cart, John carefully checked the musket.

Ninefingers! John thought. From long experience, he realized that this exposure was no mere happenstance. Ninefingers was signaling a meeting; otherwise, he would never have shown himself. The horseman would make the first move. Certainly tonight. He wanted to talk.

Sarah, having fallen asleep in the cart, was jolted awake unexpectedly early at the stop for the night. It was the south crossroads that her father had promised for days. As it seemed little different from many others, the import escaped her. With glee, she scampered off to inspect the pool while her father tended to Emily and the night's bedding. It was a perfect stream, warm, clear, and deep. Trotting back, she fetched the pail and announced, "I shall bathe, but in my shift, and wash my skirt as well."

"No, it would not be wise." For an instant, she thought she had misheard. However, her father's expression was clear and brooked no argument. No more than a feeble "but . . ." escaped her lips. With pail in hand, she slowly walked toward the alluring but now forbidden pool. Stopping only once to look back, the words of anger, outrage, and confusion boiled in her mouth, never to find an outlet.

The near bank of the pool was capped by a large, flat stone, so smooth as to make a bench. But the first touch of her foot caused it to quiver, and she only just managed to regain her balance. The weight of the wildly gyrating pail was nearly her undoing.

When the stone decided to quiet, Sarah eased her feet into the stream, idly splashing and watching the ripples race away. In accordance with a firm decision made last night, she flexed her right leg out of the water and carefully nibbled, trimming her toes of their jagged nails. The packed dirt under her toenails made a grinding noise on her teeth as she gnawed off the nails. Later, she realized that a good, long soak would have softened the chewing. The left foot was a more awkward go of it, which was a puzzle. Only afterward did she look around with some embarrassment, hoping that there were no witnesses.

Sliding slowly, either from guilt or a sense of caution, Sarah eased her body into the water, nearly up to her shoulders. And there she wallowed for some time until John summoned, "Sarah, come." He had already built the night's fire, and as she approached she realized that he had put on his squint eye. She knew it only too well. Although silent, it spoke: *What is the fable on this day? I believe not a bit of it!* Water still dripping from her skirt and clinging close to her, she explained, "The footing was bad."

"Some good came of it. Your skirt is clean. And most of your upper."

"Some of the stones were not fast and my balance was lost. But I nearly—"

It all ended quickly with a sharp retort: "Sarah! In such matters, the less explained the better!"

Through much of the early evening, her father's attention was focused beyond the arc of the firelight. He didn't seem inclined to talk. Sarah stared into the flickering fire drifting into her private world. It was not that she pondered important feelings. The truth of the matter was that she was thinking of nothing at all. Her empty mind was a state of great comfort, she found. No worries, no decisions, just a blissful float in a void.

∙∙∙

Her father's sudden movement caught her attention. Following his line of sight into the shadows beyond the light, she saw a tall, sinewy Indian dressed in worn leather. Incongruously, he wore an elaborate blue satin hat flagged with a long white feather. Such an apparition in Westfield would surely have provoked gales of hearty mirth, likely being compared to a ringlet of flowers about a goat's neck. But here, at this time, at this place, it clearly portended a serious purpose. Although the whys and true nature of it escaped her, she knew it as a truth. Important things would unfold this night!

John nodded and the shadowy figure entered the camp. Even in her quivering fright, she realized that they had exchanged signals of intent. The Indian approached only after presence and purpose was clear.

Sarah's voice was thin and warbling: "Father?"

"Remember what I said."

"I will try, Father, but my heart has a wildness!"

The visitor stopped before her, and with great effort she met his gaze. He studied Sarah carefully, deciding the extent of her mettle. There was not a flicker of meaning in his eyes nor on his face. He was likely her father's age, but taller and pine-tree erect. The story, repeated to her children many times in the future, stressed that she would never again feel so cold in her long life. Not the cold of snow, or a bitter wind in January, nor even the raw damp of a November gale, but an icy grip on her soul that no quilt or fire could soothe.

The Indian's interest satisfied, he turned to her father and dropped two squirrels at his feet. Side by side, they dressed out the meat and mounted them on spits hastily procured from a nearby maple sapling. Not a single word passed between them. Each knew the ritual. Her father mounted them on notched supports and cautioned his daughter, "Sarah, mind the meat."

Carefully, she slowly turned the little carcasses, which now appeared very much smaller. At home, the clock reel would perform the task of turning; with the weights wound up, the device would turn the spit 'til it ran down. "Mind that the spits don't burn through, Sarah. Else the meat is in the fire."

She reckoned the brace might sate a single person if of modest appetite. She suddenly realized that this had very little to do with food. The purpose here was very different. In spite of her fears, she minded each interaction of the two men with rapt fascination.

Everything was so quiet that the sprites gamboling about in her stomach had largely settled. She turned her attention by turns from the turning spits, now charring, to the two men. Their shared comportment seemed almost . . . gentle.

John retrieved his tobacco pouch and poured tobacco into Ninefingers pouch without a word passing between them. Ninefingers then filled two pipes from his newly filled leather sack. They spoke softly in a dialect entirely lost to Sarah. The family had been aware that Father spoke their language, though she had never heard him use it. She now realized how foolish she was not to have learned some of their speaking. The even, quiet tone of the two men revealed no readable feelings. When she heard her name, the flutters in her stomach revived.

Reverting to English, the Indian inquired, "You are coming amongst us?"

"Yes, and my family."

"And others?"

"Yes, many others."

"Bears may live in a cave in all their memories. Then wolves come and say, 'You must leave. Our need is greater.'" He devoured the sparse meat quickly, nodded to her father, and disappeared into the darkness without a departing word. His coming was more an apparition than a visit.

The abrupt departure of the Indian startled Sarah. The leaving, lacking any parting acknowledgment, unnerved her. This could not be a good omen. Speaking to the direction of the Indian's disappearance into the darkness, she spoke an obvious truth: "You know him."

"We have met before at Fort Orange and elsewhere. Many times. He is called Ninefingers."

Mulling over the meaning of Ninefingers' words, John at length became aware of Sarah's puzzled expression. Holding up both hands and splaying out his ten fingers, he slowly retracted the right thumb.

"The cause was not natural nor an accident. It was a directed mischief inflicted many years past. I never learned the particulars."

"You knew he would come. Or such like him." With her father's nod, she continued, "Why didn't you warn me?"

"But I did. I certainly did." Thinking back over the day's events, Sarah began to see his cautious behavior in a new light.

Continuing, she asked, "And the hat? The feather? Such a beautiful hat! If it was in Mr. Austin's possession, he would surely be much torn between setting a hard price on it or having a grand auction for more." They both smiled at this amusing but true observation. She did wonder why he would wear such a treasure on the move.

"I would not dare wear it on travels for fear of spoiling it."

"He dons it with a purpose. Did you not notice the decorations? Symbols of France."

"To frighten us, then?

"To remind us of the high regard that he is held by the French. Such a splendid gift is not bestowed lightly. This affair requires great care. Our footfalls must be delicate and measured. But now we retire and shall sleep well. A most satisfactory day."

"Father, why did Ninefingers start to speak in English for a short time?"

Barely opening his eyes, he advised, "To tell you what you should know."

...

True to his prediction, he was fast asleep moments after climbing into the tent. Sarah's mind boiled to make sense of the day's happenings, confused that he could snore so loudly so soon after all that had unfolded. Sleepily, she decided that something of great importance had happened, although the exact nature of it was not clear to her. She now knew that her father was not only expecting such a visitation but welcomed it and was somehow relieved. The outcome was happy enough that he could sleep with little worry. *Would the white horse come to her this night?* was her last thought before her day ended.

The night passed quietly for Sarah. If the nightmare haunted her dreams, it left no memory. When she was assured that Father was still asleep, she stirred and gathered her writing tools. Determined to record her thoughts of the previous day, she carefully opened her father's account book, beginning to write as soon as usable daylight opened.

An Indian visited us late last evening. He appeared as if a phantom from the dark. I served him while shaking with bumps on my whole body. A cruel savage and yet so composed and noble in his countenance. Named Ninefingers. I am befuddled and awry. He harbors me no particular ill, but I feel he would kill me in an instant if he felt that needs must. I am a traveler, a pilgrim, entering into a world not my own. I must be all eyes and ears.

Gradually as she scratched out the letters to form her thoughts, she became aware of the noise of the quill dragging across the paper. Glancing up at her father, she froze, seeing him looking at her with curiosity.

"Sarah, why do you write from right to left? From bottom to top, all backward?"

"You will need all the remaining front space for your new book accounts. Once started, writing from bottom to top backward seemed quite agreeable . . . And I hoped by doing it, you would not read my thoughts. Did you read them?"

"I misplaced my spectacles. And private feelings, scribed in private, are private. A cipher, then? If it is another of your new notions, I fear it will not be popular."

The spectacles were not misplaced, that was always accepted by both of them. While easing the account book from the pouch, Sarah had to push the spectacles aside to tease the book out. This was a stagecraft then of soft pretending; her father acting out that the glasses were lost and the journal unread. Sarah happily accepted his lies with silent relief. She was grateful but troubled. These were soothing tales that spared feelings and cooled any strife but were also mere figments of the truth. What else may not be true?

CHAPTER VII

June 16, 1707

The next dawn greeted their early start. The cart, ungreased since Westfield, gave out creaks of protest as it rolled along the dark path. No crisp breezes stirred the forest floor. Sarah was intrigued by the fragrance. Each breath was filled with the warm smells of life. Sarah was familiar with the unique smells of each season. Winter, arid and sharp like old cider. Spring brought warm, flowery odors even before the first blooms had arrived. In summer, the passing smells of growth hung in the wet air wafting along as in an unseen river. Autumn, a favorite time, a sweet ripeness nearing decay. The smell of this deep forest was all its own. She couldn't put a finger to it. Her simple friend Eleanor came to mind. Her dwelling had a singular smell identical to her person. How is it possible that every house has a different redolence? And how do others judge my smell?

Her father was playing out his own silent train of thoughts. With perseverance, he judged that they might reach their new settlement before nightfall. Sarah had lately taken to occupying the seat next to him more and more. She was increasingly reluctant to venture far into the darkened woods. Caution was difficult without clear light.

Sarah finally broke the silence, questioning her father as to the proper English name for their new home. Certainly not the Indian one of Weatanock! John supposed that they would find out when they arrived. Since so many of the proprietors hailed from the port town of Milford, perhaps they had settled on New Milford.

He mused aloud, hoping that, "Today makes an end to it. Our pitch is very near that river." Motioning to the river close by to his left, he spoke louder so as to be heard over the music of the water.

"Around the set-out common green, the sites are all long finger lots. I have hopes that ours runs down to the river. It would be a great convenience. And the fare will improve. This river teems with fish."

Prompted by her father's mention of the river, Sarah wondered that he had firmly advised that she must not swim in it. "Why am I not allowed to swim in it?" Her father, from long experience, explained that the muddy bottom hid many dangers and snags. The eddies and currents were bewitching.

Sarah finally opened a question that had been on her mind since Ninefingers' alarming visit of the previous day. "Last evening, Ninefingers gave us meat and you gave tobacco. Yet each took something back. It was not trading, yet not quite sharing. What does it mean?"

John hesitated, examining what the proper words might be. He paused long enough that Sarah feared that this was his reply: silence. Finally, he said, "Look upon it as a dance. Yes, a dance. The steps are set and known. Each move in union or apart to create a harmony. A misstep spoils the unity and makes ill will. It is a ceremony of great importance."

"Ninefingers. What is his nature?"

"Hard. A man to be treated with care. But a man of great honor in their own lights."

Her father was speaking in riddles again. Their own lights? Different than us? After deciding that she was being left to tease out the meaning of the puzzle on her own, she continued, "His stare unsettled me. The eyes were as awls boring into my very soul. What was the purpose?"

"Reading an unknown book? Or perhaps taken by your colorful hem?" John's broad smile signaled that any serious conversation was at an end.

Further probing would merely elicit further witticisms. Sarah, from long experience, accepted that when her father did not care to pursue a notion, silence or humor was his shield.

∙ ∙ ∙

By early afternoon, the mare was nearly spent, obliging them to stop so that both horse and riders could refresh. The trail coursed very near the river and little grass was at hand for Emily. She was doled out the last of the oats.

When her father disappeared down to the riverbank, Sarah unwrapped her writing tools with the thought of continuing her journal. But her mind was mute. The ink on her quill dried before any thoughts came to her. Was there really nothing of note to observe, or was the task less urgent now that her secret was known?

Scrapping the sticky ink off her pen, she joined her father at the river. He was perched on a most singular rock formation. Descending from the trail, a great flat slab of stone at least a rod wide plunged into the water. Canted at an angle, it was not so steep as to prohibit walking on but sufficiently tilted that rain kept it clear of debris. She carefully descended the smooth rock and sat next to her father at the very edge. Peering into the murky water, she observed, "The water is quiet here and deep."

Father added to her thoughts: "Good fishing, but if you slide in, you'll be obliged to swim downstream a bit to get out. There will be no climbing up the underwater slope."

"Father, you have been here before. You know this place." With his slight nod, she continued, "You have lived in this different world. When younger? Long time?"

"Much of my youth."

Smiling, she teased, "And you moved back and forth between them. You are like the eel, living in water mostly but able to slither across a dry meadow on occasion to find a better stream."

With her father's changed expression, suddenly she realized that she was being quite impertinent, even though the words were meant as wit. By slow, almost imperceptible degrees, the informality between them had ebbed away. He stood up abruptly, announcing, "Time to move on. Avoid the mossy patches on the way up."

The journey resumed in an awkward silence. Occasionally glancing at her father, Sarah mulled over the knowledge that he once lived an earlier existence quite separate from the family. Without much thought, she had always accepted that the path of our lives was an arrow, certain to arrive at a fated end. But of late she realized that this was not the case. Sadly, she came to know that there were recesses in her father's life that were forever closed to her. And the secrets?

• • •

A buzzard lazily circling above the water in search of a well-rotted fish would have noticed two groups on the river at once. The Nobles: their packed wagon continuing the slow trek south; some miles ahead on their path, a young Indian, known as Tawsume, with a fishing spear waited patiently in the shallows.

With a quick jab, he lunged at a fish but missed a large prize. From the corner of his eye, Tawsume became aware of the approach of a second young Indian man called Nawas. Tawsume was annoyed that his visitor did not approach carefully but capered noisily, jumping from rock to rock. It was commonly known that, while having no ears to hear with, fish could catch sounds somehow through the water. Hard footfalls on stones were heard even underwater, causing the fish to dart away. Such was the case here.

Finally settling on a large boulder, Nawas inquired, "What's the harvest?" Seeing Tawsume's expression, he allowed there was "Little to show for standing in the mud all this time I see."

"More English are coming. Trapper Noble's tribe."

Tawsume, in curiosity, wondered, "How do you know?"

"Can't you smell them?" Nawas, pleased with his words continued, "I saw them yesterday in the north, moving slowly as turtles."

Tawsume didn't answer directly but was instead eyeing a large, aged snapping turtle nearby in a quiet stretch of river, cautiously sniffing the air with a hooked maw. This ponderous creature was a sometime companion, loitering in the shallows hoping for an easy meal. He kept a wary distance just beyond spear reach yet close enough for a dash at a wounded fish. Tawsume, when his fishing twin first appeared, originally had some hope of a full turtle feast. Gradually, he discarded the idea and the two adversaries settled into a series of wary, predictable meetings. When Tawsume appeared, the old reptile knew that food might be at hand.

Turning to Nawas and nodding toward the turtle, he inquired, "Like that?"

Quietly, Nawas admitted, "They bring much that I like."

"Like?"

"Women with yellow hair." As was common to his nature, Nawas passed off his flippant observation as a jest, but Tawsume, from long acquaintance, knew well the truth.

"And Takhi?" Nawas merely shrugged and smiled. Annoyed at the spoiled fishing and heightened by Nawas's answer, Tawsume grew heated.

"Nawas, what are you thinking? You are soon a father! You are bonded with Takhi yet show no constancy or faith. When will you act the man? You shame yourself. You shame us all. Do you not care for anyone?"

Nawas smirked and scampered off, jumping heavily from stone to stone. Tawsume was never in doubt that Nawas was little changed even from their childhoods. Always smiling but just the same. He was more agreeable seen at a distance. From his youth, he was always the fleetest of them, and his throwing arm never seemed to miss a target. Gathering smooth river stones, he would launch them at a safe distance at the young boys, only rarely missing, and only for sport. And always his soothing words never failed to soften the hurts. That such a manly father such as Ninefingers could spawn such a feckless boy was often a topic of comment. But now, his childish behavior might not be healed with words. Soon the bonds of their longtime acquaintance would no longer hold.

Gazing into the water, he realized that Nawas's distraction caused him to lose the light. For a short period, both before and after high noon, the sun cast its light perfectly into the water in such a way that the fish were clearly visible. This slim opportunity was past, and the fish were once again safe under the shimmering water, hidden from his eyes. The old turtle, the more perceptive of the two, was nowhere to be seen.

Trudging back to the village, Tawsume was disappointed with his catch. Nothing very large or red and sweet. The bag was half full of the usual namebin fish. Quite presentable as fare once the odd sucking mouth was accepted. When they moved into small streams in the spring to spawn, the tribe gorged on them. They would have starved without this bounty. But the fish had far too many tiny little bones for his liking.

Tawsume smiled at the stories that he used to pass on to younger children who still believed any tale offered. In a serious, grave tone, he might caution wild-eyed babes to be ever careful of such fish when in the water as they might use the great sucker mouth to attach themselves to their bodies. There were two endings to the fable, each tendered according to his wont. The first described great holes rasped into the flesh; the second, less fearful, had the sucking mouths cut away in time, leaving only large red welts that were lifelong marks.

• • •

The Nobles' moaning cart, complaining more bitterly with each passing day and at a slower pace, reached Tawsume's fishing spot many hours later. John had miscalculated their progress, and it was now near dark when they approached their final destination at the new settlement site. The Indian village on the high ground to the right was readily visible from the numerous fires.

Surveying the grassy meadow near the river, he chose a low site near the water. A large buttonball tree would provide some shade while this particular ground was unlikely to be of any interest to anyone. The inhabitants of the area, of course, were forewarned of their arrival. It could hardly be otherwise. Noble thought it carefully diplomatic to keep their presence cautious until a more formal arrival was announced the next morning. For this very reason, he selected a secluded wet site.

"We're here!" With that John leapt off the cart, tending to the horse. Untacking the harness, he led the weary old animal down to the river to drink its fill. He fetched the longest rope so that the mare might have the greatest play to gather forage. Surveying the ground, he decided that they couldn't remain on this site for long. Too long here, and the mare would have foot rot.

Sarah climbed down from her seat more gingerly. Most of the day, she had dozed fitfully next to her father, awaking in starts when the cart shuddered over a log. She was sore and stiff, moving as gingerly as an old woman. Stretches and most unladylike grunts soon restored her to some working order. While setting out the bedding and tent, her assigned task, she surveyed her new home as best she could through the fading wet light. She was both dismayed and surprised in equal degrees.

Lately, she had taken to talking to herself on puzzling occasions such as this. Her father might answer her or not depending on the mood. "This is it? We've come all this way for this?" The grand adventure now seemed a dreadful mistake. Overwhelmed for the first time by yearnings for the home she knew, she just managed to wipe away the tears as her father appeared.

"Father, I am so weary. Might we sleep under the cart? I can scarcely see to set the tent."

"Yes, but no fire. Biscuits will do for dinner." Without the formality of a fire, both father and daughter gnawed on the stale biscuits under the wagon box.

"It is so low and wet here. The pests will feast upon us. Even now, I hear their songs." Sarah's words slowed and softened as they tumbled out. John chose this site for the gentle slope of the riverbank so that the horse might not risk a mishap while drinking. A maimed mare would be a disaster. But the mosquitoes were only a minor problem. The soil was all sand and soft for breeding clouds of sand fleas. He rolled over but saw that Sarah was fast asleep. Just as well.

• • •

The next morning, Sarah only gradually became aware of daylight noises: distant voices, animals braying, and river sounds. At one point, with eyes still closed, she wondered if this were a dream. Opening her eyes revealed a bright sunlit morning enhanced by a pleasant breeze off the river. Staring at her, a mere few feet away through the wheel spokes, was a large pair of black eyes. She saw not the owner of the set of unblinking pupils, but just the stare.

Lapsing into the dreaded memories of her night terrors, she bolted upright, banging her forehead on the cart bed above. Later, her Indian acquaintances occasionally vied in competition to recreate her anguished howl.

There was never universal agreement on the most authentic of the various imitations that the young women offered. The young boy garnered some reputation amongst his peers for this feat.

"What! Who are you? Leave me alone!" The words meant nothing of course to the little imp. It was her shrill, warbling tones that impressed most deeply on their memories.

Gingerly exploring the bump on her head, she looked through the spokes only to realize that the terror was an Indian child of six or seven, now nearly out of sight.

Carefully climbing out from under the cart, she could better see the nature of the land. There were broad, flat meadows on both sides of the river. To her right on higher ground was the Indian settlement set at the foot of a steeply rising hill. The meadows were lush and of long standing. No stumps obstructed a clean, straight plow path. Some parts were cultivated, some were grass but without a clear order. She decided that it was the wet ground. Certain parts were unprofitable to cultivate and left to grass. The river seemed placid now, but the banks were low enough to allow mischief if the water ran wild during spring thaws.

While she was mulling over the nature of the low ground, she was absently rubbing her left forearm. When her scratching raised a sting, she noticed a line of small bites marching up her arm. Fleas!

Sarah was intrigued by the nearly continuous comings and goings to the river. The Indians were mostly women, but some clearly elderly men. The bank of the river was alive with children sporting about, paying little heed to the adults.

Many of the women passed quite close by to the cart, and she decided that a show of friendliness was the most judicious action. The passing women often stared at her when walking near, but when she offered them determined smiles, they only paused for a moment before resuming their ways. Her smiles were never returned. Part of Sarah's mind took the other part to task. This was a foolish misstep! She should have heeded their father when he counseled, "When in doubt, do nothing."

Even years later, Sarah never worked out why she had not noticed her father's absence immediately upon awakening. The knowledge came to her in such a sudden rush that it stopped her breath. After only a moment, however, the throbbing in her breast started to calm. Time to think! Not only was her father gone but so was Emily. He was making rounds, she decided, visiting the other settlers' encampments. Of course, he was! She was soothed by the knowledge that they were not alone after all.

Climbing up onto the cart seat for a better view, Sarah gazed at the tattered harlequin strip that her mother had attached to her cast-off skirt. "Yellow is Mary's favorite color. Perhaps less notice is better." Frayed at the bottom and so embedded with dirt that a cleaning was hopeless, she began to unravel the threads, which pulled out easily. With a hard jerk, it was free. Carefully, she rolled up the strip thinking that it might have a useful purpose yet. Jumping off the cart, she nestled the soiled fragment next to her real treasure, the green silk.

She settled as she heard her father's familiar voice: "How long have you been about?"

"Not long. Where have you been?" Her tone was accusatory. She had never considered that she might be left entirely alone.

Her father either didn't hear the reproach in her voice or simply ignored it, responded lightly, "Arranging things."

"Planning with the other settlers? Are there any girls my age? That would be a great comfort to me."

Father studied his daughter for a moment before admitting, "There are no other proprietors here yet. We are the very first."

To allay her surging fear, Sarah quickly changed the subject. "Is this our allotment?"

"No, this section is too low. This part of the river has a wild nature best avoided. We are across the river on high ground." Pointing to a distant oak rising above the canopy, he mused, "Just there. This low ground is fondly held by the Indians, and the families that elect it may learn to rue their choice. I have a meeting with the elders this evening. That was my purpose this morning."

This whole adventure since they left Westfield had taken on a storybook quality. It might be exciting or frightening, perhaps even pleasant, but it all ended when the cover was closed. But now, for the very first time, she knew that the story was flowing and could not be turned off so lightly. They were truly adrift in another world.

"Why are you meeting with the elders?"

"To announce our coming."

"But they surely know that we are here."

"To soothe and soften feelings, then."

"And the other pro . . . props . . . proprie . . ." This was an unfamiliar legal word that her father had used of late and for reasons quite unclear to her was always stubbing itself over her tongue.

"Proprietors."

"Yes, that. Will they do the same when they arrive?"

With a frown, her father finally admitted, "Doubtful."

"Then why do we?"

Father answered not with words but a slow, gravelly exhale. She immediately knew that this was a silent show of annoyance and that she should work it out for herself. Her mother handled such a situation entirely differently with a torrent of sharp words decorated with many exaggerated finger pokes.

One winter's night while the sisters were warming their back parts on the chimney before climbing into the featherbed, sister Mary complained that Mother was far too fond of threatening her with the "finger wand." In some unchristian fashion, Mary appeared to endow their mother's dramatic gestures with a magical quality. Sarah slowly smiled. It was not the quick, open smile of glee nor the curled lipped satisfaction of sweet revenge but that of sudden comprehension.

"Of course! The dance." Father nodded with a smile of satisfaction.

"Am I to come?" John was quite taken aback at first. It never entered his mind that Sarah would even consider entering into this world at all, much less this soon. But all to the good. Examining each word carefully, he spoke slowly.

"If you wish. But you must remain outside the firelight and say nothing. Ears and eyes only but no words. We have no voice here." Sarah felt the veins in her neck throbbing as was the nature of her fears, but there was something else now, something new. She was excited and, to her surprise, curious.

"May I converse with others outside the circle? There will be others?"

"Yes, but . . ." The caution was in her mind before her father even spoke it.

"I will respond but not prompt. Silent until bidden."

They both watched the passing parade of Indians on their daily business to and fro at the river. Sarah glanced at her father, who had fallen quiet, wondering what he was thinking. His look was far away, and his lips were softly pursing as though speaking to a ghost. From long watching of her father, she could read that he was far away in time reliving an earlier life. A time before Westfield, a time before them.

"Father, before, I smiled kindly when the Indian women passed by, yet they had faces of stone. Did I do wrong?"

"They may judge the smile without a reason as the mark of an addled mind. Such a smile from an 'other' rings of deceit or a clever ruse."

An immediate thought sprung from her lips, an imp having a mind all its own quite uncalled: "And we are the 'others'."

Throughout the day, John was constantly away on what he described cryptically as needed meetings. Since there was little that needed her instant attention, she explored the riverbank looking for a likely spot to wash their undergarments. Surveying the turbid, muddy water, she doubted that they would be any cleaner after than before.

Sarah was now beginning to regret her initial enthusiasm for attending the meeting that evening. She was not aware at first that the gathering would be after dark. The idea of walking into the Indian village after sunset, the object of curious eyes, stirred feelings of unease that had plagued her all day.

The dark itself never provoked fear in her heart even as a very little child. Fetching a tool from the barn after dark gave her scarcely a pause. Poking Elizabeth over her night frights was perhaps unkind but great fun. But this was different. Very, very different. This edged far too close to her unwelcome dreams.

The evening meal was silent and strained. When they spoke at all, the words were carefully crafted concerning simple trifles. The point of every comment was to tread lightly in order to avoid touching the real thorn. Fresh fish and a gloriously oily duck were the evening's welcome fare. After weeks of hard cakes and salted pork, this should have been a giddy, noisy relief, a true deliverance. Instead, it was worse than any funeral meal—glum and solemn but without the bracing relief of strong spirits.

Sarah studied her father as he smoked his pipe. All appearances suggested that he was in complete ease. She marveled at how he so composed himself. But this was surely a mask. He guarded his thoughts with all the jealous ferocity of a testy old hen determined to sit on her clutch of eggs until hatching. As the day darkened, he occasionally glanced at the fires of the Indian encampment. Then, as if by a hidden signal, he stood and announced: "It is time."

• • •

The distance from their camp to the Indian village was little more than half a mile, and Sarah was dismayed that her father was striding so quickly. If they walked slower, she would have more time to compose herself. It would delay even briefly this ordeal. She considered grasping her father's hand but decided against it.

As they drew near, the shapes of the dwellings were familiar. She had seen such Indian houses in Westfield but never this close. There was no cause to mingle with the Indians, and their huts were only observed at a safe distance.

The Indian dwellings were clad in great sheaths of hemlock bark closely fitted together. The tanners at home valued the bark for curing hides into leather and was in some demand. The dye extracted from it gave cloth a pleasant rust-brown color.

Set apart from the smaller wigwams was one much larger, and Sarah guessed that this was their destination. A large fire was flanked on either side by long tree-length logs set up as benches. In the flickering light beyond the circle were stationary figures, barely visible. This would be her station. The village had sifted itself apart as the men were on the firelit benches while women and children sat in the flickering shadows behind.

Sarah was taken by the silence of the children. Their forays to the river were a cacophony of screeches and shouts. It now was clear to her that the native children's loose tethers had boundaries. John, while not looking at her, signaled with a raised hand for Sarah to stop. He continued on and took a seat next to an older man whom she took to be the chief. She noticed immediately that the chief's bench towered over her father's. Bowing to the awkwardness of her situation, she retreated into the shadows and lighted on an empty bench.

The gathering became quiet. There must have been a signal, but she noticed nothing. It felt like the silent pause was very long, although it was doubtless not more than a moment or two. Sarah wondered, with growing anxiety, when the first word might come. Finally, the chief spoke: "John Noble comes to us. He will soon dwell amongst us. He seeks our care and warmth. Who will speak?"

Sarah was curious that the chief did not rise when he spoke. At the Meeting House at home, for both Sabbath services and town business, all speakers rose to address the listeners.

It was only later, gradually over many years, that Sarah sorted out and understood the forms and signs of this most memorable encounter. The placement of her father's seat below the chief's: he was as a humble supplicant. His silence throughout the entire evening was a part of this role. The native leader spoke in English, surely a sign of a great curtesy. Many of the tribe were quite innocent of English, kept informed only by quick, sketchy translations.

Ninefingers rose first and strode to the center near the fire. Sarah was surprised at first as she hadn't noticed him. From their past meeting on the trail, it was not difficult to guess the nature of his thoughts. He was not wearing the elegant hat that had sat atop his head in the earlier visit. She noted to herself that she should think upon the significance later. Composing himself, Ninefingers carefully met the gaze of a number of men, clearly men of importance in his eyes.

"We are now entering into a place that gives no way out!" Sarah marveled at his rich and commanding voice. His very figure spoke authority. If he were English, he might attend Harvard College and aspire to the pulpit of King's Chapel in Boston. Staring at a selected few in the audience, speaking to each of them in turn, he continued.

"How long has it been since you gathered from the great waters? When did you last see the lands of your past in the East? We become fewer each year as the English increase. With every year! They bring nothing but ills. Their sicknesses fall on us. They are nothing but lice upon the land." Pausing, he swooped down dramatically and pulled up a plantain lily growing at his feet by the roots. He made a slow circuit of the circle shaking it, exclaiming over and over. "Even now, they crowd our feet!"

Sitting in the shadows, Sarah's rapt attention to the speech of Ninefingers was broken when an Indian girl abruptly sat down next to her. The log that Sarah sat on was nearly empty. That her visitor sat so close by unnerved her. Instinctively, Sarah thought to slide away only to realize that she was at the end of the bench. For a few moments, the two girls sat side by side and Sarah took the girl's measure with brief side glances while her companion ignored her. The Indian girl was perhaps a few years older than Sarah. In the darkness, it was uncertain. Indian youth seemed to lose the softness of childhood much sooner. What was certain was that she was very pregnant.

The prolonged silence between the two girls sitting so near, almost as fast friends, gradually fueled a growing sense of embarrassment in Sarah. She thought to introduce herself, but then decided no, she would wait and follow the girl's lead.

Suddenly her bench mate speaking softly to herself observed, "Small people. Always small people. Their judgment is small. And foolish."

Sarah did not intend to speak but her puzzlement surged out as, "Small people?"

The young girl only now turned to Sarah and explained. "I am Pequot. We were not small people. The far south and the east were once all ours." Casually looking around, she continued, "Here we were feared and respected. Before they came." Turning to Sarah to stare directly into her eyes, she spit out an accusation: "Before you came."

Ninefingers' speech was greeted with a chorus of murmurs. He slipped seamlessly back and forth between English and Indian. From her vantage point, Sarah could make out only a few immobile dissenting faces. The animation of the remainder spoke that Ninefingers' feelings were the consensus. After a pause, when no one else rose to speak, the chief replied in slow cadences.

"All of his words are true. We all know it. But they offer no end path. We cannot change what is. The autumn leaves will fall always." His words slowed to a pause.

Gazing down at the meadow on the river's edge, he continued: "We are as the morning dew. At full sun, we leave not a touch. But we can . . ." Sarah's concentration on the soft voice of the chief's reply was broken when her companion abruptly sprang to her feet.

With clenched fists, the girl spoke with an angry intensity in a hiss. It was a kind of oath. "They are all the unknowing dead, but still talk and talk, only talk!" She quickly turned to leave and, as an afterthought, turned and announced to Sarah, "I am Takhi."

Sarah instinctively offered a hand. "I am Sarah, Sarah Noble." Takhi stared at her for what seemed much longer than it actually was. Nevertheless, it was long enough that the outstretched hand became an embarrassment. A decision made, Takhi quickly clutched the hand and just as quickly disappeared into the darkness.

Business concluded, the crowd thinned quickly. Women and children first, then the men gradually drifted away. Sarah was amused at how similar it was to a town meeting in Westfield. There were the stay-behinds in small groups deep in conversation. Her father went from group to group making an appearance, just like in Westfield.

Despite the similarities, the feeling of this meeting was different somehow. She knew it but not how or why. That knowledge would come to her in later years when lost hopes and dreams became closer acquaintances. Sarah waited until her father came to fetch her.

Walking in silence down the slight grade to the river and their camp by half-moon light, Sarah waited for the proper moment to prod her father regarding the night's proceedings. Sensing that he would desire to sleep not talk, she chose the moment.

"And the decision?"

"Decision? A decision wasn't required. Or expected."

"Why did Ninefingers pluck and show the fever herb to the assembly? What did it mean?"

"It is an herb that we brought many years ago from England. They call it Englishman's foot. Wherever we tread, it grows." When Sarah didn't respond, he continued, "All of the flowers in your mother's garden came with us as well. The longtime blooms of this country fail before them. The bees that nurture our crops and give honey are also ours."

Sarah had already lost interest in this somber thread of words, coming boldly to the concerns that had pestered her since this morning. "Can we move our camp? Do we have permission to starve the fleas?"

If her father was not so tired from the night's events, he surely would have frolicked with Sarah's sense of gentility, but as it was, he simply replied, "Done in the morning."

"You talked with Ninefingers? Why?"

"Talk is better than the other."

• • •

He made good his word. A few days later, farther from the river, her father had cobbled together a small wigwam. Lightly built, it was intended for short-time habitation only and used the tent for much of the roof. Sarah was grateful for being able to stand upright after weeks of hunching over in the tent. Noticing her father saddling the horse, she inquired, "Off?"

"To speak to the chief and then organize our crossing to the home lot." Pointing to the wigwam, he continued, "We will need more than this very soon."

Sarah frowned in confusion. "Crossing? Is that a problem?"

Father, clearly annoyed, carefully explained the difficulty as well as the procedure needed. "Our lot is across the river on high ground. We need a guide to show the way. If we attempt to ford blind we may lose wagon, horse, as well as our implements. The high-water level this time of year requires careful knowledge to wend around the snags and hidden deep pools. They know the way; we do not.

CHAPTER VIII

Later the Same Day

Scratching an angry rash on her arm, a gift from poisoned ivy, Sarah watched her father as he rode toward the Indian village passing three figures approaching their little camp. Usually, they veered off at this point to visit the riverbank, but as the figures neared the camp, she recognized the Indian girl Takhi, whom she had met at the meeting, and two young men.

Only Takhi spoke. "Come, gather with me. These are Tawsume and Nawas." Tawsume was the more muscular of the two with a broad, open face that inspired confidence. Nawas was the more intriguing. Shorter and lithe, he was much the prettier of the two. With a face too quick to smile, she was instantly wary of him. His manner was nothing but friendly, even gracious. Yet there was something about him that caused her unease.

Sarah had become comfortable with the guarded masks of the Indians. She nearly smiled until she suddenly realized that Nawas was acting almost English. His masks were mixed! Standing very close to Takhi, they were coupled as a family in Sarah's eyes.

Takhi handed Sarah a basket as they walked toward a shady wet patch of trees. Passing a bushy thicket, Takhi suddenly stopped, pulling up handfuls of tall, watery weeds. Responding to a sharp command, "Sarah, sit!" she obediently dropped to the ground where she was standing as if in a sudden faint. Bunching up the stems, Takhi squeezed the sap of the soft stems onto the red rash on Sarah's arm. Rubbing it in, Takhi applied a second dose.

With little fanfare, Takhi continued toward the shady glen casually tossing back further instructions, "Do it often." Sarah had to admit that the sap did lessen the itch and stinging. She was well acquainted with the weed. The orange flowers, while intricate, were far too small for any interest. The long, wet stems were so weak that a strong wind often blew them over. The lowly touch-me-nots did have a use then. As Takhi receded into the distance, Sarah mulled over Reverend Edward's belief that all things in God's creation fulfil their assigned purpose.

•••

Running to catch up to Takhi before she disappeared, Sarah rued the wearing of her precious shoes when the wet ground sucked at her feet. Sarah stopped to allow her eyes to adjust to the deep shade of the forest. When her eyes could focus again, she was left looking at the largest patch of Jack-in-the-pulpit plants that she had ever seen. It was an eerie, dark meadow, a foreign place that might appear in untoward dreams. Her mother, with disgust, called them "witches' pulpits." Widely accepted as deadly poisonous, they were avoided or uprooted and replaced with more familiar plants. And yet Takhi, on her knees, was plunging her hands into the soil, rooting out entire plants.

Takhi discarded the foliage, placing only the bulbs in her basket. When she paused, giving a nod, Sarah knelt and joined in the harvest. Lately, Sarah was more likely to consider these new experiences as through her mother's eyes. With the image in mind of her mother watching her youngest daughter in a dark, godless place, gathering up poisonous witchy bulbs, she smiled. With her mother wailing to the very heavens and wringing her hands, Sarah laughed out loud. Suddenly aware of her company, she glanced over at Takhi, who was staring at her. "I was thinking of my mother."

Her basket filled, Takhi abruptly rose and retraced their steps; Sarah followed her. This was not a place of lonely comfort. And the harvest was not to her liking. Sarah's curiosity about the two young men finally prompted her to break the silence as they walked back to the camp.

"Who is Tawsume?"

"The chief's son."

"And Nawas is your . . . husband?" Sarah hesitated, but only for an instant, in assigning the proper title to Nawas. She feared that offence might be taken if she misspoke. She chose caution. But the pause was long enough. Takhi turned and smiled at her for the very first time.

"Yes, he is mine. Your thoughts are shared by some."

They reached the Noble camp quickly. Sarah was disconcerted that Takhi's natural walking pace was a double-quick. Lagging behind, she had to break into a trot several times to stay in place. Sarah was at a loss for a proper farewell and blurted out, pointing to the basket of corms: "You eat many of these?"

"Yes, but prepare them well. Raw, your belly will be full of knives!" For the second time on this day, Takhi smiled. Watching Takhi walk away, Sarah wondered out loud: "How does Takhi walk so rapidly whilst so great with child?"

Sarah regarded the basket of pulpit bulbs with distaste. They appeared ominous, nothing like potatoes. At first, she decided to do nothing but await her father's counsel. It was quite unlike her to make such a decision, but impulsively she dumped the pulpit bulbs into the kettle and nestled it onto the embers. Eat them or not, her father would decide.

She wondered what was keeping her father. It was always the same when she asked: "Organizing things."

• • •

Half a mile distant, John sat close by the chief as both peacefully savored the tobacco in their pipes. Absent was all the formality of the earlier tribal meeting. This was the soft touchings of old friends. Words were few between them as the many years together made them all but unnecessary.

"John, it has been a long time since we roamed together. We had many happy times then. Little did we imagine this future."

John had to agree, admitting that, "Sometimes I think those were the happiest days, before sorrows and the years dulled life's flavor. They pile up and become irksome."

The chief smiled and suggested, "It is not the sorrows but the regrets. Sorrows like a wound do heal. They may leave a mark always to remember, but they ease over time. Regrets fester and weigh us down. With each year, they become bigger, and we stoop under their weight. When does your family come?"

John answered as best he might, "By and by. Before the first snow. My sons have much business to wind down. Their youth will make them cautious with the details."

The conversation had slipped from the many details of the river crossing to this quiet, somber raking of the past. He knew that there was too much idle time each day. The trees on the lot were down, but without strong hands and tackling, the logs lay askew and undressed. Without hard and purposeful work, his mind often wandered into thoughts best left shelved.

He was awakened from his reverie by the chief's bland question. "Do you think of Wawetseka?"

"She often comes to my thoughts at quiet times. And always unbidden."

His friend was right. The regret, slight in years past, was a millstone now. The chief swathed in a cloud of tobacco smoke reflected, "She felt that she was ill-used."

"I gave my actions little thought . . . none at all, to my shame. My mind was set and closed." John stood up abruptly, deciding to do what he always did to banish these memories: work. Any work no matter how slight.

"I have to attend to my allotment." Nearly out of the door, he turned with the query, "Do you hear of her? Where is she?"

"Gone for a few springs now. And her daughter." In quiet moments on the trail, from Westfield, he often thought of what news he might hear of Wawetseka when they arrived. Marriage and children certainly, but this never occurred as a possibility, even in his most outlandish dreams.

"A daughter? When?" The old friend's silence answered the details.

"John, you are now in a different world. Your world. You cannot be in both. Let it be. Let them be." John knew that he was right. While loud words spoken with hard eyes have great conviction sometimes, perhaps undeserved, the soft, gentle words of his old friend were far more requiring of attention.

John stood in the doorway with his back to his friend before slowly walking toward the river. He remembered clearly the last meeting with Wawetseka, though he scarcely realized then that it would be the very last. The conversation so seemingly casual attained pregnant meaning only later.

She asked quietly, "John, when will you come again?"

Without a thought as his schedule was firm, he promised, "When it pays my business."

"Not sooner or for longer?" Answering with a shrug, he left with a soft caress. But he never came again. The bonds with Mary, though silken, were too binding.

• • •

During the weeks that followed, the Noble belongings were gradually walked over the river following a zigzag trail of hidden shallows. Although the water was far too muddy to see the safe shallow areas, the Indians had, over time, learned them all, committing them to memory.

John decided that the first house would lack a cellar to save time. The digging of the cellar hole would not pay. The timber mudsills would rest on substantial stones at each corner. It would be erected quickly before the winter descended in earnest. When the proper house was raised later, this building would serve as a ready-made barn or workshop.

Despite her fears, Sarah settled into her new world far more quickly than she ever thought possible. She encountered Takhi quite often, sometimes by accident, other times by design. Takhi was aghast at Sarah's lack of what she deemed useful household skills, undertaking to teach her how to fabricate a proper basket. Protestations were waved off with a wrist's flick; Takhi was not to be denied. Sarah rather looked forward to these meetings as they would chat as they attended the work. They reminded Sarah of the times her mother and their neighbors in Westfield sat together working on a wedding quilt.

The fly in the gravy was that Takhi's efforts were so much more handsome than her own. Sarah was quite certain that the tight pattern of Takhi's baskets might even hold water for a time. On this particular morning, Sarah groaned when she peered into the wigwam and saw a large pile of thin willow strips on the floor. Takhi was absolutely adamant that all these fresh strips must be woven up on this very day before they dried. And there she sat amidst the pile of strips.

Takhi nodded beckoning to her, "Come and finish your work."

"But yours is so much better."

"In time." Takhi's fingers darted effortlessly while Sarah slowly struggled to command the strips to stay where she wanted them. Sarah hesitated to ask the question. She wasn't confident that she had fully worked out Takhi's relationship to the tribe. It appeared complicated. Choosing safety, she wondered, "Takhi, do you have blood relatives?"

She replied without even a pause or a glance up from her work. "No, the last was my mother's mother. All the others were lost in the great dying . . . they would take no captives."

The amiable chatter between them slowly ebbed into a silence with only the rustling of the willow strips audible. Sarah often was regaled at home with stories of the great victory of the English in the war over the Pequots, King Philip, and his people. She gnawed at her lip in chagrin for yet another of her missteps. It seemed that no matter how carefully she crafted her words, she always managed to stumble over her tongue.

Waving her hand to encompass the wigwam and village, Takhi explained, "I was adopted."

Nawas and Tawsume appeared suddenly at the door, intending to retrieve some needed gear. While the older youth rooted around for the skinning knife, Nawas stood quietly behind Takhi, watching her weave. Nearly as an afterthought while leaving, Tawsume asked, "Where is the John Noble?"

"Working on our plot. The house." As Tawsume walked away, Sarah heard him muse, "With the others." The comment was not directed to her but to Nawas, a statement of fact.

The arrival of the young men briefly distracted her from her announcement: "I have finished!"

In constant attendance in the dwelling was an ancient Indian woman that Sarah suspected was related somehow to the chief. Speaking rarely but greatly revered, her weathered face seemed ageless. Deeply lined and darkly crusty, she seemed more nearly akin to a great timeless tree. Sarah never tried to speak to her as there was no cause and they were separated, in any event, by language. She was startled then when the old woman snatched her basket away from her and examined it closely. Finally, turning to Takhi, the old woman delivered the verdict in her native tongue.

"What did she say?"

Sarah wasn't certain that she really wanted to hear. After a pause, Takhi allowed that the best translation was, "Good enough for big things." They looked at one another for a moment and both smiled.

Sarah opened a waist pouch and removed a carefully rolled strip of bright-green silk. She had mulled over this action many times during her evening thinking time. Staring at her prize for a moment, she handed it to Takhi, who unrolled its full length, stroking it softly across her cheek. Rolling it up slowly, she pulled a necklace hidden under her clothing over her head and placed it around Sarah's neck.

This was clearly not a casual exchange; Takhi arranged the points with care and slowly moved Sarah's hair aside to avoid a snag. Strung with a thin cord of rawhide, the centerpiece was a drilled six-inch deer antler point. On either side were beads and then two smaller deer points. Sarah noticed that the natural ridges of the large point were worn smooth in places, resembling ivory.

Following Takhi's lead, she hid the necklace under her top. It was obvious that this was more than mere ornamentation. Sarah fully realized that nothing more was needed. It was clear that the exchange was complete. Despite this knowledge, she felt compelled to offer the words, "Thank you for the treasure. I will keep it close to me." She arose, stiff from too long in an awkward crouch.

"I must go to prepare our meal. It is already late." Takhi made a point to remind her to take her basket. "You will need it soon."

Walking quickly down to the river, Sarah reflected on who tendered the most in their trade. On each sudden movement, particularly a change of direction or an increase of pace, the large deer point nudged her almost as a reminder. No doubt, she reasoned, it would soon become accustomed, scarcely noticed.

The cursive path wading through the shallows was now committed to memory. Sarah's first tentative crossings, when she placed each foot carefully into the muddy unknown, were long forgotten. Now she crossed the river with little thought while deciding how she might best organize dinner. She was pleased after a fashion, but the river was far different from the time before; there were no dark slimy walls of a well to pen her up.

In later years, when the stiffness of age gave Sarah more need to sit, as well as time to read, she was amused to think that the muddy river water might be her own version of the "wine dark sea," a terror described by Homer in his *Odyssey*. Fear of an unknown future. Against her husband Titus's objections, Sarah had purchased a tattered translation by Chapman from a deceased minister's estate. Worthy of study was her final judgment, in spite of the savage ending.

•••

That evening brought two days of heavy rain, raising the river enough that Sarah dared not attempt a crossing. When the rain ended, John worked at a log with his adz, smoothing two sides for a fit on the wall. He decided that a proper house was not possible in the time remaining before winter.

There was not yet a sawmill in the settlement. The notion of traveling to Woodbury or elsewhere for boards and siding was out of the question as too expensive and time-consuming. Neither the old horse nor the groining cart was up to the task. He quickly calculated the cost of hiring out the haulage to an out-of-town jobber but gave it up. The tariff for driver, ox team, and wagon over a round-trip of some days would cost more shillings than he cared to part with.

His wife, Mary, would have something to say no doubt about the cramped, homely new house. In her younger days, she lunged at a new challenge with spirit, but lately she more and more craved tranquility and comfort.

The mason, one Mr. Daloon, was to come and work on the chimney soon. John had progressed as far as possible on the base but considered the flue and fireplaces beyond his ken. Daloon was highly recommended but was an odd character. His name as pronounced had a French sound to it. A Black man, it was widely assumed that he took the name from a former master. He provoked wide curiosity amongst the Indians. For the English, he was of interest only for his skill.

John regretted the money and time that the chimney would absorb, only to be quite useless in the end when the old house became a barn. Directly in front of the unfinished door was a white pine stump nearly six feet across. Milled down by hand and nearly flat, it would serve as a future doorstep to the house.

Pausing to wipe away the sweat that blurred his eyes and tickled his nose, he noticed a tall, lanky Indian man approaching from the river. Even before he could make out the features, he reckoned that it was Tawsume, the chief's son, who had lately taken an interest in Sarah.

"Sarah, you have a visitor." Sarah peeked from their wigwam, nodded at her caller, and slowly approached.

Staring at the fallen pine, Tawsume explained, "I heard the felling." He slowly walked the length of the fallen giant. The branches that might be regarded as twigs on a normal tree were the size of a man's leg, He was looking for something; he looked at a branch, sighting it toward the river, and passed on. At a sudden point of recognition, he plunged his hand into a large, hollow crevice. The knot was empty.

"This was my secret place. For my special things."

"It was too close to our door. It needed to . . ." Sarah's voice trailed off in irritation with herself. When was she going to let go of her feeble explanations or missteps? They meant as little to the Indians as the grunting of hogs might to us. Acknowledge the slight and learn from it.

Tawsume was looking closely at Sarah's necklace, seemingly no longer concerned with his childish den of treasures. She froze when he unexpectedly reached for the necklace centerpiece hidden against her throat, teasing it out.

She had met him many times in casual commerce since their arrival, but this was the first time that he had touched her person. In Westfield, this light touching by an English boy would count as nothing, scarcely noticed, but here, for some reason, it portended a great step. Tawsume gently rubbed the large point and abruptly walked away without a word. Deflated, she walked over to her father and sat heavily on the stump, now doorstep.

"I did not dare to say anything. I could not hazard any words that might not cause offence or ring false."

"Sarah, you are beginning to think as a careful woman. But your dress will not like the pine sap of the stump."

Her attempt to stand up was not a clean escape. She slowly peeled the back of her dress off the sticky stump without opening up the strip seams. The flowing sap, clear at first, was now congealed to a white paste. Pulling as much of the dress around as was modest, she slowly worried the globs of hardening sap off one by one with a bark fragment. So intent was she on her task that some moments passed before she noticed the shadow of Tawsume directly in front of her.

Unseen, Tawsume had turned around when he remembered his original errand. In the very few seconds after she raised her eyes to meet his, she thought to strive above all for composure. With greater will than she credited herself, she greeted him with her disarrayed skirt, still casually flicking the sap off the cloth.

"Tomorrow, we will go to Tauba-konomok to gather fish. Come at dawn with a basket."

"What kind of fish?" Sarah was puzzled. She had watched the fishers along the river and was puzzled that she might be of any great use. Tawsume frowned, not from anger, but annoyance that the proper words escaped him. With gestures more confusing than descriptive, he surrendered. "All mouth. Little face. They are long like snakes." Business done, he turned toward the river, stopping only briefly to caution, "On the second turn of the crossing, there is a new snag. Watch for it."

At the evening meal, Father noticed that Sarah was unusually quiet. At this time of day, she was by nature all a bubble with observations and chatter. But this night she was still. He wondered if the dress or some distress over the fishing expedition of the next day was her night's chew. He knew that she would either bring it up or no. He would let it be until she was ready. In such cases, she would silently argue with herself the pros and cons of the affair sweeping over her face in turn. If a decision was reached, her face would take on a steely determination. And so it was on this night.

"I have not had a single night horse since we have come here. And only one on the trail! And then I wasn't even asleep. A vision came to me during an idyll while bathing in the leaves and branches of a tree. But none since we came here. Are they gone?"

"Maybe. Or simply not recalled. A good omen nonetheless. Sarah, we are all stuffed with memories, more so in years. Some are fondly recalled; others plague us because they can. This, too, for dreams." After only a slight silence, Sarah veered on another path.

"Father, a small boat would be of service. Then I might cross dryly like the Indians." Speaking out these concerns seemed to free her from a burden. Her thoughts slipped on to other matters.

"Sarah, when the family is here and the house is up, you will have less need to cross the river. Soon, there will be a bridge, and canoes will cease. That will be the progress of things."

Later, curled up under a tattered quilt, for the night air was sharp, she reviewed the happenings of the day and put them in their proper places. The two encounters with Tawsume were clearly in the "needs betterment" category. The fishing for tomorrow could only be in "maybe" as it was yet a riddle as to its nature. She knew the savory eels well, but what was Tawsume's description of "all mouth"? The discussion with her father thankfully belonged wholly to the "state of grace" cupboard.

She had come to believe that a happy life was crafted and attained when most of the daily parts were nestled in the best slots. Frowning, she mused that much work was still in order. Rubbing the large deer point of her necklace, she drifted off. Bit by bit, by degrees so subtle that Sarah was unaware, the smooth fragment of a buck's antler had become her thinking talisman.

•••

Unusually, Sarah awoke before her father the next morning. With her basket in hand, she was at the riverbank at barely daylight. In the dim light, the mist drifting over the water obscured the safe route to the other bank. Impatiently, she waited for the increasing light to reveal the markers. As Tawsume had advised, there was a nearly upright log snag. Not a danger in itself, it was liable to confuse the way to the unwary as a false marker.

Her father had dismissed her notion of a boat too lightly in her judgment. Being soaked to the skin several times each day had quickly become irksome. Soaked to the waist, her dress was a great weight becoming heavier with the mud that she attracted as she trudged along. Just at the point that it began to dry and lighten, she need wade back to her side of the river again.

Sarah was surprised at the large number of fishers, as many women as men, gathered at the river. She recognized the two men Nawas and Tawsume as well as Takhi. They were in the midst of many others and neither approached nor beckoned. This was to be a communal effort, that was clear, but the nature of it escaped her.

The fishing destination was a shallow patch of water below a rocky waterfall that in low water became a hindrance to fish. Two lines of stones barely breaching the water formed a wide V shape with the wide end upstream and the narrow, open point downstream. She had passed it many times before but dismissed the letter as a queer fancy of nature. Now she knew its true purpose. They had constructed and maintained it faithfully over time. Yearly, the spring floods surely would have washed it away.

Plodding along behind the rest, Sarah noticed that the women all carried baskets with an even looser weave than her own faltering effort. A number of men barely visible in the dim light, however, appeared to carry bundles of sticks. These were not bundles of loose sticks as she had originally surmised but flexible lengths of saplings woven together to form a fence. Unbundled and joined together, the women were wading through the water to create a holding net at the bottom of the open V. A line of spearmen at the wide upstream end of the weir below the falls stamped and splashed about, slowly driving the enclosed fish into the wicker trap. Of course! It was simplicity itself.

Without even removing her shoes, Sarah waded into the river to help with the unfolding of the net. It is perhaps the nature of divine humor that such improbable events so often befall the hapless, but Sarah unerringly stumbled upon a glacial sinkhole that the Indian women wisely sidestepped. While only a few feet across, it was far deeper. From wading in safe thigh-depth water, she suddenly disappeared into an abyss far over her head. All thought, all logic and reason, were overwhelmed by stark, shrieking terror that flooded her breath with water.

Sarah's fear reminded her of a time when she was six years of age. Near the old barn in Westfield was a low, wet spot that was muddy for most of the clement seasons. A shallow well was dug in the middle of it to take advantage of the groundwater to sate the cattle. Not very deep and lined with rough stones, it was useful for much of the year. Only in the driest months did the level drop so low that the drawer had to lean far into the well to fill a bucket.

It was Sarah's task to keep the nearby watering trough filled. The trough was a modest affair, a hollow split sycamore log that she usually filled with three buckets. Late in a dry October, she leaned into the well to hear the splash when the pail found water. Jerking at the filled bucket, she lost balance and fell headfirst into the shaft. As Providence would have it, she landed at the bottom with her right side up. With arms and legs splayed against the stone walls, she was at knee depth. She never dared explore how much water lay beneath her feet. In this state, she feared that she would tire quickly and sink into the dark abyss. In truth, there were only a few inches of water below her feet.

With care, Sarah, by handfuls of stone, pulled herself up a few inches at a time, locking her feet fast at each interval against the walls. Crabbing her way up the shaft, after exhausting effort, she reached the warm daylight. At first, when Sarah entered the kitchen in a wild state, her mother assumed that she had tripped and fallen into the trough. The family's reaction to Sarah's teary tale was muted, although the expected attempt at mirth by sister Mary blessedly was absent. The next day, her father knotted an extra length of rope to the bucket.

Finally, the memory faded. Sarah was oblivious to the river current that almost immediately flushed her out of the sinkhole into shallow water. Curious, some of the fishers broke off from their tasks and gathered around Sarah in amazement as she thrashed about, gulping in the knee-deep water. A strong hand pulled her upright by the hair. Sitting in the shallow water surrounded by an amused audience, she heard Tawsume's deep voice. "Sarah, go and attend to Takhi."

She was only too glad to flee this sight of her humiliation and slogged through the water, climbing the muddy bank only on her third try. Nawas and Tawsume were distracted by the drama. Pensively leaning on his spear, Nawas shook his head as he wondered: "She finds favor in your sight?"

"She has a large hidden spirit. She has hands and will be useful."

"Hidden spirit? Hidden forever! And useful for fishing?" Nawas laughed aloud at his own wit.

"You no longer look to colored hair?"

"But not the rest. Delights afar always become sour when nearby."

Sarah collapsed in a wet heap next to Takhi and slipped off her shoes. Shaking her head with only a sigh, she scooped the mud and sand lodged in the toes. Takhi had watched the spectacle unfold from a distance, incredulous that Sarah could have so unerringly stumbled into the only misstep near the weir. Glancing at her curious friend, Sarah yielded to the urge to explain.

"I can swim, but I was gripped by a terrible fear and my mind was lost to it." When Takhi remained silent, Sarah continued, "As a very young child, I fell into a well." Unsure if Takhi had ever seen a well, she explained. "It is a deep hole dug in the ground filled with water. The sides are steep and often impossible to scale. It was so very dark. I climbed handful by handful toward the light." She spread her legs to mimic the act of anchoring her body while acting out how her hands as claws groped for secure rocks to grasp. "Several times, I faltered and almost fell. Many of the stones came loose, falling into the water. I thought I would die surely."

So absorbed in the telling of the tale, Sarah never noticed that Takhi became more animated as the peril was recounted. Leaning in to Sarah, nearly touching faces, Takhi nodded nearly in triumph: "And yet, you are here!"

Sarah was often confused that Takhi regarded the world with such an unchanging demeanor. All events simply were the same to her, neither evoking anger, joy, or even amusement. Life was of a single flavor. But with Sarah's tale, Takhi's face became alive. Her eyes lost the dullness and sprang to life. Only once before, at their first meeting with the village, was Takhi's spirit so fierce. For a moment, Sarah feared that she might have stumbled once again but soon realized that this was a glimpse of another's dream.

"Takhi, you should not be here when so great with child."

"Life does not stop. And the fish will come soon."

Sarah motioned toward the group of women squatting on the riverbank with their baskets and spoke with exasperation: "And the fish will come?"

With outstretched arms, Takhi promised, "From the sky."

"And your eyes jest with me yet again!" Sarah was quite unaware that Takhi, as they spoke, watched the fish trap being closed. Women were leaning over the wicker barrier scooping up baskets of fish, the water draining through the loose weaves. The spearmen stood guarding the open end of the net, jabbing anyone trying to escape. Only now did the long shanks come into play. With a quick, muscular overhead flick, the fish sailed through the air in graceful arcs toward the riverbank. Takhi's timing was truly uncanny, for no sooner had she raised her arms than fish fell around them with thuds as if from heaven.

These were a type of fish that Sarah had never seen before, a type of eel. River eels were common fare. Her brothers caught them in pots and wicker cages with funnel entrances. Baited with foul, inedible offal, they were sunk into the river at dusk and retrieved in the morning, with four to six the expected catch. For her mother, these were delicacies. She rarely failed to mention that they were long treasured by the nobility at home and how lucky they were to have them.

They did seem to take an uncommonly long time to die, however, which her brothers found very amusing. A freshly dressed eel, headless and skinless, thrown into a hot skillet and quickly salted, would wriggle about with vigor. Her sister Mary often poked at her plated portion with a knife, explaining that she preferred her fish truly dead.

As the eels rained down from the canopy, the Indian women scampered to fill their baskets. Takhi, even in her condition, moved quickly to fill her basket. She turned to Sarah with a caution: "Fill your basket quickly. They will escape."

Sarah was, aware of the slippery nature of eels, reached for a handful of sand. It was only when she picked up a still writhing fish that she realized that this was something very new. The creature had no jaws. In its stead was a large, gaping open mouth ringed with rows of yellow teeth. Rooted to the spot, she could do nothing but stare at the pulsing maw as in a trance.

Sarah had seen this vision once before. In a sermon, Reverend Edwards described the Devil perched in his Hell. Sinners dropped into his grasp and were devoured by a drooling mouth ringed with foul yellow teeth. Sarah's clutched the lamprey more and more tightly until the grit of the sand failed. With a slurp, the fish popped out of her grip, colliding with her face.

Takhi dispelled her lingering torpor with a warning: "You will not care for a good bite from them." Wiping the slime from her face with a sleeve, Sarah pursued the hapless eel. After a smart wrap with a stick, it became docile. For the native women, this was a seasonal rite repeated yearly. The pace they set was measured and assured. Sarah, by contrast, scampered from eel to eel, thrashing them all in a frenzy. Finally, the empty weir was once again disassembled. All except Sarah had filled baskets. The women watched her wailing away at the last eel.

When she sat, Takhi observed, "Warriors in battle, blood high, are like that, as you. These are my favorites. You do not eat them?"

Sarah shook her head. "Father will expect them. Do you salt the surplus?"

"We eat them all."

"But surely, many will spoil before that?"

"We eat them all."

Sarah remembered her father recounting that Indians, rather than putting food by salted, tended to gorge on the excess when available, fattening up as bears do for the coming lean winter.

An occasional eel slithered out between an open weave of Sarah's basket only to receive a sharp blow and a return to the basket.

"Sarah, you need a closer thatch."

"No, I need bigger fish."

Sarah didn't credit that it was possible, but the trek back was surely longer than this morning's pleasant upward leg. Earlier, she was distracted by curiosity. What use were the sheaves of sticks? Catching fish in baskets?

Trudging south was by no means a lark. She was wet and heavy; the basket of devil eels grew in weight with each mile. And they were even less comely dead than alive. Peeking into the basket presented nothing but a coiled mass of teeth. Takhi walked beside her for a time but at length increased her pace to catch up to Nawas. Without a companion to set the pace, Sarah gradually lagged behind the group.

As a result of her thrashing about in the river, a pebble had worked itself into her shoe. When it migrated to an unbearable spot, she sat down on a fallen log beside the trail to remove her shoes. Well worn, a crack in a sole allowed a river pebble entrance unnoticed. Slowly, she peeled off her sodden stockings. These had no holes but were caked with mud.

The constant wetting of the stitching of the dress by her river crossings was causing rot to the seams of the strips; the bottom strip the worst of all. Fingering a large gap, she briskly pulled on the strip that separated with scarcely any complaint. Of the two bands of cloth that she had pulled off the dress since they left Massachusetts, this was the larger. The hem was rising with the passage of time. She laughed softly, thinking of her sister Mary's likely explanation for this state of being, a miraculous surge of growth.

As her fishing companions disappeared from view around a slight bend, Sarah debated with her more farsighted self whether she should consign either the cloth or the fish to the river. The debate back and forth being indecisive, she added shoes, stockings, and rolled cloth to the basket of fish and continued on the trail home barefooted.

Her shoes did not survive the trial. Brittle with the crack in the sole widening, they were put aside. Takhi, some days later, presented her with a well-worn pair of Indian moccasins with a cryptic, "She won't need them." Since the right was larger than the left, Sarah knew that there was a larger story. Not so very long ago, she might have read Takhi's cryptic remark to mean that the former owner acquired a new pair, and these were cast-offs. Now she thought about how the former owner died. And the mismatched set? How many wore them before?

CHAPTER IX

June 27, 1707

The following run of days were all mirrors side by side. Sarah settled into a comforting pattern of chores, meals, and predictable encounters. While the adult Indians took little interest in her, the children became emboldened, running up to her but veering off at the last in loud giggles.

Sarah was engaged in just such capering with a little boy, perhaps the phantom of her first morning, on that memorable day, a day seemingly like any other but which would deflect her life path to its final direction. She was waving a handful of shimmering turkey feathers in the air, enticing the boy to try to snatch them away. This was a game that she rarely won. And today his little fingers again snatched them out of her hand before she could pull away. Sarah watched the victor scamper off waving his booty in triumph.

Sarah then noticed a figure approaching. It was so unexpected that she doubted her own eyes. Only when the figure was in hailing distance did she credit her senses.

It was a gentleman clad in the most opulent attire that she had ever seen. The coat was blue silk with golden trim. The weskit was the white of snow. He was not wearing common overalls but real breeches and stockings. He would have stopped conversation even in Boston or Newport. But here in the wilderness? Sarah would scarcely have been more astonished if angels from Heaven had suddenly appeared.

A small figure behind him was partially hidden by his master. As they came abreast of Sarah, she saw that the trailing figure was a small boy of perhaps eight years. He had the blackest skin that she had ever seen. His very person seemed to shimmer in the bright sunlight. The boy's skin was like a raven's, nearly iridescent. Although not nearly as grand as his master's, his clothes were rich enough so as not to cause embarrassment to his owner.

They walked past her with no acknowledgment, intent on approaching her father. John was sitting on a drum of wood, dressing a turkey. Hovering out of sight a few yards away was a red fox. Only when John tossed the offal in its direction did it dart close to snatch the easy meal. It was an uncommon day that the fox didn't show up, waiting or not, depending on the possibilities. Clearing his throat, the man addressed her father.

"I am seeking John Noble. Are you the man?"

"I am." The grand figure waited for her father to look up from his work. He continued awkwardly when John continued his gutting task.

"I am Benjamin Henshaw. I've been led to understand that you know the way to Fort Orange."

"I do."

"I wish to engage you as a guide."

"One way or a return? It is a long journey. A challenge."

"My business will decide. What is your rate?"

"Two and six per diem plus one for my horse. Extra two if the wagon is needed. And provisions."

"How many days will the journey take?"

"It depends on your pleasure, your horses, and your baggage." Eyeing the well-dressed Black boy, he inquired, "Just you, then?"

"No, Neptune will attend me. You will gather the necessities?"

"It will be plain fare and must be paid forward in hard money before we leave."

Henshaw pondered the transaction and asked hopefully, "Will you accept my note of hand?"

"No, you are not known here; the note has no value. Five pounds now as a premium and the total sum later in salt pork."

After a quick mental calculation, Henshaw boomed, "Done and done" and extended his hand to seal the bargain. When Noble offered his right hand, after wiping it clean of turkey offal, his new client slowly pulled back his closed fist. He had no desire to soil his soft hand with filth. With a gracious nod making do for a handshake, Henshaw and the boy returned to their camp near the river. Sarah, listening nearby, caught just a few fragments of their conversation. But talk of per diems and payment was enough to stoke her fears.

"Father . . . what?" Gesturing toward the receding Henshaw.

"A stroke of good fortune! The river god needs a guide to the post at Fort Orange. We will eat well this winter." Wealthy merchants from seaport towns were very early tagged with the derisive "river gods."

Sarah thought it best to wait until after the evening meal of turkey before voicing her concerns. Would she go? Her father's excitement at the prospect suggested not. But would she then remain alone? The meal was another silent affair. Waiting for the perfect time to speak became such a torture that she finally blurted, "Am I to remain here alone?"

He frowned at her question. How could she even think of such a thing? "By no means! I will arrange with the chief for your safety. You will stay with the chief's family: the mother, Tawsume, and Takhi."

"How long will you be away?" Her fears wiped clean her carefully marshaled questions and objections, leaving only the most telling. John gestured to the unfinished dwelling.

"A month, no more. I can afford no more time. The house must be erected by late fall."

In a tone unusually grave for her father, he warned, "You will obey the chief as you would me. Do you understand?" Sarah nodded numbly. She was now quite without senses, in an abyss without thought or will. "While I am away, you are a part of his family."

Later he talked lightly of the coming trip, thinking that it was good that she had some time to judge the Indians before he left. Though strange still, they were no longer cold strangers. Sarah realized that her father was sugaring the news, but his words were mostly reasonable. And she might return to their wigwam, from time to time, for needed wares. This was a comfort. Her thoughts turned to the grand merchant and particularly his servant.

"Father, did I hear rightly that the boy was called Neptune?" Continuing at her father's nod, she said, "That is surely not a proper Christian name. That is not a name at all. Why? What is the reason?" John slowly shook his head. She knew from close watching of her father that this might have two meanings; either he truly didn't know, or he was disappointed by the query.

"To mark their differences from us perhaps."

The journey south on the trail was now another life in Sarah's mind. In that distant time, she had asked her father why the family animals were never named. His words now suddenly sat up in her mind.

"Or to avoid creating an unprofitable memory?"

As was her custom, Sarah mulled over the day's happenings as she drifted off to sleep. The night was warm enough that sleep was difficult. Her father's imminent departure was baked hard and unchangeable. Fussing over it was to little avail. She would bring just enough possessions to the Indian village to excuse trips away to the house site, but not so few to arouse her father's suspicions. The fine hopes for her journal were gone. The entries, as she now realized, did nothing to light her way but only reminded her of past errors.

The night promised no cooling. If anything, it pointed to an even more liquid dawn. If Sarah had still been in Westfield, she might have shucked off the blankets and slept in her shift. Following Mary's example, perhaps even less. At last, fatigue was the victor and she slept.

Sarah awoke early, even before her father, in a sweat, but a cold one. Her skin was patterned with bumps, her heart pounding deeply. Try as she might, she could not know the cause of the deep sense of dread she felt. The dream must have come to her again. That was the only explanation. Yet she had no memory of it.

Two days later, the caravan of horses left for Fort Orange. Sensibly, the river god wore plainer ware as did his servant. The finery of days before was for show only. Sarah was surprised at the abundance of baggage.

In addition to his three horses, Henshaw insisted on renting the cart to carry his essentials. Her father tried to dissuade him, explaining the cart was slow and would hinder their progress, adding more cost for the party. But the man was adamant. He demanded his comforts and could well pay for them.

John knew, as did Sarah, that the extra time on the trail was not welcome. Too much needed their attention before autumn. As the worn cart, wheels still howling for bear grease, vanished north following the river, Sarah reflected that her father's departure wasn't as difficult as she feared. It was a sensible diversion to ensure a plentiful supply of meat for the winter.

• • •

The chief's large wigwam provided far more comfort than she enjoyed in the hut that her father had hastily built. Rather than lying in the dirt, the native dwelling had raised platforms for sleeping. Best of all, it was proof against wind and rain. Sarah need not move the blankets during a rain to remain dry.

The first night, Sarah remained fully clad under her bedding quietly observing her hosts disrobing ritual. Only a feeble moonlight played over the darkened interior, but it seemed to her that they slept in nothing but their skins. She listened attentively as the breaths gradually became more sleeplike. Tawsume was the last to doze off. Judging that they were safely asleep, she shed her dress under the blanket and slipped into a shift.

Sarah was, by turns, surprised and amused at how easily the days became routine. Takhi acted as her guide, patiently laying out the order and procedures of her daily life. Women often brought nuts and strange plants for Takhi. They were deemed necessary to ensure a healthy child. Despite admonitions to take more care, Takhi remained active. She never accepted that she was not as agile, however. At times, she viewed being with child as a great inconvenience.

Three days after her father left, they were working in a garden rogueing aggressive plants that threatened the planted mounds. Sarah was aware that the Indians comingled different plants together but had never seen it. And they grew no wheat. She would miss bread.

Takhi struggled to her feet in a series of grunts.

"How long until the day."

"Soon."

"Can I attend on that day?"

Takhi answered with a sharp, "No." Seeing Sarah's frown, she continued: "Pequots birth alone. Come." Taking her by the hand, Takhi led Sarah to a hidden grove a few feet from the river. In the midst of a circle of clean sand, there was a miniature shelter carefully wrought, a small wigwam. Inside, the sand floor was covered with mats. Takhi inspected the ground, carefully removing errant weeds and sticks.

Finally, she announced, "This is the place of beginning."

Thinking out loud, Sarah wondered, "And the closeness of the river?"

Settling heavily on a convenient log, Takhi explained, "For the ritual cleansing."

"And you will be all alone so far from the village?"

Takhi smiled at Sarah's alarm. "There will be a midwife nearby that I may call if needed." Takhi raised her right arm, waving her hand casually. Sarah, using both hands, pulled her up off the log. By this time, the gesture was automatic. Waving hands signified a vigorous pull was needed.

Walking back to the settlement, Sarah's conversation with Takhi was interrupted by a persistent deerfly. Buzzing incessantly around her head, she swatted at the air in futility, even slapping her head when she suspected an imminent bite. Takhi faced her and slowly raised her right arm. Sarah was quite perplexed, as she was already standing. Takhi raised her eyebrows sharply, a telling sign of exasperation. Sarah meekly extended her right arm above her head. She was entirely at a loss to fathom the purpose. Instantly, the fly settled on her forearm, dispatched with a brisk slap.

Takhi shrugged. "With deer and horses, they favor the high body parts with much blood."

Within minutes of reaching the settlement, Takhi presented Sarah with a soapstone bowl and what she took to be a pestle. In the shade of the dwelling, Takhi raised both arms. Sarah knew the sign. For a minor recline or raising, one handhold was sufficient. To sit on the ground or to leave it, two hand pulls were the rule.

Sarah often used the mortar to pulverize herbs and medicine, but never for Indian corn. Back in Westfield, the corn was delivered in bags to Gillette's mill and returned as fine meal, lacking, of course, the miller's tariff.

Takhi, with greater experience, milled the corn quickly, dumping the finished flour into a coarse earthenware vessel. At times, she inspected Sarah's efforts, shaking her head. More work was needed.

This was very like the thoughtless task of carding wool that Sarah had so dreaded at home. With her sisters, there was chatter and gossip to sweeten the work. But Takhi, pounding the corn was nearly mute, pausing only briefly to judge Sarah's efforts.

Sarah was reminded of a box turtle that she adopted as a companion years ago. The turtle soon lost interest in Sarah, no doubt grouping her with other creatures of no interest. Excepting for eating the forage provided, it was maddingly inert. When prodded for some sign of life, it disappeared behind its trap door. Sarah did not sense that her chuckle was audible until she noticed that Takhi stopped her work to stare.

•••

Sarah's travel journal, begun with such earnest enthusiasm a different life ago, was long abandoned. The flood of recent experiences, some sensible, some perplexing, others unsettling, washed away her former intentions. She judged them now as quite childish. She had decided instead upon compiling a list of maxims that might prove useful for young girls such as herself. Takhi, this very instant, provided lesson number eleven: If a friend means you to know a secret, she will confide it in her own good time.

Sarah's attention drifted to a group of young girls in exuberant pursuit of a leather ball. Armed with curved sticks, they cuffed the ball back and forth with an energy clearly ferocious. In a flurry of sticks slashing in a blur, legs and shins were violated.

Startled at the frenzy, Sarah could not resist the query: "What are they doing?"

Wistfully, Takhi explained, "Preparing for the event."

Quite confused, Sarah asked, "Event? Is it a game, then?"

"Yes. But not a game as you know. Also called 'little brother of war.' But it has a greater purpose: to become one with the others. To prove your worth."

Beginning only now to follow Takhi's reasoning, Sarah slowly spoke, "To prove yourself to others!"

"Yes, but to oneself most of all. My first event was my blossoming time. After, I felt at home and at peace. I had a place. With the men, it is more serious and dangerous. Even with us, there are marks." Takhi lifted her garment, tracing a faded scar on her left knee.

The girls eventually tired and drifted off the field, a great number of them limping. Sarah ground her portion of corn lost in thought. Of course, this is a test! To prove what you might become. A trial by a sort of combat with deep fears and the feeling of being an "other."

Sarah's reverie was interrupted as Takhi emptied the last of her meal into the earthenware vessel. Takhi was curious that Sarah's portion was only a fine powder. During a double-handed pull to raise Takhi, Sarah impulsively announced, "I would do it also!"

Her pregnant companion was not immediately sensible of what she meant. Sarah often spoke to herself, shifting from this notion to that in an eye's blink. In such cases, the only intended audience was herself. No response was expected or welcomed. But clearly, this was not one of those times. Sarah was suggesting the impossible. Takhi was so surprised at first that she doubted that she'd read Sarah's thoughts correctly.

"You cannot. You are not one of us. The others will never permit it. Each group has a closeness. You are an outsider." Turning to Sarah after a silence, Takhi revealed the obvious, "You will always be. And they will use you badly."

"I would do it and gladly bear the cost. Until my father returns, I am a member of your family. The chief has said so in open conversation. If what they say is true, it is my right!"

Finishing, Sarah was careful not to reveal her satisfaction with her logic. Takhi was perfectly aware that Sarah could clutch at the slenderest reed of truth and weave it into nearly any vessel that she chose. The further that she was allowed to venture into the tale, the more difficult it was to refute. But this time what she proposed was dangerously sensible.

With a sigh, Takhi raised her arms for an elevation and entered the wigwam. Motioning to Sarah to remain behind, she approached a tall girl that was clearly the leader of the players. Takhi pointed to Sarah, and an animated conversation ensued. The captain shook her head vigorously as Takhi spoke. Dejected, Sarah knew it was a refusal, blushing that she was so mindless that she never foresaw the wider circle of ripples that her request might create.

Takhi's plea was, by all indications, over. While the two women stood with their backs to Sarah, Takhi handed something to the captain. Sarah couldn't see what it might be, only that the tall girl turned to regard her briefly. Takhi then walked toward Sarah at a surprising pace.

"It is possible. You will not find the chief as easy a catch as Takhi. He will decide. I will guide you only since I have become so slow. Sarah, this is a serious doing. And hurtful. Do you understand?"

Far too quickly, Sarah responded, "Yes, I do."

Takhi did not believe for a moment that Sarah truly understood. "You could be hobbled forever!"

"What are the rules?"

Takhi was speechless. "Rules! There are no rules! Have you not learned anything?"

• • •

The evening's meal was uneventful. Guests came and went. At length, only the chief, the old woman, and the two girls, Sarah and Takhi, remained. Tawsume was nearby, busy at some task, but working very slowly so as to make only the slightest noise. Sarah recognized the ploy: pretending to be busy but really only listening. The atmosphere was so easy that Sarah feared Takhi had not yet brought up the matter to the chief. She considered making the request herself but finally thought better of it. The old woman folded her hands and stared at the chief. The conversation between mother and son was very long and very quiet.

In a voice tinged with irritation, the chief queried, "Takhi, how can you come to me with this? I did not raise you in such foolishness. She knows nothing of this. John Noble does not expect that his Sarah will have this ordeal in his absence."

Takhi could only confess, "We have talked. She knows the way."

Sarah could never decide if it was the import of the issue at hand or the chief's commanding voice, but Sarah sprung to her feet when he turned to her. "Sarah, do you know what this is named?"

Without even a hint of a pause, she answered as she might a penetrating query from Minister Edwards: "Little brother of war."

"Sarah, it is a warrior's game, to build trust, to show courage and bravery. To endure pain as it should be. To teach about life. Why do you wish this?"

For the first time, Sarah was beset by doubts. Why was she so certain before? Was this another of her foolish fancies? The eyes upon her were hard and demanding. She was the rabbit frozen under the hawk's gaze. But unlike the hare, she had to make a move.

With tears beginning to flow down her cheeks, she confessed, "To banish my childhood fears. I wish to sleep untroubled by demons. I wish to become."

The chief quietly looked into space, a sign that even Sarah read as a demand for no more talk. He was torn between his given word to trapper Noble and the old legends of outsiders, running through his mind that entered the tribe in the long past and were blessed. Rising noisily, the old woman caught the chief's attention and, almost unseen, nodded. Bowing to the inevitable, he sighed, "Join, then. Little good can come of this, and I fear great sorrow."

Sarah's spirits soared with the chief's final pronouncement. His demeaner and tone during the deliberations foretold a very different judgment. When she learned that the contest would be played out on the following day, her courage sagged. She had hoped for more time to prepare. She chided her own cowardice. The thought of a conjured illness to avoid the game flitted across her mind. Upon leaving, Takhi informed her that they would begin before sunrise to help her prepare. With a well-considered plan, even a weak player such as Sarah might even the odds.

"We must turn their strengths against them. Harry them."

Takhi's matter-of-fact evaluation of her chances washed over her. Takhi was correct, of course, as she often was. Sarah decided that she would place herself in Takhi's hands, trusting that her friend knew best. It was as if she were a small child once again. She fell asleep surprisingly quickly while still considering into which of her three mental slots the day's events most nearly fit. Roused only once by a wolf's wail, she slept soundly until Takhi roughly shook her shoulder.

"Come! We must prepare." She waited for Sarah to slip into her dress and exit the dwelling before handing her the crosse stick.

"It has served me well. Show me how you hold it!" When Sarah gripped it two-handed in a natural stance, Takhi smiled in satisfaction. "Yes, that is good. The nub on the blade is useful on ankles."

A hard boil had formed when the wood was still young and was now a sharp, hard spike. Until the sun cleared the trees across the river, Sarah was tutored frantically on the basics of the game.

As the two teams filtered onto the field, Takhi, evaluating her charge, made a decision. "Sit!" Sarah dropped to the ground as though stunned. Takhi produced a short, thin knife and deftly started to cut away the lowest strip from Sarah's skirt.

"Sarah, you are slow, and all your movements are open. You will be hindered less without this. Remember what I have taught. Do not play to your enemies' strengths. Hang back and seek an advantage. Look to their eyes to tell the next move."

Sarah carefully rolled up the strip that Takhi undid. Now she had three rolled strips that needed reattachment before her mother arrived. She would have to fashion a needle from a thorn; the stitching would be so crude that a likely tale needed conjuring to pacify her mother.

The Indian girls' garments were all longer than hers, yet they seemed to move as gracefully as a languid stream. Sarah knew that she was clumsy; perhaps this was Takhi's attempt to lessen her awkwardness. Whatever the purpose, Sarah felt only half dressed. The ordered world of Westfield was long past.

Takhi, motioning to a group of females to her left, cautioned, "The tall one must be treated with great care. She becomes possessed by a ferocious spirit. She looks for blood." Takhi touched her left eye. "Looking in her face full, this eye sees mostly to the side. Use that as your approach."

Pointing to the right side of the field, she explained, "They are for you." Sarah approached the group, who eyed her suspiciously. She wished that the distance were greater. Anything to delay, however slightly, the coming reckoning. The leader was the same girl that Takhi had spoken with earlier and who sported a green silk headband with a flowing double tail.

• • •

The skirmishing began cautiously at first with little advantage to either side. Each was eyeing their opponents and judging their strategy. Sarah followed Takhi's direction. She hung back awaiting an opportunity, mentally deciding which adversary to challenge first. At a promising opening, she dashed at the ball only to be deftly tripped by an unseen opponent. By the time she stood and dismissed the bruise on her leg as minor, the company was far down the field. As the play rapidly moved back and forth over the course, Sarah gradually lagged behind.

Sensing an opening when three players were engaged in close quarters, she darted in only to receive a blow at her hairline in a flurry of crosses. Although she experienced a flash of light when the stick hit her, she felt no pain and continued the pursuit.

Like her teammates, Sarah took measures to avoid the tall leader, who suddenly now controlled the ball. With such a long reach, she could only be bested by guile. In addition to a wandering eye, she signaled her every change of direction with her shoulders. When she sensed a move to the left, Sarah summoned the remainder of her flagging strength for an all-out charge. The engagement was little more than a collision as the two girls with sticks held at the ready rebounded from the impact with a clatter of wood and bone.

By all accounts, it was a piteous mismatch. Her native opponent towered over Sarah by better than a head's height. Yet both lay motionless in the grass. The tall girl finally rose and regarded Sarah for a time before trotting off in a limp. They had fallen near the edge of the field where Tawsume was observing the game.

When he reached her, Sarah was making choked gurgling noises, trying to regain her breath. The deep breaths came only to be followed by prolonged vomiting. He stood over her while watching the game nearby. As she tried to rise, he grasped her by the shoulder to help her upright. The slight head wound was opened more when she fell on a stony outcrop; now the whole of that side of her face was covered in blood. The cuffed ankle was swollen of a curious blue color. Tawsume's only comment was, "On this day, you are finished here."

Takhi took her in hand and helped her move haltingly off the field. Even rubbing the blood out of her eyes with her sleeve, the world now seemed entirely pink. Seated on a sleeping platform, Takhi probed Sarah's foot. "Sore, but you will heal. You will not be lame." Feeling the ankle, Takhi suspected that, "This may not ever be the same size as the other. The color will fade, but this shoe will be tight."

Takhi washed the clotted blood from the head wound. The news was perhaps not welcome. "This will leave a mark to remember. Near the hair. Easy to cover."

Sarah scarcely heard Takhi's prognoses. Her errors during the game banished thoughts of her wounds. "I have acted as an addled fool! I had every advantage. I caught her blind. The day was mine. But instead, I went for her!"

Takhi was arranging flaps of skin over the cut, hoping the scar would be less. Sarah's heated review of her errant moves was not a surprise. She had heard this many times before, what should have been. The complaint was age-old.

"Rising blood betrays our better sense. Even you have it!" The old woman, always a lurking presence just out of sight, suddenly loomed out of the shadows. Holding Sarah's head in both hands, she roughly moved it about to better judge the wound in the dim light. After several painful pokes, she returned to the preparation of the evening meal. As a parting shot, she casually commented in what was a clearly dismissive tone her opinion of the whole affair.

"Takhi, what did she say?" Takhi, clearly groping for a proper meaning, paused, finally advised what the old woman's thoughts were. "You are a sparrow who believes that she is an eagle."

• • •

Sarah's sleep, in name only, that night was intermittent. She was plagued in turn not only by her throbbing ankle but by the previous day's events. She spent most of the night trying to conjure up a rebuttal to the old woman's truth. But in the end, she knew that she had stepped out of her place. She carelessly put herself forward in a serious business as thoughtlessly as she might pluck a flower. She could only ponder what the fruits of this rash caper might prove to be.

The foot was swollen more, taking on hues of red, blue, and purple. Sarah was hard put to even see the ankle bones. Rising from her sleeping platform, she found that walking was possible but only gingerly and with slow decision. The forehead gash was healing already. Without a looking glass for a reflection, she anxiously peered into a still bowl of water to judge the nature of it. Breathing through her mouth so as not to ripple the still water, she decided that the scar would likely resemble a capital W. The result of Takhi's ministrations in arranging the loose skin wrought a curious result.

Takhi appeared later that morning, giving Sarah's foot and forehead a cursory glance. Everything that could be done was attended. Time and fortune would determine the outcome.

Sarah had barely settled when Nawas entered without the normal courtesies. Veins bulging from his neck told his mind all too well. "I will speak to Takhi alone. Leave!"

CHAPTER X

July 16, 1707

As was customary at this time of day, only the three women, Sarah, Takhi, and the old woman, were at the residence. Even Sarah was shocked at Nawas's gross breach of protocol. To enter the chief's quarters unwelcomed then ordering his family member and a ward to vacate was an ominous declaration. With the old woman's nodded assent, Sarah lurched toward the door. Close behind, the elderly woman paused to deliver hard words to Nawas. Sarah, not knowing the words, clearly understood the quiet threat.

Nawas turned to Takhi, still seated. "You spend too much time with the English. You must attend more to us, to me. I command it!"

Takhi slowly shook her head, as much to say *no* as to express her disbelief that he had done this. Their union was never an easy blend. While their bodies melded, their two souls barbed. His foolish actions would not be soon forgotten. The consequences would wash back and forth over him as a tide. His standing would lessen in everyone's eyes.

"No! I will not. She has a spirit as my own. We are as twins."

"You say no? Who are you to defy me?"

"I am Pequot!"

He drew himself up to full height, responding with a sneer. "A Pequot? Better than us you think?" Growling in his throat, he gathered up phlegm and spat on the ground. "See you now! No longer mighty Pequot! You and your kind are now nothing but wandering beggars."

Drawing the same short-bladed knife that had earlier trimmed Sarah's dress, Takhi sprung at Nawas. But even her rage could not give her the needed speed. A powerful backhand caught her full in the face. As she lay sprawled near one of the platforms, Nawas delivered several sharp, well-aimed kicks.

At a distance, Sarah, as well as the old woman, heard the muffled shouts from the domicile. What finally caught the entire encampment's attention, however, was Takhi's piercing scream. Whatever duties may have claimed their earlier attentions, every soul, in unison, paused as if one in response to her cry. As Sarah later recounted the tale to Elizabeth, it was the loudest scream that she had ever heard. Quickly correcting herself, she admitted that perhaps it wasn't the loudest after all. But the pitch was so high, the tone so pure, that it caused her to have to swallow hard to clear her ears.

Those listeners within earshot converged on the chief's residence. Some were far away, some nearby, some were fleet, some were plodding. But they all shared the same quest. Tawsume entered the wigwam ahead of all the others.

Nawas exploded through the door as though thrown, followed by Tawsume. At each attempt by Nawas to stand, he was cuffed to the ground by Tawsume's fists. Finally, Nawas crawled away on all fours. To stand and fight would invite the greater beating. He chose the lesser punishment of only kicks as he four-footed away. Finally, Tawsume allowed Nawas to rise and walk upright, limping through a gauntlet of children and women with faces of stone throwing hoots and catcalls. The less expressive of the youngsters preferred small rocks.

Sarah and the old woman did not witness this public trial and punishment of Nawas. Hurrying into the residence, they found Takhi on the hard-packed dirt floor. Bleeding heavily, she was still quite conscious. Pains of childbirth were obvious.

Kneeling next to her, Sarah plaintively pleaded for directions. "What must I do?"

THE SEASONING

Before leaving to gather the needed essentials for the birth, the old woman directed Sarah, "Stay near and give her strength through the trial."

In the excitement of the moment, Sarah was completely innocent of the fact that the elderly woman spoke to her in English. It was only very late that evening that this realization suddenly came upon her.

Takhi gripped her hand. "Stay and bear witness for me." Nodding a promise, Sarah instinctively tried to aid Takhi as she struggled to rise. It was a hopeless quest, and she collapsed like a dropped stone. "I must go to the place I prepared."

In a clipped tone, the old woman brooked no debate. "No, it is too late. The time is upon you!"

At near dark, it was at an end. Sarah was only aware of the intensity of the contractions when Takhi's breaths caught short and the viselike grip on her hand increased. But there was scarcely a single sound. The labor was so long that, despite her steely intentions, Sarah's mind wandered between the spasms.

She recalled her mother's accounts of the births that Mary had attended as midwife. Most had some telling point of interest: stillbirths, twins, or an extraordinary length of labor. Of particular interest were the shrieking curses and imprecations occasionally hurled at the waiting fathers nearby. Invariably, these statements were discussed in private with friends to tease out any particular meaning. It was piously admitted, of course, that these were insights into private lives that strangers should never be privy to. They were avidly relished, nonetheless. Several times Sarah had to pull her face out of a smile at the memories.

The packed earth floor of the residence was long ago made impervious by thousands of footfalls. Any liquid did not sink in but ran in rivulets seeking a low spot such as a child's footprint. Sarah now knew the purpose of the sand bed that Takhi had so carefully crafted. With the child born, Takhi's countenance seemed to change. As a leather water bag sinks inward as the liquid is drunk, Takhi's very body drew back into itself. Sarah, now an observer, watched Takhi cradling her daughter. Very carefully, she ran her fingers over the little girl's every feature, examining the infant's body for defects.

"Watch over my girl, dear friend."

Protesting, Sarah explained, "There is no need. You have come through the ordeal."

"No. I am fading away, like all my kind. Promise me that you will."

When Sarah persisted, Takhi smiled thinly and cautioned, "Speak only the truth. You have no skill with the other." When she closed her eyes, Sarah feared that she was gone. After a short pause, she opened her eyes, pleading, "Please! Guide her. She must be Pequot."

"But, Takhi, I have no knowledge of how to teach her."

"Teach her to be strong and proud."

And then she was gone. Her eyes remained open after she died. The old woman gently closed them.

"Will you honor your pledge, Sarah Noble?"

"I must and I will." Her promise was more a fervent hope than a real plan. Sarah had no idea how she might affect what she had just vowed. All that Sarah had learned and acquired over the past months was suddenly washed away in a great wave that was, at once, both irresistible and so very familiar. She broke out in loud sobs. When the flow ebbed sufficiently that she could speak, she made eye contact with the old woman. "I know it is not her way. But it is my way."

...

Within minutes, it appeared that nearly every woman in the settlement was in the residence to prepare Takhi for her final journey. Working alone and in groups, they presented a blur of movement that addled Sarah's every attempt to make sense of it. As difficult as it is to single out a particular bird in a wheeling, swoping flock, she gave up the attempt, making for the river and the Noble camp.

Tawsume was waiting with a canoe when she arrived at the river's edge. Whether through the gift of foresight or insight, Sarah was grateful for the dry passage. Her quest was to reclaim her journal at the back of the account book. After a long pause, she decided to write of her friend.

In their tent, everything appeared generally in order. However, she knew that the Indian children couldn't help satisfying their curiosity by poring over such exotic English things during her absences. No doubt, some things would remain missing. Her father, usually in jest, referred to such loses as "wastage."

Sarah was surprised that Tawsume was still waiting for her by his canoe. The return passage was also silent, excepting two words. Leaping onto the riverbank, she turned to him with a soft "thank you."

Later that night, lying on her platform, she carefully marshalled her thoughts. Left to themselves, they ran amok amongst each other in utter confusion. Only by organizing each thought in turn could perfect sense be made of them all.

Sarah realized that she had never before seen someone in the very act of dying. Almost alone amongst her friends, she had witnessed none of her siblings' deaths. She had, of course, viewed the dead at various funerals, but they were dressed in the solemn composure of sleep. The minister often counseled in his sermons the true path to a proper death. He even had a name for it, the *Ars Moriendi*, the art of dying. But it was mostly about how to prepare one's soul for resurrection. He gave no guidance for the dying on the finer points of farewells to kin and family.

The past was unavailing to explain Sarah's current quandary. She finally settled upon a scenario, an ideal ritual that would announce that a soul had departed this earth. The eyes would slowly close, followed by a deep exhale. And finally, the limbs would gently sag. All in unison, an aura of dignity would prevail. But Takhi was denied this final gift. Her eyes remained open, and she gave no other signs of death. She just stopped, never to begin again. Sarah took some scant consolation that Takhi's death was serene and not macabre like Grandmother Goodwin's in Deerfield.

Her friend Eleanor, when in one of her melancholy states, mused about her own grandmother. When struck by smallpox, Eleanor's grandmother was walled up in her room with her husband. Provisions and other necessities had been provided through an open window. As the disease progressed, two holes were dug behind the barn. One was for the grandmother's body, the second for all the furniture, clothes, and any other object that the sick woman touched, including the family bible. Tearfully, Eleanor had wondered if her grandmother on her deathbed might have heard the scraping of spades digging the holes. The tale always ended haltingly with sobs for the grandmother being interred in the makeshift grave before her body was even cold. A Christian burial in consecrated ground was rarely observed in pox cases. Mourners feared the contagion. Eleanor's sobs became wails during her confession when she admitted she stopped waving to her grandmother through the window when the smell became more than she could bear.

• • •

When the notch between the hills to the east turned the slightest orange, a harbinger of dawn, Sarah collected her writing implements and walked to the river. Settling on a favorite rock that offered a depression to hold her ink, she wrote:

It is dawn by a dead fire. It has been a night of such loss. My sister Takhi has died. A Pequot mother suffering as much grief as me, even more. But her baby lives. I promised Takhi that I would protect her and I pray that I may honor my pledge.
I am sick to my soul. Her ceremony will be today.
I feel the weariness of the ages.

Hearing the growing murmur as the village awoke, Sarah dipped the loaded quill pen in the water to rinse the ink clean. Only later and gradually did she learn that she was not to be part of the ceremony. Amidst the funeral activity, none of her temporary family mentioned a role for her. She reckoned that Takhi's family was against it. Nawas was of slight importance, but his father, Ninefingers, held great sway over the village. As the upholder of the old ways, he was adept at pricking the tribe's conscience. She watched and listened at a distance across the river. In the face of the hostility of Nawas, she feared that redeeming her pledge to Takhi would be all but impossible.

• • •

During the weeks that followed, Sarah's life took on a curious sense of normality that never seemed right. She worked in the fields as usual. The children were no less exuberant than usual. But there was a dark abyss. She childishly expected that Takhi's absence might be marked by signifiers, permanent changes wrought by her passing. At night, she chided herself on her silliness. Surely, she should not expect that the death of one girl should cause the river to stop flowing or the sun not to set. In her heart, however, she felt that it was unseemly that Takhi's death carried so slight a meaning.

Gradually, she spent more time at the Noble's home site. The chief's family was as attentive as ever. Tawsume warned her that she was not to spend a night there but must return to the lodge. He had taken over Takhi's role as guide and mentor. Both were aware of the difference. He was more formal and circumspect: the friend became the chief's surrogate.

Her father's extended absence crowded more insistently into Sarah's nightly review of the day's happenings. The family would not be able, unaided, to finish the dwelling before snow. He had been gone too long. They would have to hire a crew to undertake the house raising. If one could even be found.

Fortunately, more proprietors were arriving by the week, all men with needed skills. If the money be found, surely one might be engaged. Almost daily, she saw the daughters of new arrivals at a distance. She had no desire to embrace them; they could teach her nothing. Always lurking behind her thoughts on the dwelling was a fear that her father might not return. He may have disappeared as Takhi.

On a particularly uneventful morning, Sarah sat grinding corn in the great soapstone mortar. She faced the river as the rising sun cast a pleasing, sparkling glow on the water. After high sun, the view was merely water. But at this time of day, there was a nearly magical aspect to the silvery ribbon of the river. She had come to enjoy this mindless grinding of the corn. Similar to her chores at home, it was at once a useful release, allowing her thoughts to wander.

Such was her empty trance that she failed to notice her father approaching. Even when he dismounted and tied off the tired mare, she was heedless, lost in a painful emptiness.

• • •

Kneeling behind her, Father wrapped his arms around her. Recognizing her father's hands, she scarcely flinched. A boat-shaped scar on his left hand, the memory of a youthful mishap, comforted her. Carefully putting her work aside, Sarah rose and embraced him.

"You were gone much longer than you promised."

"The high and mighty set their own clocks," he explained with a shrug.

Noticing only the tethered horse, Sarah was alarmed. "Where is the cart? What shall we do without it?"

"Calm yourself, Sarah. The Henshaw merchant was delayed against his will and grew tired of paying daily for guide, horse, as well as cart while we lounged. We were dismissed. The eccentric nature of the cart caught his fancy, and he paid handsomely for it. Likely the horse was relieved of the return burden."

Mulling over the transaction, Sarah couldn't help but wonder, "But will we not have need of it?"

"The great wagon that your mother brings will be of greater profit." With a contented smile, John allowed that, "With a full pouch of Spanish milled dollars, the house will soon be goodly raised." At Sarah's frown at the mention of Spain, he laughed. "Sarah, money has no religion."

Approaching the residence, he became aware of her limp. When it became apparent that she had no intention of volunteering the cause, he probed casually, "What has happened?"

With no hesitation, Sarah admitted "the game." Growing increasingly irritated over his absence over the weeks, she was newly emboldened to tell the truth without honey. Startled, he paused for a moment, digesting the news. "The little brother of war?" Nodding, she held up both palms, signaling that she wanted to speak first, to explain her actions.

"Father, all my life I have been fearful. Of the Indians, the dark water, the storms of hidden demons. The fear dragged like a great weight upon my soul. It never left me. I decided to embrace it. The real pain of discovery might be worse, but it would bring an end. It has to end. I will never be whole . . . and my friend Takhi has died."

The chief and the old woman, his mother, listened to the conversation between Sarah and her father. The words were sufficiently muffled that only the general tenor of the exchange was clear. John had barely launched into a reprimand: "You have disregarded my clear wishes in this matter . . ." when the Chief and his mother entered the wigwam.

THE SEASONING

Greetings and shared news between the old friends would have to wait for a calmer time. John, his anger only just under control, glared at the chief. It was the old woman who broke the silent impasse. Speaking in perfect but curiously accented English so that the girl might follow, she calmly explained their actions. The tone of her voice admitted no embarrassment or regret that his wishes were not followed. In her thinking, she had the right.

"John, your eyes in this matter are cloudy. No matter how soft the nest, it must be abandoned in time. The woman's spirit must find peace. This was needed for her to come into being. In all these years, have we ever led you falsely? Sarah is here!" When he did not burst into a repost, she continued, "She did well. Your family was not shamed."

With a sharp gesture, he signaled to his daughter that it was time to return to the homesite. Turning to the chief, with the slightest of smiles, he promised, "We shall talk of the matter again later when I am rested and of a sweeter mind."

Approaching the river, her father, at length, mused, "She is probably right." Sarah, with relief, realized that the matter was settled. The heated scolding would never come.

"It was only when Takhi was dying that I realized that the old woman spoke English, and very well."

Glancing at Sarah, Father added, "And French."

Sarah plodded along silently for a moment before finally venturing, "She kept it very well hidden. To her clever advantage."

They led the horse down to the river rather than mounting the beast. She was nearly spent from the recent exertions and would need some coddling to regain her strength. John coaxed the mare through the shallows while Sarah paddled a lent canoe directly across. An indulgence from the chief, Sarah had long suspected that it was a ploy to allow him to know her whereabouts. It leaked some and required energetic paddling to reach the far bank while still afloat. But she remained mostly dry.

John was well pleased that the site was in such good order. Failing to give Sarah explicit directions, he feared that their belongings would have suffered a thorough pillaging. She must have been in attendance regularly. A campsite even slightly unkempt would tempt visitors with fingers of burrs.

Sarah, watching her father looking over the camp, was moved to assure him. "All the tools are safe, as far as I can see. There was some wastage of minor trifles. A pair of my hose has gone missing."

The evening meal was only corn mush. John had passed on to the chief the remaining salted pork to even out his debt to the tribe. He looked forward to some fresh meat. His victuals at Fort Orange had been meager indeed. He had avoided the plentiful salted beef as it was streaked with green.

"The family will be here soon. How are we to present you? Is your best dress in good order?" Sarah nodded, startled by the question. Her father was talking as though she had recently shucked off a cocoon, becoming a different person.

"Your mother will be pleased in my way of thinking. But you must present yourself as . . . cleaner. And more demure. She will be watchful at first; soothe her with her old daughter."

Sarah grew more anxious as he spoke. Her own father spoke as if he scarcely knew her. "Why would mother be displeased? With shoes and my proper long dress, I will be in her eyes what I was."

"Your mother is ever fretful and worried. The fruit never strays far from the tree. When we left, you were her worrisome child. It will be unsettling to her when she meets the woman. And a mindful one. Prudence might dictate a slow revelation. You are on the mend?"

Sarah, with a startling enthusiasm, explained, "Yes, the leg is almost fine. Weeks ago it was a bloated black squash! I hobbled about like our lame cow." When her father frowned, searching his memory, she refreshed his recollection: "You remember, the one we ate.

"I foolishly let down my guard, and she caught me with her stick." He assumed that something of the sort was the cause of her limp but was quite happy to remain in a state of ignorance of the particulars. Noting his alarm, Sarah pulled back her hair, exposing the scar, hoping to offer a bit of cheer.

"And I can cover this with just a wave of hair. Takhi tended the wound and arranged the flaps of loose skin this way and that, according to her fancy."

Sighing, John ended the conversation with a terse, "Are you done?" He knew that there was more but wished for a later revelation.

As the flames of the fire slowly turned to glowing embers, John sensed an unusual change of mood in his daughter. Sarah's moods were ever mercurial and changing; she might shift from rage to mirth in the space of a long yawn. However, turning pensive always signified a storm soon to break. He suspected that she was kneading her anger over Takhi's death into a fever state. Sometimes, in these cases, it was better to let it cool; other times, a more direct path proved more fruitful. He finally decided to prick the boil.

"The chief made me privy to Takhi's end."

Sarah in a voice so mild that he was perplexed, asked, "But why Takhi? She was the best of us all!"

Without waiting for a reply, she sprung to her feet and stomped around the fire with clenched fists. Raging at the darkness just beyond the fire, she cursed Nawas with words that he had never heard her utter before. Her shrieks echoed through the forest. Even the old horse was roused from her somnolence, shifting nervously. As quickly as she erupted, she was spent. Collapsing heavily next to her father, she offered amends. "I have acted like a petulant child."

"Sarah, deep feelings are not often easily managed." Taking her tear-stained face in his hands, he kissed her scarred forehead. This was not in his character. For Sarah, such a kiss might well be a glistening pearl for all its rarity.

Continuing, he said, "My little warrior mouse, all pages must turn or else the book might not continue. Only Providence can decide."

Sarah confessed, "I feel that I am less since she died. Part of me is missing. Is that sensible?" He paused so long before answering that Sarah wondered if he were really listening.

"Sadly, very sensible. But these things are not thinkable. They are merely to be endured."

• • •

The house site from its vantage point far above the river offered a twinkling nightly view of the Indian village on the far bank. As more trees were felled, the view expanded to expose more of the meadow below. Leaning against a comfortable curved stump, Sarah watched the clouds of fireflies drifting in and out of view. There was no moon on this night; their lazy lights seemed much brighter somehow. What struck her most was their silence. The multitudes flashed and traveled here and there without a sound. In her experience, movement always had sound. Their silent lights appeared to her as a telling omen.

"Father, I believe . . . well, no, in truth, it is only a hope. Each of the flashing fliers is a departed soul. In no great hurry, they drift about in silence in search of their kindred."

She waited for her father's observations, but unlike before, he was not listening. He was fast asleep. Watching her father's sleeping form in the silvery light, a question suddenly came to life in her mind. It was so obvious now that she puzzled why it had never occurred to her before. Surely, it must have been sleeping in her mind all the while only to awaken now: Why had her father chosen this place above all others as their new home. Why not the Hampshires or Maine? And why this particular time?

Sarah knew perfectly that she was simply crafting an argument, tidy and clear, in her thoughts so to clinch her point. Her father came here because he had a need. He had known these people for many years; something in his life of many years ago drew him back. Sarah tried to visualize what his life encompassed all those years ago, but she was missing too many pages. Her last, drowsy thought of the night was she should have listened more keenly to her father's conversations of the past.

CHAPTER XI

September 16, 1707

It is a well-known truism, scarcely needing any comment, that seasons in New England are each and all fanciful teases. Winter approaches amiably enough bearing mild temperatures with blankets of glistening wet snow just sufficient to color the dreary brown land. With not a warning, the cold descends with an icy grip, unrelenting until spring. Summer glides in with promises of dry, warm breezes that stoke the ardor of men and beasts, only to be sapped and enervated with the coming of the wet heat, a suffocating quilt not easily kicked off. Each morning now, the river was veiled by a dense fog that was only burned off at midmorning. Dreams of dry, crisp fall days were thwarted upon awakening each morning.

John was surrounded by piles of stones crabbed out of the plot. He was nearly finished laying in the foundation to support the great chimney. He didn't feel safe beyond working up the stout base. The fireboxes and flue construction were past his skills, for something of artistry was needed so they didn't smoke. The only advantage to the still, wet air, however slight, was that the mortar was workable longer.

A passable well for drinking water had recently been completed. The stream running off the high ground was too unsteady, and the water would soon be fouled by roaming livestock. The first well was a dry hole. It would serve as a privy once partially filled in. Mishaps were common enough that overly deep privy shafts were discouraged.

Sarah busied herself, as she had for some days, piling forest debris on a bonfire. She had been at this business for nearly two weeks, gradually clearing a plot that would be plowed in the spring. The fire never completely cooled. A few quick rakes every morning was all that was needed to rekindle the flames. The sooty ashes swirled into the air each time new debris was added.

Every morning, Sarah became caked with the ash, sticking like a paste to her sweaty face. To her delight, nearly every time she added fresh fuel, little dust devils spun off the burning edges, dancing and capering before disappearing as they entered cooler air. When one nearly as tall as herself was spawned, swirling leaves and sticks in a funnel vortex, she impulsively stepped into it. The little storm vanished without providing the slightest sensation.

Nearly every day, new settlers arrived only to crush Sarah's hopes when they proved to be strangers. Her father explained that most of the proprietors would likely arrive from a southern direction. The new town would, at least at first, have strong connections to seacoast towns. There was some vague talk that the owner grandees from Milford were set on establishing a new Milford. After many interruptions to his work, he ordered her not to bother him again unless the newcomers came from the east or north. Stung by many false hopes, she gradually paid less heed to a strange wagon's coming.

On a particular day when the fog seemed stubbornly reluctant to rise above the river, Sarah's ears were pricked by the low rumble from due east. After a number of errant rushes to greet mere strangers, she cautiously waited until the great wagon lumbered clearly into view. Her father mentioned that the family would arrive in the biggest of all wagons. This would not be a gradual move but all at once. Still too distant to identify, she noted an armed man preceding the wagon with another at the rear. Other figures, apparently women, wandered along the sides, one leading a cow. She had just decided that the wagon driver was also skirted when she caught sight of the great white feather pinned to her mother's best bonnet.

"Father! It is them. They have truly come." The scream had barely died before she was at a full dash toward the wagon. John, at first, shook his head thinking that this was another of Sarah's inventions. Recognizing the man-high wheels of the machine he had bought earlier, he started off in a limping trot. Both of his knees were becoming troublesome these later days, limiting his speed. Sarah, with more mirth than consolation, counseled bear grease for the squeaks in his knees.

Stephen, in the point position before the wagon, watched a lithe Indian girl closing the distance at a full run. Unarmed, this mere slip was no danger to anyone. Amused, he wondered what her business might be. Too late to react, he realized that he was the intended prey just before Sarah leapt at him. Her arms about his neck and legs wrapped around his body, he was in a full hug.

"Brother, I am so happy that you are finally here. I have missed you greatly." Exploding into a strange babble of rushed thoughts, Sarah finally paused. Taking a deep breath, she wrinkled her nose suspiciously. "You smell oddly. Was it always so?"

Recovering from his shock, Stephen looked closely at his sister. She was all but unrecognizable. Stripping away the streaked dirt from her face as well as her odd mix of attire, he suddenly blurted, "Sarah, it is truly you! You have certainly become the wild one."

Stephen briefly thought of passing on cautioning words to Sarah so that she not alarm their mother unduly. After inspecting her closely, he decided that this was a fruitless hope. Her appearance was impossible to soothingly explain.

In the end, he simply advised, "Mother has fussed and fretted about you during this entire journey, growing more snappish by the day. I tire of the nips. This very morning, she donned her favorite bonnet. She will be much taken by the change. Go, Mother is waiting."

Taking Stephen's last words as a command, Sarah sprinted off toward her mother. Entirely abandoning his watchful duty to guard the road ahead, Stephen turned to see Sarah running to the wagon. He feared that this would not be a joyous reunion. However, if everything settled down for the better, surely this day would provide a mirthful family tale. Little doubt that her quite Indian demeanor would be long discussed in family circles. Shaking his head, he smiled, muttering under his breath, "And I smell oddly?"

Mary reined in the oxen when Stephen stopped to engage the Indian girl. Alarmed at first that her son was being attacked, it soon appeared that the contact was even more puzzling. What business had she with him? After what was certainly an unseemly delay, Stephen untangled the girl's clutches and gestured toward the wagon. She was at a loss to fathom what interest the Indian waif had with her family. Her son had unaccountably pointed herself out to this young creature. The little imp, while dirty and shabby, covered the distance to the wagon with amazing dispatch.

Without pausing for an introduction or even slackening her speed, Sarah leapt onto the wagon in a single bound. Mary shrunk back in disgust, attempting to escape from the girl's unrelenting hug. This foul creature buried her face into Mary, sniffing deeply. When she was able to catch her breath, Mary screamed to the children, "Stephen! John! David! Help me, I am beset by a heathen!"

Ignoring her mother's alarms, Sarah calmly explained, "Mother, now that you are here, everything will be as it was! We shall be happy again."

Mary was stunned that this creature spoke so nearly in her daughter's voice.

Probing hesitantly, she finally asked, "Sarah, is that really you in this body? You have changed. You are thin . . . and soiled. Where is the rest of your dress?" Mary picked at the hardened sap spots on Sarah's dress in dismay, mentally numbering up the missing strips that needed replacements.

Sarah dryly replied that, "The first was lost to wear and mud. The other two I peeled away for convenience." She described the shortening of the dress in a giggling tone as if recounting a childhood prank.

Sarah knew that her mother needed time to slowly sift through the events of this day. Too much unwelcome news offered in a rush aroused only her obstinance. Sarah went quiet, offering her mother what the family called "cud time." As a beast placidly chews at leisure, her mother would need a similar respite to make things palatable.

However, instead of calming, her face screwed up to match her wail. "Oh God, preserve me! You have become a changeling. Like the babes of Deerfield, you have become a savage. You are lost to us forever! I would die before I endure this."

THE SEASONING

Sarah had rehearsed for many weeks what she might say to her mother when they met, different speeches according to her mother's particular humor. Lining up her words in battalions had always failed her in the past, but on this late summer's morning, they marched in perfect order. "Mother, I do what needs must. I am still your Sarah, no less. Not a changeling nor lost to you. And I no longer dream the dream. The glowing horse is gone. I am free! Whatever else I have become, I am still your Sarah."

Mary didn't reply, too mortified at the spectacle she might make in such a public place. Of course, she reasoned, without her own kind for guidance, Sarah had no choice but to use the tools at hand. With proper clothes and a good scrubbing, she would soon again be on the right path. "What happened to your shoes?"

Wiggling her toes, Sarah admitted, "Long since spent."

Suspiciously, Mary tugged on the strip of rawhide around Sarah's neck, exposing the deer point necklace. "And what is this?" Sarah was surprised that her mother's tone was more curious than angry.

"A gift from a friend."

"Do you have need of it?" With Sarah's nod, Mary decided to let it be for the moment. She would deal with it later at a proper time. Too much had transpired over these months that she was not privy to. Best to wait until John limned in the details. For the first time, Mary noticed a fresh scar near Sarah's hairline. It was in the shape of a cursive W. Gently tracing the outlines with a finger, she inquired with a rising voice, "And the cause of this?"

Carefully affecting a casual air, Sarah answered, "An adventure."

"Is the tale a long one?"

"Yes," Sarah replied tersely. She was reluctant to offer more that might rouse her mother's ire.

"Would the knowledge trouble me?"

With a sigh, Sarah confessed, "Yes."

After some thought, Mary decided, "For another time, then. It has the queer shape of a W. Were you branded by the court for some crime?"

When her mother pulled back her flowing hair to examine her ears, Sarah giggled. She knew that it was common practice in New England to brand felons with the letter of their crime on the forehead as well as cutting off an ear. A counterfeiter, for example, would live out his days with a C branded into his forehead. Her mother making jest of it was a great relief. "Not an A, thank the Lord. Perhaps the W describes your wayward nature."

Mary was suddenly aware that the family was clustered expectantly near the wagon, all excepting her husband. He was only now coming into view, easily identified by his lope. She sorely missed the sight of his deliberate pace as well as his springing up on his toes with each step. "See the others. They are eager to hear of your adventures. And then we shall dress you properly!"

Sarah turned to dismount the wagon, halting when noticing a cradle tucked between her mother's feet. So, her baby sister, Preserved, did not die! Looking closely, the child bore little resemblance to the baby she left. The improbably large white garden grub that she recalled was now a plump and rosy girl. While in Westfield, she never picked her up, preferring only to gently touch the little creature's nose. It never raised a response. Repeating the touch now, Sarah noticed a thin smile.

"Mother, she has weathered the passage well. Her name accords with her improved situation. She has indeed been Preserved."

Leaping from the wagon, she was soon surrounded by her siblings; there were hugs and lively banter. Mary was amused despite herself. Her Sarah might be half naked, unshod, and dirty, but her tongue was as active as ever. Still, there was something unsettling about her, a difference not quite clear. She couldn't as yet put a finger to it. She mused that the W perhaps signified that she was, indeed, her Wonder Child.

The reunion of the siblings was a bedlam, a cacophony of competing voices each determined to own the stage above all others. Somehow, perhaps from long experience, it all made sense to them. Sister Mary's greeting were the only words held in family memory. Carefully inspecting Sarah, Mary Jr., affecting a look of disappointment, muttered, "You still sport your hair, I see!"

As Mary dismounted the wagon, John stood quietly, a rod's distance away. Despite the long separation, they didn't rush together headlong in a run but, with locked gazes, approached each other at a measured pace. The memory did not rise consciously in the mind of either, but they acted out once more the courting dance of many years past.

Mary was the first to speak. "My wandering in the desert is finally over. We are one again. This is a strange new world, and I fear starting again. It seems that, even now, I have been outstripped by my youngest daughter. She is a wonderment. Your judgment has proved true. "

"Mary, we have much to talk about."

"John, not now. Slowly, later. And tender the easy parts first to soothe my soul. The hard parts will come soon enough from the children's idle chatter."

When the party reached the home lot, Mary was quite pleased. The Indian-style domicile seemed serviceable for the time being. The second structure nearby was unfinished, but she was confident that her sons could strip off great peals of bark from the hemlocks nearby to finish it quickly. Even the partially raised log house met her approval. "Yes, stout, warm, with few drafts" was her comment.

She was even more pleased when she realized that their dwelling house would front the future village commons at a high corner. They would no longer, as in Westfield, be distant from the Meeting House in a wet, low farm. The village would unfold below on the slight grade.

The only disappointment was that her husband didn't recall where the surveyor's map placed the minister's and Meeting House lots. Hopefully, farther down the commons that they would be spared the shabby Sabbath-day houses nearby and the drunken revelers.

On the appointed days that the militia mustered at the Meeting House, after marching about and the discharging of muskets, there was serious imbibing. Election days could be even worse! By the time that the results were announced, the taverns were ripe with money. Partisans, bellies filled with rum, were likely to dispute the results noisily for some hours afterward.

The chimney was up to ground level, and sufficient logs were in place to trace the house outline. Other timbers dressed on two sides were scattered about where they were felled. More hands and tackling would be needed to set them in place.

• • •

The following day, Sarah's excited attempt to show her siblings the safe path across the river came to naught. When pointing to a large flat stone projecting from the riverbank, she cautioned that the path was unsafe if water flowed over it, Mary abruptly cut her off. "Why would we want to risk the hazard and get half wet? We have no interests over there!"

Sarah was nearly set to advise gripping the shoes between the teeth when crossing, allowing the hands to better balance over slippery stones. She went silent when she saw that Mary's opinion was common. In that moment, Sarah began to doubt that she would ever return to the calm certainty of the routines she knew in Westfield.

John soon engaged a housewright, Stephen Kelsey, to raise the house. Along with the added hands of the growing numbers of settlers drifting in, it would soon be accomplished. At Stephen's advice, John made the slow uphill trip to Woodbury in the great wagon to procure the boards needed for the roof. Leaving early, he returned after dark on the next day. He had shared a mattress in an inn with a gouty gentleman who groaned at every turn. Nevertheless, it was pleasant to spend the night in a proper dwelling.

Three days later, Mary was roused by the sound of strange voices before dawn. They were conversing in suspicious whispers. Nudging her husband in alarm with an elbow, he sleepily assured her that there was no cause for fear. It was only the undertaker Kelsey and his sons to work on the chimney. As the dawn spilled out more light, their voices became all the louder. She was increasingly skeptical of his decision once she could see Kelsey in clear light.

"John, he is an ancient old man! Our dwelling house will be raised by a revived Methuselah?"

She was not assured by his jesting response, "He need only live a week at best." He had to admit that she did have a point. Kelsey was nearly sixty-nine.

Despite Mary's misgivings, the chimney rose quickly. When the masonry neared the second floor, old Stephen Kelsey ambled over for a talk.

"Mr. Noble, John, a word. Earlier, your young daughter advised with much determination concerning the flues above. She wished that separate flues flare into the upper chambers, each passing through large flat stone tablets. She reckoned that they should be featherbed size. I guessed that this is not your will?"

"No, it is not, Stephen. Did she maintain that it was my wish?"

"No, but she was so clear and almost commanding as to give me pause."

"That would be Sarah, then. Proceed as usual, sir." As the visibly relieved Kelsey walked away, John could not resist raising the question, "Would it work?"

Kelsey scratched his forehead in thought for a moment, then moved his hands in the air, mentally mapping out the smoke's path. Finally, he admitted, "I believe so but with difficulty. And it would devour much space and materials."

As good as their word, the Kelseys finished the chimney after only a few days. It looked ominously naked arising upward with no house around it. Carelessness or untended fires often caused the loss of a family's shelter. Mary had seen on more than one occasion the blackened chimney rising out of an empty cellar hole. The lucky few lost only their dwelling. There were stories of a man and his wife visiting friends on a winter's night only to return to the loss of their children. Mary would be calmer when the stack was suitably clothed.

Sadly for Sarah, the chimney rose with scarcely an angle. Backside warmings in deep winter would not be possible in this house. The masonry finished, the site was soon an anthill of activity since the undertakers were keen to move on to the next house.

•••

A scattering of new neighbors arrived for the house-raising in something of a festive mood. This was the first meeting where strangers might take one another's measure. Evaluations made during the following days, as each man judged the other's worth, would mold the future town relationships for years to come. Who to trust. Who had the best sense. Who was most skilled.

It was an unspoken custom that neighbors toiling on the raising would be suitably fed and kept far from the pangs of thirst. After explaining to the crew that the rot-safe chestnut timbers were to be laid up first on the foundation and only then the white pine, John paused, walking over to his wife, critically observing the work from nearby. "Mary, is there brandy enough laid in?"

She assured him, "More than sufficient for this mob!"

"You have never seen one of these. When the brandy slows, so does the work."

"John, we shall all eat well. That I promise."

"Mary, the engine behind this enterprise is not the victuals but the exhilarating fluids."

After two days of frenzied preparations, there was little left that needed Mary's attention. Sarah sat out of harm's way, watching the timbers being hoisted into place one by one. She was intrigued that these men, who never worked together before this morning, clearly knew their appointed tasks. She decided to put this curiosity away for further thought.

The wives gathered in shifting knots as they carefully weighed the merits of their new neighbors. Manners of speech as well as deportment provided important clues. Did a particularly fine gown reveal a true state of worth or merely an empty show? Were there clever mends on a well-worn skirt? Did coarse homespun signify a lack of means or merely a sensible woman not given to puffery? Sarah remained apart as her older siblings carried out their own dances of introduction. In her eyes, they were all sifted out into the very types that she knew in Massachusetts: the quiet, the watchful, the followers, and the puffed-up flounces.

A few of the young men engaged with varying success with the older daughters present, including Mary and Elizabeth. One immediately caught Sarah's eye. Handsome, well-formed, and confident, he glided from group to group as an East Anglia squire might while dispensing largess. While she accepted as fact that each should be judged singly, surely, she felt that the Lord must have created creatures that were meant as repellant at a mere glance. This was such a creature. Laughing softly under her breath, she decided he was the perfect match for sister Mary.

Most of the young men, however, stood about in groups scuffing their feet in the dirt as though working on traction for an introduction. In the distant tree line, she became aware of young Indians visible in the dappled light. Springing off her convenient stump, she approached them. Some she knew slightly from her time under the chief's protection, but most were strangers. For the first time, she was aware of how slight her communion really was with the village across the river. At her nod of greeting, the group stared at her for a moment and slowly walked down to the Indian village.

After an evening meal of the slight remains of the workmen's midday rest, John announced that, before dark, he intended to collect the various tools still outstanding. When the midday repast was declared, many men simply dropped their tools where they stood, hastening to the food and drink. He feared that in the leaf litter and clutter, the valuable iron tools might go lost. Sarah followed, inquiring what tools were missing. Most particularly, her father was concerned for his best broadax still at large. Sarah soon found it nestled under a partially dressed timber.

"Father, when this day began, I was giddy at the raising of the house. I found watching the people and the busyness very satisfying. Some of Takhi's tribe were nearby, but were all solemn, even the wee children. They were mourning a loss?"

After a moment's reflection, he admitted, "That seems to be the nature of things. Not just now but through time."

Sarah wondered sadly, "Are differing hearts always destined to be weighed on some great steelyard?" She mimicked a balance scale with both palms as the trays. "My gain is always your loss?"

When he shrugged, she fell into reviewing her favorites from the Book of Proverbs. They were terse and clear in meaning. She hastened to remind him of the verse, "A man's heart plans his way, but the Lord directs his steps."

"It is a promise, is it not?"

Her father softly replied, "Many things are promised, Sarah."

• • •

As John had promised Mary, the house was sewn up tight and warm before winter arrived. He had taken a great risk buying the expensive wagon and bringing the brace of oxen. New towns had only limited pasture to support livestock, and it was common practice for new settlers to rent oxen for needed tasks, sparing the cost of feeding them. John did very well in the following spring, letting out his pair of oxen to farmers desperate to lay in their crops. The beasts rarely had an idle day. John's rate was sufficiently lower than market to ensure that his animals were kept busy. One stipulation held that the oxen would be well-fed at the very time of their rental. After a particularly contentious dispute, John insisted on viewing the feeding.

The great wagon was also in demand. One canny newcomer by the name of Boardman hired both the wagon and oxen on several occasions, hauling full loads of sundries from Woodbury with the intention of establishing a store when the settlement numbers were sufficient.

Sarah's father's account book rapidly filled with entries that would soon crowd his daughter's journal.

The old horse that carried John and Sarah south was a topic of conversation one evening over supper. The mare, tethered at the edges of the Indian meadow, steadily declined from the scanty fare. The age-old farmer's dilemma, balancing the cost of feed against the return of service, was becoming more insistent. Sarah, using a heel of bread to scoop out the last bit of gravy from her trencher, one evening quite matter-of-factly added, "At the end, the Indians eat them."

The family fell silent, though they were hardly shocked. Even her mother had grown to accept Sarah's occasional peculiar observations. It was common belief that Sarah's tongue was a permanently open sluice gate passing along whatever floated by.

Young Mary, as was her nature, was always ready to poke a hornet's nest or bait a likely bear. She couldn't resist sharing an observation, "Much meat is to be had from them."

John spoke first. "It is not our custom."

Glancing at her husband, Mary added in a soft, even vague voice, which was hardly in her nature: "To treat such a longtime faithful servant in such a manner lacks any charity." The whole topic aroused a sense of unease in her.

Attempting to soften the mood, in a studied, jocular tone, she admitted that, "I have no knowledge of their proper cooking. I have no recipes. So, Sarah, how would it be accomplished?"

Licking her gravy-coated fingers, Sarah, without a pause, counseled, "Long, slow, and wet. Not enough fat to soothe the tongue. But a fullness of flavor."

THE SEASONING

•••

With the arrival of her family, Sarah's contact with the Indian village over the river became less and less. Takhi was dead, and there was little need for her to cross over to the other bank. Takhi's child was secreted away from her at the insistence of Nawas. After the chief's family discharged the promise to her father for her welfare, Sarah never saw them again. Even Tawsume didn't guide his canoe to her stream side. The blended parts of her life, briefly joined, had separated.

With the coming of spring, the Noble farm burst with activity. The men burned off the debris left from the felling of the forest. The ashes were believed good for the earth. The remaining stumps were so large that they were left be and the brace of oxen labored at pulling the plow amongst them to break the ground for wheat and Indian corn. It would be some years, when the pressing farm needs eased, before the stumps would be laboriously grubbed out one by one. Until then, the growing fields would be studded with teeth.

Mary was determined that her kitchen herb garden should be done this very week. The white pine, whose stump served as the doorstep, had encountered rocky obstacles in growing and sent out spidery aboveground buttress roots on top of the ground for support. Initially dismayed, she soon realized that they were perfect for the fancy divisions of her garden.

The goodwives that Mary encountered up to now were very pleasing. Hailing mostly from the seacoast towns, they were well versed in all the sudden news from England as well as the newest fashions. Graciously, they provided the necessary seeds: sage, tansy, and marigold. Two women, with whom she got on particularly well, kindly shared their hoarded boneknit and fleabane seeds.

The latter would soon be useful as her husband was eyeing the purchase of a shaggy hound with blue spots. Strewn betwixt the sheets, the flowers and leaves of fleabane discouraged nightly biting visitors. And given David's hapless nature, the clasping leaves of boneknit would surely be needed at some point for a wrapped poultice to mend a broken bone.

Hoeing with vigor, Mary realized that Sarah had been absent for a while. This in itself was of little concern. Sarah was not a slacker or an idler. If she went missing, it was for a determined purpose. It was when the near noon sun caused her to turn aside that she noticed Sarah, at the lower edge of the clearing, in animated conversation with a young Indian boy. Only when the sun's glare faded from her eyes did she see that he was surely not a boy but a young man. Her quick strokes of the hoe slowed and finally stopped. The wind rushing up from the river over the now cleared land drowned out their words.

Sarah, true to her nature, was gesturing excitedly. Mary knew at a glance that they were not strangers but were of long acquaintance. Looking up at the Indian man who towered over her, Sarah held her hands straight at her sides in fists. Mary would talk to John this very evening after her thoughts were calmer and organized.

Long before her mother took notice, Sarah smiled at her approaching visitor. Rather than waiting for Tawsume's careful beginning, she spoke first. "Tawsume, it has been so long! I miss our times together."

Tawsume, in the peculiar inflection that he preferred to attach to her name, mused, "Sarah, our lives are on different paths now. You seem well . . . new clothes and shoes."

"I am returned to my own world now. How is Takhi's girl? And you?"

"Both of us are well and strong. Nawas takes great interest in his daughter."

Surprised, Sarah asked with hope but little real conviction, "Nawas has changed for the better?"

Dismissively waving a hand, Tawsume admitted, "Nawas does not change. His soul is long set. Only his purposes change. He is good with her but stern. She is greatly tethered. Too much. Almost like the English." A nodding smile acted as a slight apology.

Tawsume carefully watched her mother's movements during this brief meeting with Sarah. "Your mother's head bobs this way and that in silent watch. Like a great beaked bird before a meal."

Turning quickly, Sarah flushed red at her mother's disapproval. "Yes, Mother must have need of me."

With a broad smile, Tawsume confessed, "I have someone to meet."

Watching her friend recede into the shadows while she approached her mother up the gentle slope, Sarah wondered whom it was he was to meet.

He had many friends, but none so close as to cause such a lightened mood. Although her mother's face portrayed much of her thoughts, she uttered no words of reproach. Sarah's face also formed itself into an empty mask but not from any chastisement that her mother might feel. She now became aware that she would never know the name of Tawsume's secret friend nor perhaps ever be privy again to his life.

• • •

On this day, Mary departed from her accustomed self at dinner. Her typical narrative was a catalogue of daily events interspersed with pithy thoughts on new residents who stopped by to pay their respects. This lively chatter was replaced by the dreary melody of clattering dishes. But, this time, she was unusually quiet. As John feared, she would expose the nub of the matter in their sleeping chamber. And it so unfolded later that night just when his eyelids were fluttering to a close.

"John, Sarah was speaking to an Indian man this afternoon very earnestly. I have seen him before but always at a distance."

After only a half try yawn, he suggested, "Tawsume, I would think. And?"

"John, I find this communion unsettling. To what good purpose?"

"Mary, not all happenings have a portent or a meaning. Many are will-o-the-wisp encounters as untoward as drifting leaves."

"Do not make light of it! You were not a witness. They stood close with great smiles. And she stood with her fists closed held against her sides, drumming them against her body."

"Mary, it signifies nothing."

"It speaks of hidden thoughts."

Despite his resolve, he sighed. "You are conjuring up demons from thin air. She is a good lass; leave it. Don't try to mingle into her feelings."

"John, why can you not see the temptation? It is so clear. You above all should be mindful of the peril. Your own life should counsel caution."

"Mary, for years now, you have examined this part of my life, poking and prodding, mining for new insights. When may we close the chapter? No good will come from picking at it. It is in the past. It cannot be changed, and the constant turning of it causes you nothing but pain."

Gently touching her husband's arm, she softly added, "I fear for her, John. I wish to spare her the remorse."

• • •

The house was a near twin to the old one in Westfield, the daughters' sleeping chamber being directly above their parents. The moist, green floorboards were already beginning to dry, the cracks widening, allowing more sounds to filter into adjacent rooms above. John and Mary, knowing how their voices carried, spoke so softly that the girls caught only fragments.

The daughters knew from experience that when their mother spoke quickly at a run, in hushed tones, serious matters were at hand. Straining to identify names, only Sarah's came up. Sarah closed her eyes, feigning sleep, responding only with annoyed grunts at Mary's pokes. Sarah refused to be drawn out of her sleeping ruse. Finally, Mary's tugging on Sarah's ear provoked Elizabeth to laugh, and she gave it up with a sharp, "Be that way, then." These antics rarely angered Sarah these later days. Rather, they seemed merely a childish waste of time and words to be patiently borne. As the years fled past, young Mary lost interest in the game.

• • •

Even though she had little contact with the Indians as in time past, an occasional mood sent Sarah down to the river. She watched the children sporting about noisily on the other bank. Those that she knew years ago were grown and attending to other cares.

Settled on the sunny flat rock slab, the beginning of a safe passage into the river, Sarah was startled to see the figure of Nawas approaching. After all the years, he was still as handsome, perhaps even more so, and led a young girl. Making eye contact, she rose to allow them passage. In the cold and clipped voice that changed little over the years, he warned, "No, English, you are not for her. You will never be for her. You undid her mother. You will never do the same to my child. Or you will pay with your life."

Before her father pulled her away, the solemn child asked the very question that Sarah dreaded, the one that haunted her thoughts.

"You are the Sarah?"

Nawas quickly pulled her into the river. "This one is not for talking. I forbid it!"

Countless times during the passing weeks, Sarah considered over and over again this brief encounter, trying to tease more meaning out of it, but to no avail. Was this some omen or predestined meeting? Many times, she compared Takhi's person with this little girl, side by side in the looking glass of her mind, vainly looking for the slightest correspondence, some sign that a fragment of her friend lived on. She could not.

CHAPTER XII

Spring 1714

Walking out through the front door, Sarah stepped onto the pine stump step. With years' use, and as many feet scuffed across its surface, depressions wore into it. Two sunken footprints attested to years of boots being scrapped clean. It was better than seven years now since her father had dressed it flat in 1707. The stickiness was long past. The other edges were slowly wearing away. Soon, becoming spongy, the worn stump would be covered by a great flat stone. It was too close to the house for a grubbing out or a burning. The house, built with hopes that it might be temporary, was even now still the family dwelling.

The laid-out house lots abutting the town commons were slowly filling up, but there were still large empty gaps between dwellings. There were many new faces in town, but the exact number was something of a mystery. The new minister kept a careful tally of church members who owned a full membership in the congregation. But the larger number of Sabbath-day attendees without a full membership was of some concern. And the recent policy of allowing sober dissenters freedom to follow their own inclinations made a true count of the population difficult.

Since Church of England followers were allowed sufferance out of political necessity, other dissenting congregations demanded equal consideration. The Baptists were grudgingly accepted, but the Quakers aroused great consternation. Refusing even sensible militia duty, they were of a world apart. The general feeling was this was the inevitable result of too many foreign types drifting in from seacoast towns.

Sarah, as she often did, reflected on her father's passing this past spring. Seemingly hale and hearty as he was all those years ago on their adventure here, John was found one morning slumped over his workbench. With bubbles of foam around his mouth, the clear verdict was apoplexy. The probate court in New Haven sliced up the slender estate as best they could amongst the heirs, but only a biblical miracle of the loaves could have provided anyone a proper share.

John Noble's marker was a thick wooden slab. Her brothers carved a winged death's head at the top with a fanciful vine of life curling around his name. Sarah's sister Mary was heated in her intention to place a substantial stone over his grave. The wooden stele would soon disappear, leaving him lost to posterity. Grandchildren might still remember the location, but the grave would eventually be forgotten. The money for the expensive stone carving, however, was not yet forthcoming.

The widow Noble early on announced that she had no intention of remarrying. She would make use of her dower share of one-third of the estate during her lifetime. She saw no reason to forfeit this security for the unknown perils of a new husband. As a now single female, her money was once again hers alone. It was widely noted in town that she was the most stalwart of women, a visible inspiration. A newly made lady friend confessed to her that she lectured her own daughter whist she was in a whine to, "Steel yourself up like the widow Noble."

And to all eyes beyond the Noble's door, this was the clear truth. Beyond the threshold, the gospel was on another verse. While Sarah grieved over her father, she believed that he died as he lived. A quick death busy at his trade was as it should be. Although he was taken far too young in her eyes, this was often the nature of things. She was grateful that she had no unsaid words to give him. Everything between them was settled before he passed. This was a comfort to her.

Not so her sisters. As the homely matters of each day gradually crowded out the grief, Sarah came to believe that life must above all seek out life. It was the purpose to us. Young Mary felt their father's death most keenly. Sarah less so. There was little left unsaid between them to grieve over. Mary settled into a state of regrets, things left unsaid and gestures not tendered.

While Sarah's mother was still hale and hearty, her passing would be crueler and more played out. Unseen by nonfamily members was the fact that all that made up her soul was slowly ebbing away. It was a topic that all Sarah's siblings avoided, even Mary. As though the mere spoken words might conjure up some evil witchery, the taboo was silently agreed upon.

Their mother was a willful, hardheaded woman all her days, the family shaping and honing their world to conformance. Neighbors, whom she lectured sharply, were known to refer to the Mrs. Noble as "the knothead." A next-door neighbor, Penelope, who became a fast friend, was known to raise her arms, pleading, "Mercy, Mary, mercy," during one of her scoldings. Her mother could be as impervious to argument as a white oak knot was to the saw. And now her will, which was, in truth, her being, was gradually leaving her. Decisions became more difficult. She more and more deferred to the judgment of her sons.

Sarah shook off these profitless musings before resuming her walk down the commons. But not before speaking out in a loud voice, "Quicker is better."

Sarah had scarcely begun when she spied old Prudence Philpot determinedly nearing at a trot. Her gait could not be mistaken; the left leg, long ago injured, spayed out clumsily with each step as she walked. Being a small woman with a long body and oddly short legs, her curious carriage was rarely mistaken. Most particular about this woman was a prodigious mole on her nose. Only the most gracious person didn't stare at the large, puffy spot. A tuft of black hair, which seemed to vary in length by the season, crowned its center. Brother David mused aloud over supper one evening that the widow Philpot let it grow in winter for added warmth. Even more curious was that her head tufts were snow white.

Moving with some dispatch, the widow Philpot drew abreast of Sarah. "Sarah, on your way to the Meeting House to dress the pulpit for this Sabbath?" Without waiting for a response, she continued, "An honor to be selected. You are a great credit to your family."

Sarah smiled and offered the pleasing answer. "I am indebted to the congregation for their choice. It was most unexpected." In truth, she knew clearly that this was not the honor that it would be in a long-settled church.

The unfinished structure was usable only for part of the year. Swallows flew with abandon into the open window holes, which lacked glass, swooping about the heads of the faithful. Winter nor'easters left shoals of snow on the floor beneath the windows. Bitter weather often forced services into private homes. When the Meeting House was done and properly appointed, Sarah suspected that older, more worthy ladies would be chosen for the altar committee. Her reply had been crafted less to mislead but more to avoid an unpleasant argument.

The widow Philpot, trotting breathlessly by Sarah's side before her wind gave out, finally revealed her purpose. "And is it not time for you to ponder a match? My nephew Sylvester might suit you. He is a dear lad, and you are not getting any younger. When next you accompany your father to Woodbury, I will arrange a . . ." Her voice suddenly trailed off as she recalled that John was gone, dead some months past.

Tersely, Sarah promised, "All in good time." She accepted that the old woman did have a point. The sons of the settlers were in no position to offer any time soon a future to young girls until achieving a productive estate of their own. Marriage into well-established, out-of-town families was the accepted means. The lady with the mole had family in Woodbury, but her inquiries were usually more circumspect. The fear amongst the mildly interested young women was that perhaps her kin bore some resemblance to the matchmaker. The offer delivered, the matchmaker scampered off in her distinctive gait. Sarah walked down the commons rather enjoying a humorous reverie, wondering if the dear boy Sylvester shared any of his kin's more curious attributes.

• • •

Perhaps it was that she was paying so little attention that caused Sarah to notice too late the small Indian girl blocking her way. The girl suddenly appeared as though an apparition. Though reedy and slight of stature, she struck a willful stance. Feet planted firmly apart, hands clasped in tiny fists, it was clear that she had a mind for a serious talk. "You are the Sarah?"

"Yes, and you are . . ."

Before Sarah could finish her thought, her tiny interrogator interrupted, "Takhi's daughter. You made a blood pledge. Will it be remembered?"

Sarah was still quite startled by the unexpected confrontation and briefly was at a loss for any response. Pausing to regain her wind, she finally quietly asked, "You know of the pledge? How?"

The girl frowned with impatience at the question. Her explanation was colored with contemptuousness. "It lives as a common memory with us."

Sarah stared silently at the girl for some time, though perhaps not as long as her later memories spun out. Likely only now approaching her seventh year, Takhi's daughter already wore the mask. Sarah saw nothing of her dear friend in this child except perhaps for her will. And yet, here she was, a haunting fragment from the past. Unlike the glowing horse of her past dreams, however, this vision was not ethereal. This specter demanded a resolution.

Finally collecting her wits, Sarah ruefully admitted, "Yes. It is a memory that I have long since avoided picking at. A gnawing fester. Come tomorrow at this time and place, and we shall make a beginning. And your father?"

The mask briefly slipped aside in a smile as the girl promised, "He will be elsewhere."

•••

Later in the peace of the featherbed, Sarah parsed out how she would redeem her long-standing pledge to Takhi. She wondered whether her ruse would hold up long under the watchful eye of Nawas. Even if undiscovered, the plan would take months until fruition. Would the girl even see any purpose to it? If she expected a decisive stroke, the subtlety of Sarah's intentions would be lost to her.

She could almost hear her father's words of caution: "Too ornate a plan.

Too much could go astray at any time." Finally, he would pose a question that had no answer: "Is settling your conscience in this manner what is best for the child? Should she be drawn into the English world?"

Sarah was still nestled, after all these years, in the center of the featherbed with Elizabeth to one side and Mary to the other. So it would remain until one or the other married and left. Elizabeth would surely wed, yielding for the first time an outboard spot to Sarah. With clever coaxing, Sarah hoped that Mary might trade her side for Elizabeth's. For reasons quite without explanation, she had long cast a covetous desire for Mary's side of the bed.

Listening to the soft breathing of her older sisters, Sarah wondered what secret thoughts and adventures filled their minds. They shared the same blood, the same house, and even the same bed, but each dwelt in separate worlds. While Sarah might predict how they would each react to sundry happenings, she felt no comfort that she really knew their souls.

She found herself suddenly in a pleasant state of composure at last. Her mind made up and the plot's details assembled, Sarah slowly drifted into sleep. She could feel it approaching gradually, lapping over her body as a comforting, warm tide.

Walking quickly down the commons the next morning, Sarah, for the first time, realized that she would have to conjure up many excuses stretching into the future to explain her regular disappearances. By clever evasions and coy smiles, she would lead Mary to suspect that she was meeting a young man. That would appeal to Mary's nature. Smiling, she quite savored the notion of Mary as an unwitting accomplice. Mary's sly, cryptic words over supper would convince the family that Sarah sported a swain. Sarah realized that she would be pressed to name the man at some point, but she would deal with that problem as needs must. For a moment, she considered conjuring up a tragic but serendipitous drowning in the great river. A perfect man but not a swimmer. Perhaps a tale of unrequited love?

Entirely absorbed with her intricate plotting, Sarah lost track of her purpose until she noticed the Indian girl amidst a stand of thorny blackberries that had sprung to life on the green as soon as the great trees were felled, flooding the ground with sunlight. She scrapped away a patch of dirt with a foot, drawing a large capital **A**.

When the girl eyed it suspiciously, Sarah explained, "I propose a journey. It will be long and hard. The worth of it will be clear only at the end. And even then, you may spurn it. Thus, I will redeem my vow. As your family was always true to me, I will be true to you."

After a moment's reflection, the girl hesitantly demanded, "What is it? The meaning?"

Fearful that the girl would change her mind, Sarah continued quickly, "It is both a sound and a symbol. The sound must come first. There are two sounds: the hard *man* sound and sometimes the softer *woman* sound. The *woman* sound is more changeable to agree with its neighbors but for later." Sarah was unsettled using such an argument to explain the letter sounds but hoped that such a shared page might prove a useful beginning.

"Practice the shape and the music. Know it perfectly that you don't have to think upon it. There will be much more, many others." Sarah continued down the commons, loudly repeating the sounds.

The meetings stretched over months, often held in abeyance by Nawas's untimely appearance. Otherwise, the girl was dogged, even relentless, in her quest.

Mary's curiosity was heightened as the weeks passed. On at least one occasion, Sarah noticed her sister following at a distance. Mary had carefully evaluated the local inventory of likely men, eventually reaching an impasse. She reluctantly dismissed the whole affair as one of Sarah's fairy tales.

The meetings between Sarah and the girl on the town commons quickly became very brief once the girl learned the pattern. Sarah would pause only briefly to scratch a symbol, speaking the companion sounds. When the girl nearby repeated the music, Sarah would continue down the commons. To a casual observer, Sarah merely paused to button her coat or arrange a scarf.

By late autumn, Sarah needed to push away the fallen leaves to carve out an *R* in the dirt. This dusty spot was raked over so often that it was nearly the only spot where weeds could not take root. Sarah hadn't addressed the girl directly in some time. There was no need.

The next sign was given at the time of the first wet snow. The wet ground, not yet frozen, was a scrim of mud. Sarah was amused that it seemed like the painted blackboard used to instruct Elenore in Westfield. Not so many years ago, but in truth a different life ago. How would the person she once was judge her present quest?

If her father were still alive, Sarah knew well that she would not be standing here. Her path would be elsewhere. Only her father's passing allowed this path. Breaking away from her waking dream, she was aware that she had paused too long. Hastily, she ploughed an *S* in the soft mud with her stick and started to walk away. She turned so abruptly that the girl was nearly at the letter. Startled, she froze, awaiting Sarah's next move. In the largest letters that fit in the muddy spot, Sarah incised the signs *S A RA H*.

To the confused girl, Sarah promised, "You have all you need. Marry them together. Roll them over your tongue until they are sensible. The last sign with the posts and cross has no voice at the end." Continuing her pace to the church, Sarah couldn't resist turning to see what her pupil made of this latest lesson. The girl was still hunched over the letters, mouthing them. While she was silent, her eyes had, for the first time, the fierceness of her mother's.

Sarah decided that she would add a word in addition to each of the last few remaining letters. Delayed by stormy weather, it was a fortnight later that below the letter *T* she scrawled *T A H K I* in the drying mud. She only narrowly missed Nawas's appearance. She feared that their long-playing game had been found out. However, the girl, noticing the looming shadow of Nawas shading the letters, with feigned innocence answered her father's angry demand. "What are you doing? What is this?"

"The English left them. A grown girl with a stick and a basket. I am curious why they do this."

"Banish them! They have no meaning for our lives!" As they walked down the grade to the river, Nawas watched her intently in an aside. She was into something; that much was clear. He was sure that careful watching and her tongue slips would, in time, reveal it. She was as solitary in her thoughts as the shelled mussels in the streams. He would wait 'til she opened up in her own good time.

Nawas allowed his daughter to end the silence. She was most revealing at these times. "Father, do the English signs tell you anything?"

"No, they are as muddy as the river. They mean nothing to me. And they hold as little to you."

After winter's teasing, playful pauses of warm and soft snow, the hard season finally had sent its icy fingers in earnest. It seemed that even the season grew tired of games, finally deciding to reveal its nature in earnest. Avoiding the steepest, slippery banks, father and daughter followed a rounding path. The bitter wind in her face caused the girl's eyes to water. If Nawas was watchful, he would surely have been puzzled by the tearful cheeks married to a broad smile.

•••

Sarah was relieved that the long effort was done! She reflected in her accustomed spot nestled between her sisters in the featherbed during the night's quiet. This was the time and place when her mind was clearest and her thoughts were best. This was her thinking place.

Everyone had their own sacred place. Brother John held that his mind was keenest on horseback. Elizabeth's thoughts were sharpest while carding wool. Mary, ever contrary and puckish, held that her place was seated on the privy.

But Sarah was thankful that it was over. Over the weeks, the doubts grew that she was doing a good. At the end, she feared that this was a feckless quest, the blind on a hopeless journey leading the blind toward a ditch waiting to swallow them both. Gradually, she realized that lacking a primer and a tutor to guide her, she had set the girl on a path of failure and frustration.

As the weeks rolled by, her father's silent cautions became louder. Was what she had done really best for the girl? Perhaps the old woman would guide her! She was a creature of mysterious talents! Was she still living? Sarah realized that she might never see the last stitch in this garment that she had crafted.

CHAPTER XIII

January 12, 1762

Over the course of almost a half century, Sarah had told the tale many times over. The children particularly were enchanted. For her grandchildren, as well as grandnieces and grandnephews, the distance of time and place was so great, it was as though she was relating a biblical epic.

The little girls plagued her with questions about the mysterious Tawsume. They were thrilled by tales of this handsome, laconic stranger who was always there when needed. Invariably, the boys demanded more details of the gory game. Was everyone bloody? Did anyone die? And, of course, a close inspection of her W scar, now quite faint, was the final flourish. Admittedly, it was a favorite diversion at large family gatherings. It was passing into family lore, doubtless each listener would pass on the version that clung to memory.

And Sarah was not in the least reluctant to play out the various roles. After all, it was the exciting pivot of her life. The children's delighted squeals drove the narrative. Imperceptibly over the flagging years, she became more hesitant, yielding only to increasing pleas for "The Story." What once seemed as clear as a pane of glass, the truth in her mind became cloudier in recollection.

Did Takhi really mean what she'd said? And was Nawas as evil as memory recalled? What did he profit by attending to the girl so closely? And the purposes of Tawsume. The same pebble cast into the pond's middle or its edge creates different stories in ripples. The tale, once vouchsafe, now provoked unease in Sarah. In these later days, she often paused over some troubling detail. The younger kin held that her senses were slipping. In truth, she was pondering which variation of each particular memory to use. She vowed many times that this was the end of it!

Sarah was exhausted by the effort. The constant need to hone the story's bits sapped her energy. With every telling, she became more unsure of the truth. Next to the comforting fire, she stuffed her short clay pipe with tobacco, enjoying the pleasant rush of the first deep draft.

Turning to her audience, silent with agape mouths clearly expecting more, she made an abrupt announcement. "The writer may finish his book with the word "*finis*," the end. The end of this adventure? That is The Story from my memory as I know it. If the finale is written, I am not privy to it. I am quite spent. The cakes are et and the visit is over."

∴

For Sarah, New Milford was a long time past; she left decades ago when she married into the Hinman family of Woodbury. The coming to Connecticut now seemed as though a dream.

Casually waving her left hand in a practiced, telling gesture, Sarah reminded them as they slowly trooped out, "Your homes call. I can hear them. Give my regards to your families." The last child shuffling through the open door was six-year-old Sarah, one of her namesakes. There were so many Sarahs in the family that, for clarity, initials usually from middle names were added in referring to each. When mentioned Sarah B. or Sarah M., the confusion was immediately sorted out.

Sarah S., turning, demanded in a voice too loud for her stature: "But, Grandmother, it needs a close to be right." The little one was correct, of course. The steelyard's balance was askew, awaiting a final measure to true it up. Even in her old age, Sarah knew that this young girl bore watching. Just emerging from the grasping nature of childhood, she was becoming lately of some interest.

Sarah settled or rather sank into her old sleigh chair, the very same chair her mother had used, searching for the sweet attitude that gave her aching joints the most ease. While being most unladylike, it afforded the most comfort. The long story taxed her memory, but the awkward pose was more trying.

•••

Hearing the rumble of heavy carriage wheels passing by, she guessed that it was the stage slowing for a stop at the nearby tavern. Rising from her chair, she walked slowly to the window for a look. Scraping the frost off the pane for a better view, she noticed the coach pulling into the Bull's Head tavern. Letting off passengers for refreshments, the ponderous coach continued around to the livery in back to change out the team. Mail and papers would be passed on to the proprietor, also the unofficial postmaster.

Sarah would send her servant girl to collect her paper, the *Connecticut Courant*, before it was passed around and read to tatters. Returned to the innkeeper when well perused, some small consideration was expected in return from him. She hoped that her servant was too young to suffer any improper attentions, but the matter needed close watching.

Woodbury had a curiously large number of taverns, between nine and eleven at different times. The county court, providing the yearly licenses, was keen to permit only reputable men as keepers. Even an errant youthful indiscretion from years past was gravely examined.

Each of the taverns had their own temper and following. The Bull's Head was frequented by the middling sort and was mostly respectable. The King's Arms farther up the street attracted those of means and men grasping to join a higher order. Sadly, now that the war against the French and Indians was over, the stream of interesting types hurrying along the street was much less.

The famous General Israel Putnam, Old Put, was well known to the people of Woodbury, as well as most of Connecticut. He stopped to engage Sarah in conversation one summer's day. Actually, she had loudly summoned him. At her age, she did not stand on the niceties of decorum. Either through a gracious disposition or curiosity, they had an agreeable conversation of current happenings.

Watching her servant girl sweeping stray embers back into the hearth, Sarah was unsettled by her custom, quite without thought, of addressing her as "girl" rather than by her Christian name, Jane. It seemed wrong, but her daily habits always returned to it. She needed to keep the distance.

Long ago on the trail, her father had cautioned about giving names to casual creatures as creating unprofitable memories. Now Sarah mostly craved peace. She was nearing seventy, she supposed. There was some doubt. Her father thought she was born in the year that the town clerk's prize bull was struck by lightning. Mother was convinced otherwise. At her age, Sarah had no desire to join with the cares of another soul. The endings caused pain that was unwelcome.

In truth, there was no need to fret over it. Jane would soon be gone; only a matter of months at most when her reprobate father was released from service and the contract held for her service would end.

Like everyone, Sarah longed for spring. Even the mud season was preferable to the winter's bony grip. She longed to sit in her sunny knot garden, watching the interesting passersby. She quite delighted in conjuring life stories for any stranger walking down the lane. Sighing, she turned away from the window and considered the twenty paces back to her perch. Lately, she had taken to carefully considering each footfall in turn.

•••

Watching her young servant girl, a most hapless creature, attending the fire, Sarah was startled out of her comfortable doze by a loud knocking at the street door. This was the formal street entrance rarely used and only then by important callers. Casual visitors always used the nearby funeral door.

Mindful that her mistress was in a choleric mood, the girl returned to announce softly, "You have a gentleman caller. Full and very sleek." The girl's choice of words was meant as a measure of respect, but the very notion that she might have a "gentleman caller" in these times brought a broad smile to Sarah's face.

"And the name of this gentleman?"

"Daniel Boardman, mistress."

THE SEASONING

When last Sarah saw Daniel Boardman, many years ago, he was a cheerful, energetic young man of great promise. By common consent, he was a lad set to get on in the world. How long had it been? Twenty-five years? No, longer! No matter. Daniel's face would give the years. She answered in a voice as sweet as the young girl's: "Daniel . . . Well, do not keep the gentleman waiting. Show him in."

When Daniel Boardman entered, no, rather glided into the sitting room, Sarah was disappointed. She was confident, however, that her expression revealed nothing. The man standing before her bore scant resemblance to the rangy, raggedly dressed boy of her memory.

The years had layered on more weight over his frame, giving a more fleshy, soft appearance. But his attire was simply astounding: weskit of white silk, a red coat with silver buttons, and the brightest blue camlet breeches that she had ever seen. He was handsome as a young man, and he was certainly still comely now. Unlike his boyhood form, bulging forth from his fine stockings were a pair of very well-turned calf muscles, no doubt to delight the eyes of every woman.

Men might be enchanted with a female's partially exposed lifted bosom, but women seemed enthralled by men's calves. Her late sister Mary maintained with a dismissive snort that fat calves only revealed the size of a man's purse. This was often the case. A man's rounded calves were acquired generally by spending long periods horsed. And only men of means had the leisure to while away valuable working hours in the saddle.

Sarah greeted Daniel with the broadest of smiles. Certainly, this meeting with a long-ago companion provided most of the upturned curl to her lips. But a lesser amount, admittedly, was provided by the elegant wig that topped his head. She couldn't resist her imagination placing the hairpiece onto Daniel's youthful, shaggy head of her memory.

Both Sarah and Daniel were silent as they looked hard for some feature in the other that fit longtime memories. Sarah was the first to speak. "Forgive me for not rising, Daniel, but the works are in some disrepair."

Taking the liberty of sitting without being bidden, he explained that, "I have only a few moments while they change the coach. It is a short stop."

So as not to hear a list of complaints about springless coaches and wretched tavern food, she spoke before Daniel caught his breath. "I hear that you are a merchant. If your pocketbook is as full as your person, you have done well indeed."

The seams of the grand suit of clothes, still quite new, were even now being tested. He seemed to ignore her toying jest, responding with pride parading as modesty. "I have come up in the world."

"And New Milford? The town?"

"Much changed for the better. There was some hope for a time that New Milford would be the best seat for the new county. But Litchfield craved it. Very unfortunate. Courts and lawyers are good for business."

"And how is your business, Daniel?"

"Good. Save for the bad money from New York!"

"Well, the cash-at-hand trade and false money often share the same yoke."

Daniel, becoming more agitated, boomed, "These counterfeiters are as bold as brass, calling themselves the Dover Money Club. I agree with Roger Sherman. Business must have sound money! Do you know him? A man held in great esteem dressing in patched homespun."

Daniel's outburst caused Sarah's servant to peek through the door to ensure that nothing was amiss. "Such warm words, Daniel. Passion of the purse?"

Sarah was dismayed when Daniel made no answer. Instead, he chewed on his lip in rage. She had tossed out the lighthearted quip hoping to recapture some of the spirit of the jesting moments of their past. Sadly, she reflected that her friend was gone. The lively clever wit had faded. Irreverence had moved aside for decorum.

"And our Indian friends, Daniel?"

"Fewer every year. Most who remain are praying Indians. A few who follow the old ways skulk amidst the wastes west of the river in the rocks and caves. They gather with the runaways, debtors, and vagabonds. The minister calls these wilds Satan's Kingdom. And—"

Sarah interrupted Daniel's thoughts as she commanded the young servant girl nearby. "Girl, we shall have tea." Quickly remembering the niceties, she turned to her guest, wondering, "Or might you fancy Madeira?"

Regaining his gracious manner, he allowed that, "Tea would be very welcome."

In a voice sufficiently loud that her servant would understand, Sarah announced, "Tea it is then. And on the best china."

She turned to Daniel and continued in a tone so soft that he had to lean toward her to hear. "The Madeira these days is for guests and show only. It was always a fond friend of mine, but I fear that it is no longer fond of me. My enjoyment is to remember while watching others . . . I'm tempted sometimes to taste it again, but I fear the disappointment. Old memories are so often pleasantly false. At my age, I prefer to hold them fast."

In the next room, Jane, or "girl," as her mistress insisted on calling her, was dressing a silver platter with blue export china. She was a servant for some months now. Falling into debt to several men, her hapless father was bound over to serve them, fourteen months for one and sixteen to another. He was traded back and forth on different days as suited their whims. Saddled with the cost of supporting the family, the town insisted that she be indentured out to lighten the cost.

Jane signed the intimidating document with an X, as did her mother. She was never privy to the contract's length of service, merely being bundled off to the widow Hinman. Was it to be a full indenture for seven years? Hopefully not. If the widow passed on, the contract might be included in her estate. She might be sold anywhere.

Jane had no complaints of her treatment: she was well-fed and clothed. When her duties were satisfied, she had the free run of the town. The widow, whose given name was Sarah, was sharp with her on occasion but mostly out of frustration. She also often chose words harder in tone than she meant.

In the first week of her service, the mistress questioned her closely as to her "plan." At Jane's confused confession that she had no plan, the widow went silent and cast over her the baleful stare that Jane would come to fear.

"Without a plan, girl, you are a mere feather in the wind. Is that what you desire?" The old woman's eyes rolled around in thought for a moment. Finally, Sarah announced, "Make a chart in your mind. On one side line up your desires, but be practical. On the other, your God-given gifts. We shall couple them up." That was the only time the topic was raised, but Jane was under no illusion that it was the last.

The tea brewed, she nestled the sweet cakes, those too old for the grandchildren, onto the platter. In an inattentive moment, one slipped from her fingers. Hitting the floor with a thud, it rolled across the floor to the low spot directly above a sagging joist. Retrieving it, she nestled it amongst the others, admiring her arrangement of the offerings. Catching herself before she laughed out loud, she was of a mind with her mistress: a good soak in the tea would revive them.

Both Sarah and her guest were relieved when the girl settled the laden platter before them. The idle chatter reliving old times had slowed and thickened awkwardly. Now strangers, they grasped in relief at the slightest interruption, allowing them to pause the conversation. Daniel sipped slowly at the steaming tea, providing a natural excuse for silence. He graciously declined the sweet cakes. They were far too like the tavern fare offered on the return from Boston. Sarah finally posed a question that was long a source of concern.

"And what of Takhi's daughter?"

Daniel, in an act of self-control, carefully put the teacup down before gripping the edges of the table so firmly that his knuckles shifted to white. Color rose in his cheeks before the boiling words escaped from his lips.

"Impertinence incarnate! There is not a lick of ladylike behavior in that creature. Pitching with a ball of thorns is more pleasant than conversing with her. She was weaned on snarls, if you need the truth."

Sarah, from long practice, was able to choke off the thin smile that had a mind to form, but the sparkle in her eyes betrayed her delight. "I seem to recall that her mother, Takhi, had some such similar temperament."

Daniel, in less than a moment, regained his smooth composure, offering a more measured disapproval. "She has for a long time since maintained a so-called Indian school and teaches them to read . . . to *read*! Can you fathom it! With no permission from the selectmen, nor the justice court. She sought no blessing from the minister. It is unseemly. Those of her station should display more humility."

Sarah listened silently to Daniel's heated sermon. Holding up a finger to call a pause, she refilled her pipe, slowly lighting it with a flourish. Years ago, she thought tobacco a vile practice quite beneath a lady. In later times, when her other vices were denied her one by one, she took it up. If Madeira were not allowed, she would seek solace in tobacco. The pipe-filling ritual conveniently allowed time to collect her thoughts.

"We now uncover where the burr lies under the blanket, do we not? We have both become brittle over time, my young friend. I wither with the advancing years as my body becomes a dry husk. But, Daniel, I fear that your lively mind has become unyielding and hard from misuse. This should not be your appointed time."

Daniel squirmed under this unaccustomed rebuke. To Sarah's questioning expression, he blurted out a feeble answer, "I strive to uphold the divine order." Quickly changing the subject, he demanded, "And how did she attain her letters in the first place? She was long before the missionary Indian school was put into being at Kent. It is the common belief that untoward influences were slyly at work in this matter."

Reluctantly, Sarah decided against toying with Daniel about the malign influences that led to Takhi's daughter's literacy. His puckish nature was long since transformed; he would not rise to the mirth of the tale.

Daniel now regretted the impulsive decision to pay Sarah a visit. Many times over the years he had passed by her dwelling and eaten at the nearby tavern without approaching her door. He had a premonition that foretold disappointment. But on this particular run, full of satisfaction with his buying skills, the decision to visit crowded out his caution.

With her face wreathed in a swirl of tobacco smoke, Sarah finally wondered if it "was not proper that all God's children should read His words for their own attainment of grace? Haven't we always believed this even from the earlier days?"

Protesting, Daniel revealed, "Yes, but she goes too far . . . even teaching some of them to write!"

"How else are they to keep books and sign papers with more than an X?"

Daniel suddenly felt small, as if he were once again a lad. After all these years, she was doing it again. Sarah never argued but with questions. Never an honest contradiction, she poked at notions with the unsettling innocence of a wee child. Always those damnable questions! He was relieved when she moved on to another thought.

"What of Tawsume?"

Eager to impart some news that she might not dispute, he quickly revealed, "Dead, I believe. A hard sort. He became ill last spring and set out on a journey west. I believe he wished to die alone. The hardy, stout man withered away to a mere filament of his former self."

"Did he leave anyone behind? Wife? Children?"

Daniel was momentarily bewildered. Although he had noticed the silent man many times over the years, he admitted to Sarah that he had no knowledge of his life. Glancing at his gold watch, he was suddenly reminded of the hour.

"Madam, I must depart. Stay well until next we meet!" He bolted for the door, not waiting for her servant to show him out. Indeed, the door was slammed before she had time to craft a farewell.

Not surprisingly, Daniel had acquired a habit of petty rudeness as befitted his rising position. Upon entering her parlor, he sat before the usual formalities of an offered chair. The hasty retreat, however, was different. It was not ill manners but a flight, the relieved shedding of the skin of a former life. Daniel's parting words were, of course, one of those soothing little lies that oiled human intercourse. They would never meet again regardless of how many times he might step off the stage two doors down.

CHAPTER XIV

Later the Same Day

Listening to the girl in the adjacent room cleaning up the tea service, Sarah called out impulsively, "Jane, come!" The girl sighed with closed eyes. Often, a sharp summons using her Christian name was followed by a scolding for some misstep on her part. She entered the room with slow, short steps as if perhaps a demure manner might soothe her mistress's anger. Instead, the old woman pointed to a low three-legged stool near the fire and beckoned, "Sit and keep me company for a time."

Jane was puzzled. Sarah showed no anger. Perhaps she intended to talk of the future. But Sarah continued to rock, ignoring her, deep in thought. The stool was joined together for a small child. So low that Jane's knees were nearly the level of her face, she could only look up at Sarah in her high chair. The passing moments without Sarah's acknowledgment fed her unease, causing her to glance about the room nervously.

What occurred next was always far beyond her understanding. The widow Hinman abruptly halted her rocking and stared at her. Suddenly, she emitted gales of laughter that seemed, at first, nearly maniacal. Jane shrunk back on the stool, fearful that this fit would surely be followed by a spell of fatal apoplexy. When it continued, she came to know that this was genuine laughter. Sarah pointed to Jane twice, each time dissolving into spasms of laughter, before she could force out more than a few words.

"Jane, you're the bird in the boot! The little bird in the boot."

When Sarah was fourteen, perhaps a bit older, the family firewood for the winter was piled up near the front door. Logs four feet long were stacked up to chest level. The wooden windrow snaked along the top of the commons away from the door for at least a hundred feet. Her father, on different years, placed it to one side of the door or the other, seeking the best position so that the stack might keep the drifting snow away from the door. The stack was worked up and burned starting from the furthest point, gradually moving forward as the snows locked in. Closer to the house by February, it was less toil to drag the wood through the drifts.

That particular year, the cold ended sooner, leaving the last few cords near the house unburnt in May. In an accident that might well have proved serious, her father snagged his boot on the old plow, slicing it cleanly from ankle to calf. The old boots were judged beyond profitable mending, and her father tossed them on top of the wood row for later attention. He had every intention of cutting up the leather into suitable strips for hinges. On doors requiring no great strength, leather offered a less dear alternative to the blacksmith's iron hinges. Quite by chance, one of the boots partially slipped between the logs, presenting the open top protected by a beech log.

Elizabeth was the first to notice that a pair of drab birds were showing great interest in the open boot. Soon they were stuffing it with bits of straw and pine needles. These little brown creatures weren't much to look at, but how they could sing! After some brooding, she cited the old adage that things of great value often came in small packages. By general agreement, it was decided that somehow her new beau, Jacob, figured into her thoughts. He scarcely came up to her shoulder.

Oblivious to the family's comings and goings, the birds eventually hatched out four chicks. Then, day by day, the nest began to empty until only a single chick was left. The dinner table chatter offered up a number of culprits. Stephen wondered if a barn rat was raiding the nest after dark. Her father thought it was a snake hunting mice. A small bird would do just as well as a meal. Sister Mary believed that the survivor lived by hiding in the toe of the boot protected by nest debris.

With no competition for food, the remaining chick grew rapidly. It developed a curious habit of looking up at the adults with wild eyes while bobbing its head for food. When the boot was finally retrieved for strap hinges, the nest debris was filled with spider egg cases and dozens of scampering spiderlets. The thoughts were that the spiders somehow protected the hatchlings from greater pests. John, at the kitchen table, calmly supposed that even lesser creatures needed to make a living. Jane's fidgety behavior squirming about on the stool suddenly brought the whole episode back to Sarah.

Sarah regarded the young girl for a moment, teetering nervously on the child's stool. Her posture was most unladylike.

"Jane, go fetch my paper from the tavern before the ale circles make it unreadable." Jane's sprint to the door was halted by a familiar tone. "And, girl, pay close attention to where you are. You are in my care. When men's bellies are filled with rum, their idle hands would take great liberties with a girl of your station."

Jane turned with a smile before exiting.

"Set your mind at ease, mistress. I know all their tricks and ruses."

Although the tavern was only a few doors away, Sarah sent her, knowing that the girl would be away for a while. Over time, Sarah divined by tongue slips and observation that the girl had acquired a fast friend at the inn, a servant of mysterious origin, and a few years Jane's senior. The servant was very dark skinned with equally toned hair and eyes. Gossip maintained that she hailed from one of the Sugar Islands. Sarah did wonder about the girl's name: Medea. Was the name bestowed in a premonition of her later state? She attracted the unseemly interest of the tavern customers, and Sarah feared that Jane might well be swept along. In Sarah's mind, strange names beckoned equally strange beginnings. During idle moments, she occasionally remembered the slave boy Neptune, long gone now.

She remembered that Jane's indenture would lapse in a few months. What would become of her? Return to her debtor father, who was at blame for the girl's present state? Why was Sarah so reluctant to address her by her Christian name, Jane? She smiled as her father's words of caution rolled across her memory. Even after all these years, they were still as loud. The girl would need a plan, one suited to her talents, meager though they were. Without one, she would be buffeted about by events all her life. With sufficient prodding, the girl might come along. If only she could read! But surely, there was not enough time remaining to make it happen. Unless she consents to it. Then, the girl would always be just Jane to her.

Sarah, holding the chair's arms tightly, slid it from facing the warm fire a quarter circle left to face the windows. There was no danger in overshooting the mark. After many years, there was a smooth arced indent worn in the floor: one side faced the warm, the other the window. In the pale winter light, her skin was nearly transparent. In idle moments such as these, she often wondered what this might signify. Was this the slow beginning of becoming a spirit?

"Well, Takhi, my long-ago pledge has been redeemed. I may rest easy now. But I fear a new chapter has begun."

She savored the winter's sun. The light was clean and weightless. By comparison, the fireplace heat seemed cloying and heavy, like too rich a cake.

Fingering the large deer point on the necklace, she set the old chair in motion.

"We are as the morning dew. At full sun, we leave not a touch."

Printed in the USA
CPSIA information can be obtained
at www.ICGtesting.com
LVHW040817190724
785524LV00002B/5